psevdonymovs bosch

Illustrations by Gilbert Ford

LITTLE, BROWN AND COMPANY

New York   Boston

Text copyright © 2014 by Pseudonymous Bosch
Illustrations copyright © 2014 by Gilbert Ford
Excerpt from *Bad Luck* copyright © 2015 by Pseudonymous Bosch

Little, Brown and Company

Hachette Book Group
1290 Avenue of the Americas, New York, NY 10104
Visit us at lb-kids.com

Little, Brown and Company is a division of Hachette Book Group, Inc.
The Little, Brown name and logo are trademarks of Hachette Book Group, Inc.

The publisher is not responsible for websites (or their content) that are not owned by the publisher.

First Paperback Edition: September 2015
First published in hardcover in September 2014 by Little, Brown and Company

Library of Congress Cataloging-in-Publication Data

Bosch, Pseudonymous.
  Bad magic / Pseudonymous Bosch ; illustrations by Gilbert Ford. — First edition.
    pages cm
  Summary: "Thirteen-year-old Clay, a boy who no longer believes in magic, tags graffiti on his classroom wall and, as punishment, is sent to a camp for wayward kids located on a volcanic island, where eccentric campmates abound, a ghost walks among the abandoned ruins of a mansion, and a dangerous force threatens to erupt with bad magic"— Provided by publisher.
  ISBN 978-0-316-32038-2 (hardback) — ISBN 978-0-316-32039-9 (paperback) — ISBN 978-0-316-32040-5 (ebook) [1. Magic—Fiction. 2. Camps—Fiction.] I. Ford, Gilbert, illustrator. II. Title.
  PZ7.B6484992Bad 2014
  [Fic]—dc23

2014008771

10 9 8 7 6 5 4 3 2 1

RRD-C

Printed in the United States of America

---

* Oops.

FOR NATALIA AND INDIA
(NOW IT'S FAIR)

This book begins with a bad word.

Can you guess which one?

WAIT! Don't say it out loud. Don't even think it to yourself. I get into enough trouble as it is.

In fact, if the only reason you opened this book is to find the bad words in it, you will be sorely disappointed. I learned the hard way to keep my writing clean.*

Alas, when the hero of this book, Clay, first pronounced this word that I just mentioned, or rather that I most definitively did NOT mention, this swear word, this curse word, this very, very bad word, this word that I am not repeating or in any way revealing, he didn't know there was anything wrong with it; he was only three years old.

Where would such a young boy learn such a grown-up word? I have no idea. *I* certainly didn't teach it to him.

Maybe his father yelled it when his father stubbed his toe. Maybe his babysitter grumbled it into her phone when she thought Clay was sleeping. Maybe an older boy taught him the word because the older boy thought it would be funny to hear a three-year-old say it.

It really doesn't matter where Clay learned the

---

* Let's just say editors aren't the gentle bookish creatures people think they are, and leave it at that.

word any more than it matters what the word was; it only matters that he said the word when he did.

At the time of this fateful event, Clay was in a crowded elevator, leaving his first dentist appointment. As his brother would tell it later, Clay was happily sucking on the acid-green lollipop he had been given as a reward for his good behavior,* when all of a sudden he took the lollipop out of his mouth and hollered this terrible, terrible word at the top of his little lungs.

"#Ɛ*%!!!"**

Needless to say, everybody in the elevator was shocked to hear such foul language come out of such a small child. A big kid giggled. An old lady frowned. Even her Pekingese lapdog seemed to whimper in distress.

Mortified, Clay's brother, who was twelve years older than Clay and who was in charge of Clay for the afternoon, leaned in to Clay's ear and whispered, "You can't say that—that's a bad word."

Clay looked at his brother in confusion. "Why? What did it do?"

---

* Q: WHAT DO YOU CALL A DENTIST WHO HANDS OUT LOLLIPOPS?
  A: A VERY SHREWD BUSINESSMAN.
** WHY DO WE USE RANDOM TYPOGRAPHICAL SYMBOLS TO REPRESENT EXPLETIVES? HOW THE *&%*^#$ SHOULD I KNOW? I DO KNOW, HOWEVER, THAT THESE SYMBOLS ARE CALLED *GRAWLIXES*. (FOR MORE ON GRAWLIXES, SEE THE APPENDIX AT THE BACK OF THIS BOOK.)

Everybody laughed. The mood in the elevator, er, elevated.

But that isn't the end of the story.

On the bus ride home, Clay's brother couldn't get Clay's question out of his head. What did bad words *do*? What made them bad?

Finally, he had an answer: "Bad words are bad because they make people feel bad. That's what they do."

Clay nodded. This made sense to him. "And good words make people feel good?"

"Right."

"And magic words make people feel magic?"

Clay's brother hesitated. He was an amateur magician and said magic words all the time—mostly while practicing tricks on Clay—but he'd never thought about them in this particular way. "Um, I guess. How 'bout that?"

"Accadabba!" said Clay, giggling. "Shakazam!"

Sometimes, between siblings or close friends, words take on meanings that can't easily be explained to other people. They become like inside jokes—inside words, as it were. After the elevator episode, *bad word* became Clay and his brother's inside word for *magic word*. Also for *code word* and for *password* and for any other word that had some unique power or significance. For any word that *did* something.

"Can you think of a bad word for me?" Clay's

brother would ask before making a coin disappear behind his hand or before pulling a scarf out of Clay's ear.

"What's the bad word?" Clay would demand, blocking his brother's access to the refrigerator or bathroom.

As Clay grew older and became more and more adept at magic tricks himself (possibly more adept than his brother, although please don't tell anyone I said so), *bad word* maintained its special meaning.

"Hey, bad man, what's the bad word?" they would ask each other in greeting.

When they left coded messages for each other, they would leave hints about the bad word needed to decode the message.

When they did magic shows for their parents or friends, they called themselves the Bad Brothers.

Bad was their bond.

Then, around the time Clay turned eleven, his brother pulled off the biggest, baddest magic trick of all: He disappeared, with little warning and no explanation.

That was almost two years ago. And still Clay would sometimes wonder what he had done to drive his brother away. What had he said? What bad word had he uttered without knowing it?

And what bad magic would make his brother come back?

CHAPTER
ONE

MAGIC SUCKS

Clay was not the type of person who would want a book written about him. I may as well admit that now.

Go ahead, judge me. Call me names. Curse me and the horse I wrote in on. But there it is.

He wasn't shy exactly, but these days, at the age of twelve, almost thirteen, he liked to keep a low profile. He slouched in his chair. He hid his face in a comic book or skateboard magazine. He wore a hoodie, even on warm days. It wasn't that he had a big nose or funny ears or horrible acne; I may be biased, but I think he was almost handsome, in a dried-snot-on-his-sleeve sort of way. It was just that he preferred not to attract attention. Just being looked at for longer than a moment or two made him start jiggling his knee. I can only guess what Clay would have thought about being scrutinized for almost four hundred pages.

Still, it happens to everyone occasionally. Being looked at, I mean.*

On the morning to which I now turn, the morning Clay's life began to tumble helplessly out of control, on *that* morning, kids kept looking at Clay, not just once or twice, but repeatedly, and he had no idea why.

It started as soon as he got to school. The staring and the whispering. The first few kids he caught turned away so fast that he almost thought he'd imagined it. But the next few were bolder; they openly ogled and snickered. One girl he knew just looked at him and shook her head. Two boys he couldn't remember seeing before gave him a thumbs-up. And that was even more alarming.

After he stowed his skateboard in his locker, Clay ducked into the bathroom and examined himself in the mirror. There were no boogers hanging from his nose. His fly wasn't open. His hair was a mess, as usual, but it was hidden under his hoodie. He could see nothing wrong. Nothing that wasn't always wrong, anyway.

---

* AS FOR A BOOK BEING WRITTEN ABOUT YOU, THAT ONLY HAPPENS IF YOU'RE UNLUCKY ENOUGH TO MEET SOMEONE LIKE ME. BEWARE.

Had somebody been spreading rumors about him? Had he been mistaken for someone else? It made no sense.

Clay's first class, language arts, was on the ground floor with an entrance directly off the school-yard next to the basketball court. When he walked up, a half dozen kids were already standing around, talking in hushed voices.

While the others took a few steps back, Clay's best friend, Gideon, stepped right up to Clay.

"Okay, yeah, sure, it's kind of...awesome? And I'm kind of...impressed?" said Gideon. "And I know I'm always saying you should just do this, like what are you waiting for, but here? Now? At school? Seriously?" Gideon had this odd way of speaking so that it always sounded as if he were in the middle of a conversation; it was a little hard to follow, even for Clay.

"I mean, do you have a death wish?" Gideon persisted. "Or are you just totally certifiable?"

"What are you talking about?" Clay asked. "Why is everybody—?" He faltered. "What the—?"

Behind Gideon, on the outside wall of their classroom, there was a freshly painted graffiti mural, or "bomb" as they are sometimes called.

As soon as he saw the mural, Clay's leg started to jiggle. He felt dizzy. He thought he might puke.

MAGIC SUCKS!

it said, in big black bubble letters.

Underneath was a small tag, the signature of the artist:

CLAY

"Don't worry—I took a picture," said Gideon, holding up his phone. "Yeah, they'll kick you out of school, and yeah, you'll have no future, and yeah, your parents will kill you, but at least your words will live forever, right?"

The name, the lettering style, the entire mural was unmistakably, unquestionably, undeniably Clay's.

The trouble was, the mural *wasn't* his. He hadn't painted it. And he had no idea how it had gotten there.

It was as if the mural had appeared by magic.

Very *sucky* magic.

CHAPTER
TWO

A SCHOOL PLAY

While the mural might not have been Clay's, the now-immortal words *MAGIC SUCKS!* were very much his own. It was just that he'd written them elsewhere.

On paper. Not stucco.

Like many great works of literature—and for all I know, like many great works of graffiti art as well—Clay's words (all two of them!) were inspired by the greatest of all wordsmiths, William Shakespeare.

I'm not trying to impress you. Okay, maybe I am trying to impress you. But it's true nonetheless.

Allow me to explain:

Every spring, the sixth graders at Clay's school put on a Shakespeare play. Depending on the kind of student you were, it was either the highlight of your educational career or a major source of dread.

For Clay, as you might guess, it was mainly the latter.

Most years, the sixth graders chose to perform *Macbeth*, because it has witches and bloody hands; or *A Midsummer Night's Dream*, because it has fairies and a man with the head of a donkey, or, as the students always delighted in calling it, the head of an "ass."*

This year, a new language arts teacher, Mr. Bailey, had come to school. To his students' chagrin, he had insisted on choosing the play himself: *The Tempest*. He'd even cast himself as the lead!

THE TEMPEST
BY WILLIAM SHAKESPEARE
STARRING

MR. E. BAILEY
AND HIS SIXTH-GRADE STUDENTS

---

* HEY, DON'T LOOK AT ME.... SHAKESPEARE SAID IT FIRST!

It hardly seemed fair.

By now I'm sure you've read every one of Shakespeare's plays many times over. (If you haven't, I insist you put down this book and start immediately.) But just in case you're experiencing an inexplicable lapse in memory, I will remind you that *The Tempest* is about a sorcerer named Prospero who is stranded on a tropical island with his daughter.

There is a storm. There is a shipwreck. There is a monster. There is romance. There is magic. There is mayhem.

The usual story stuff.

Clay liked the play well enough. At least he liked the opening, with all the crashing thunder and lightning and with the big cardboard ship that got destroyed in the first few minutes of the show. (Somehow, the fact that he'd painted the ship himself made the destruction all the more satisfying.)

What he disliked was his part: Antonio, Prospero's conniving younger brother.

In Clay's opinion, the best roles were Ariel, the tree spirit who casts spells on everyone (not that Clay wanted to wear Ariel's green sparkle tights!*), and Caliban, the monster who is enslaved by Prospero.

Gideon played Caliban. On opening night, Clay

---

* AND NOT THAT IT WOULDN'T BE A FINE THING IF HE DID!

watched in envy as his friend, his face caked with awesomely gruesome Halloween makeup, growled and scowled his way across the stage, cursing everyone in his path.*

As Antonio, Clay didn't get to do much at all. In the play's last act, Prospero forgives Antonio for having stolen his dukedom, but Antonio never gets to apologize, or defend himself, or even curse like Caliban.

Instead, Clay had to stand on the side of the stage next to the smoke machine, listening to the old sorcerer's pompous speeches while trying to forget there was an audience watching his every move.

As the play went on and his eyes started to sting from the smoke, Clay felt increasingly fidgety. And increasingly strange.

Whenever he looked at Mr. Bailey, Clay didn't see his language arts teacher; he didn't even see the character Mr. Bailey was playing, Antonio's older brother, Prospero. He saw his own real-life older brother. The brother who had left almost two

---

* CALIBAN CURSES CONSTANTLY IN *THE TEMPEST*. AT ONE POINT, THE MONSTER, WHO WAS TAUGHT TO SPEAK BY PROSPERO, TURNS TO HIS MASTER AND SAYS, *YOU TAUGHT ME LANGUAGE, AND MY PROFIT ON IT IS, I KNOW HOW TO CURSE. THE RED PLAGUE RID YOU FOR LEARNING ME YOUR LANGUAGE!* BASICALLY CURSING HIS LANGUAGE ARTS TEACHER FOR BEING HIS LANGUAGE ARTS TEACHER. WHICH WAS QUITE AMUSING FOR THE AUDIENCE AT CLAY'S SCHOOL, CONSIDERING MR. BAILEY, A REAL-LIFE LANGUAGE ARTS TEACHER, WAS PLAYING PROSPERO.

years earlier. The brother Clay was doing his best to forget.

He could almost hear that funny humming sound his brother made—*hmmgh*—and his brother's voice saying, "How 'bout that?" His brother was haunting him—through Shakespeare!

Toward the end of *The Tempest*, after Prospero has magically manipulated everyone into doing his bidding, as if they were all puppets in his personal puppet show, the magician renounces magic forever:

> *This rough magic I here abjure,*
> *I'll break my staff,*
> *Bury it certain fathoms in the earth,*
> *And, deeper than did ever plummet sound,*
> *I'll drown my book.**

"Liar," blurted Clay. "You'll never give up magic. You don't care about anything else—"

"Shh!" Gideon whispered from the wings.

Clay blushed red. He hadn't realized he was

---

* Throughout *The Tempest*, Prospero toys with the people around him. He makes them fall in love, fight with each other, and believe each other dead, very much as if he's the writer of the play. For that reason, many believe Prospero's giving up magic was Shakespeare's way of saying *I quit!* Indeed, *The Tempest* was the last play Shakespeare ever wrote—at least, the last one he wrote by himself. I guess after Shakespeare gave up magic, he started needing help with his homework, just like the rest of us.

speaking aloud. He wasn't even sure whom he'd been speaking to: Mr. Bailey or Prospero or his brother. He looked around. Everybody was focused on Mr. Bailey. As far as Clay could tell, nobody else had heard him.

He sighed—silently—with relief.

"And stop jiggling!" Gideon added.

Clay blushed redder. And willed his knee to stop bobbing up and down.

"You're jiggling again."

A week later, Clay and Gideon were sitting next to each other in Mr. Bailey's class, working on essays about the play. It was almost the end of the year and everyone was writing at top speed, as if every syllable brought them closer to summer vacation.

Everyone except Clay.

Gideon poked him in the leg. "Dude, your knee!"

"Sorry," Clay muttered.

Clay, as you may have noticed by now, was a jiggler.

For as long as he could remember, he'd had a mysterious restless energy that kept him in constant motion. It wasn't just his knees. He twiddled his thumbs...tapped his toes...

"Clay, a pencil is for writing," called Mr. Bailey from across the room. "Not wiggling!"

...and wiggled his pencils.

"Um...thinking!"

The exception was when he was skateboarding. With wheels moving below, Clay's body relaxed and his mind was able to focus. Unfortunately, skateboards weren't allowed in the classroom.

Holding his knee down with one hand, and his pencil down with the other, Clay made himself look at the piece of paper on his desk. The paper was blank, and the essay was due in ten minutes.

"Nine more minutes, everybody," Mr. Bailey said to the room.

Make that nine minutes.

Clay glanced at the chalkboard:

> Discuss the role of magic in THE TEMPEST. Why does Prospero break his staff and drown his magic book at the end? If you had magic powers, would you do the same?

What was it about this question? Why was it so difficult for him to answer?

And why did it make his leg jiggle uncontrollably?

As the rest of the class filed out, Clay walked over to Mr. Bailey's desk, which was piled so high with books that Clay had to look over them to see his teacher.

Mr. Bailey was a short, plump man with a pink face and a mutton-chop beard. Today, as was not unusual, he was wearing a knit vest and leather sandals with purple socks. If he looked like a magical character, it wasn't Shakespeare's fierce wizard Prospero; it was Tolkien's harmless hobbit Bilbo.

Mutely, Clay held up his empty sheet of paper.

"What's this?" bellowed Mr. Bailey, standing up but not taking the paper. "Writer's block?"

Despite his small stature, Mr. Bailey had a loud, booming voice, developed, he had bragged to his students more than once, during his many years on the stage.

"Uh-huh," said Clay, bouncing on his toes (which is a double-leg jiggle, if you think about it).

Mr. Bailey nodded. "Actually, I've always thought *block* wasn't the right word. It's more of a knot, wouldn't you say?"

"Uh-huh."

"Or maybe a net," suggested Mr. Bailey, philosophically. "A net one gets all knotted up inside."

"Uh-huh."

"But the point is, young man, you are unable to write."

"Uh-huh."

"Why?" asked Mr. Bailey, leaning toward Clay across the piles of books.

"Uh-huh," said Clay, taking a step back. "Wait, what?"

"Why can't you write?" asked Mr. Bailey, leaning farther. A few books toppled over, but he took no notice. "Is it the subject?"

Clay squirmed. "I don't know. I mean, I don't even believe in magic."

"Do you have to believe in something to write about it?"

"No, I guess not," said Clay.

"Well then...?"

Clay hesitated. How to explain? "My older brother, when I was little, he used to do all these tricks—you know, card tricks, coin tricks, hat tricks. I figured them all out eventually. Magicians just say a bunch of stuff to make you think they're doing something they're not. They're liars. Cheese-wizards."

Mr. Bailey laughed, as if this were a great joke. "Cheese-wizards? I think you're confusing magic-show magic with magic in Shakespeare's time. In those days, magic was taken very seriously."

"What's the difference? The whole idea of magic is fake. It's all cheese-wizardry."

"Well, write that, if you must," said Mr. Bailey.

"I can't," said Clay. "My...brain won't let me."

Mr. Bailey regarded Clay over his desk. "I've heard teachers complain that you are developing an attitude problem, Clay. Is this what they're talking about?"

Clay shrugged, forcing himself not to look away. He didn't think he had an attitude problem; he thought he had an honesty problem. The problem was, he didn't know how not to be honest.

Clay had exceptionally big eyes as well as wild, furry, half-curly hair. When he stared without blinking—a talent he had developed at a young age to irritate his older brother—the effect was quite startling. He looked like a forest animal.

Discomfited, Mr. Bailey was the first to look down.

"I think I have something that might help—"

From under his desk, Mr. Bailey slid out a large cardboard box. Spilling out of the top was the velvet robe he had worn in *The Tempest*, and sticking out of the robe was the gnarled piece of wood that had served as his magic staff. For a second, Clay thought his teacher might give him the staff—either that or hit him over the head with it. But Mr. Bailey put the staff aside and started pulling out more props from the play.

"Ah, here we are—"

Smiling, Mr. Bailey handed Clay a smallish book covered with cracked rust-red leather. Inset in the center of the cover was a tiny triangular mirror.

It took a moment for Clay to recognize what he was looking at. Prospero's magic book. The book

Prospero drowns at the end of *The Tempest*. Clay had never seen it up close before.

"Thanks, but, um, are you sure you won't need this?" asked Clay. "What if you do the play again?"

Mr. Bailey waved his hand dismissively. "Once I've played a role, it's done. The character becomes part of me."

Clay opened the book—or tried to. The pages of the book had dried together, and Clay had to pry them apart in order to look inside. Though old and worn, the pages were blank save for a few stains and some yellowing near the edges.

Mr. Bailey told Clay he didn't have to write about *The Tempest*. As long as he wrote something— anything—in the journal, he would get class credit.

"Like what?" asked Clay, peering into the tiny mirror. His eye peered back at him. He had the odd sensation that he was spying on himself.

"It doesn't matter—I don't even have to read it," said Mr. Bailey.

"But how can you not read it if you look at it?"

Clay thought his logic was irrefutable, but Mr. Bailey just chuckled. "Believe me, I have a lot of prac-tice ignoring things that students write."

He sat down and put his sandaled feet up on his desk, satisfied that the problem was solved.

"Did I ever tell you about the time I played King Lear? Now that was a performance! . . ."

As Mr. Bailey told him about the trials and tribulations of playing Shakespeare's mad king, Clay kept trying to excuse himself.

To no avail.

CHAPTER
THREE

THE WRITING ON THE WALL

That afternoon, when he got home from school, Clay leaned his skateboard against the wall of his bedroom and sat down at his desk—which was actually a drafting table.

For somebody with writer's block, a casual observer might have noted, Clay sure wrote a lot. His desk, his skateboard, the wall his skateboard was leaning against, almost every surface in the room was covered with Clay's writing.

I say writing, but mostly it was his name written again and again. Or variations, like

CLAYMASTER

or  CLAYMATION

or CLAYDO.

Sometimes his name appeared as a simple tag. Other times it was written in twisting three-dimensional letters. In the most elaborate versions, the letter Y was depicted as a fist squeezing clay.

More than anything, Clay's walls resembled a graffiti artist's sketchbook. A talented graffiti artist's sketchbook, I would add. (I'm told hands are notoriously difficult to draw.) But as I said, I may be biased.

As to whether Clay had ever brought one of his graffiti pieces to life somewhere else—on a school wall, for example—the answer is no. At least, not yet.

He pored over pictures of vintage graffiti art. He hunted for murals beneath freeway overpasses. And lately, at Gideon's instigation, he and Gideon had started following around some older kids who had an active graffiti crew (not that the older kids ever tolerated them for very long). But whether it was due to moral qualms or fear of being caught or just his cautious not-quite-thirteen-year-old nature, Clay had yet to write on a single wall outside of his room.

Of course, that doesn't mean he didn't plan to.

Clay pulled the journal out of his backpack and took a pen out of his drawer, ready to write whatever nonsense came to mind.

As soon as he uncapped the pen, it exploded, spraying ink in every direction. A big black splat landed on the red cover of the journal.

"Aaargh!"

The pen was a "magic" pen—a gag gift—given to him by his brother four years earlier.

"Figures," Clay grumbled.

All the gifts his brother gave him exploded—whether they were supposed to or not.

Shaking his head in annoyance, Clay threw the pen to the floor, then wiped off the journal with a tissue. A smeared, star-shaped stain remained.

"Oh, great."

He grabbed a fat black marker off a shelf and opened the journal.

MAGIC SUCKS!

he wrote in swollen bubble letters.

As he dotted the exclamation mark, Clay imagined that he saw a blue flame erupt—and for a flickering second he saw the page fill with words. He blinked, and the page went blank again.

I must be getting tired, he thought, rubbing his eyes.

He tagged the page quickly—

—then closed the journal. There was nothing more to say.

When Clay arrived at school the next morning, he still hadn't decided whether he was going to show Mr. Bailey the journal. It might be wiser, Clay thought, to write something longer, without the word *sucks* in it.

The last thing he expected was that the whole school would see his journal entry blown up on a wall.

MAGIC SUCKS!

CLAY

The words on the wall were nearly identical to those he'd written the night before—the only difference being that they were bigger—much, much bigger. It looked as though somebody had scanned Clay's journal, then run Mr. Bailey's wall through a giant printer.

Clay couldn't understand it. Had somebody snuck into his room in the middle of the night, taken his journal out of his backpack, copied it onto Mr.

Bailey's wall, then returned the journal—all without waking Clay up? He couldn't think of anybody who hated him enough to go to all that trouble.

He felt weirdly exposed, as if it were a long confessional journal entry, not just two words, that had been copied onto the wall.

When Mr. Bailey found him, the bell was ringing and Clay was still staring at the wall, repeatedly tapping his journal as though it might eventually reveal the explanation for the mystery mural. He snapped the journal shut, but he was too late.

"Give that to me," said Mr. Bailey, who suddenly looked a lot less like a hobbit and a lot more like an angry middle school teacher.

Biting his lip, Clay handed him the journal. Mr. Bailey opened it to the offending page.

"I'm very surprised, Clay," said Mr. Bailey, glancing from the journal to the wall and back again. The effort to keep his fury in check was making his cheeks red and puffy. "Writing this in a journal is one thing, but on a wall...?"

"I didn't do it—"

"Is there something you're upset about? Something going on at home, maybe?"

"I said I didn't do it—"

"It will be better for you in the long run if you admit it now," said Mr. Bailey, his cheeks getting bigger and redder by the second. He was beginning to resemble a blowfish.

"But I didn't—"

Mr. Bailey held up his hand. "Save it for the Head of School—"

"Can I at least have the journal back?" said Clay. The journal was the one clue he had about the writing on the wall. The one thing that might help him clear his name.

"Administration office, now!" Mr. Bailey exploded, spit flying everywhere.

Clay walked away, his whole body quivering with anger and confusion. He was about to be suspended, possibly expelled, for something he hadn't done and couldn't explain.

Before leaving the schoolyard, he took a last look at the graffiti. From a distance, the bubble letters appeared to wriggle, snakelike, in the sunlight. His words came in and out of focus, over and over, taunting him with their message.

MAGIC SUCKS!...

MAGIC SUCKS!...

MAGIC SUCKS!...

An effect, it seemed, of the tears welling in his eyes.

CHAPTER
FOUR

A FAMILY MEETING

Other families had Friday night dinner; Clay's family had Friday night meetings.

The meetings started promptly at six o'clock and proceeded according to a strict set of rules, with each family member choosing one topic, and one topic only, for the evening.

When Clay was younger, the topics he chose most often were Spider-Man, the Hulk, and whatever magic trick his brother had most recently taught him.

Lately, he had started keeping his personal enthusiasms to himself. For the family meetings he chose more practical topics, like how he needed a trip slip signed, or how he needed new sneakers, or how he hadn't been to the dentist in over three years.

The fact that he had to bring these things up at a meeting tells you most of what you need to know about his family. Outside of the meetings, I'm afraid to say, they didn't get much family business done, or even spend much time together not getting done the business that they were not getting done.

It hadn't always been that way. Before Clay was born, things were very different. Or so Clay was made to understand by Max-Ernest. Max-Ernest, as you might surmise, was Clay's older brother, and somebody I am intimately familiar with.*

You see, their parents were convinced that they had been too controlling of Max-Ernest when Max-Ernest was little (true). They felt they had overworried, overscheduled, and generally overparented him (also true), and that as a result Max-Ernest was an overanxious person (I won't judge).

When their second son, Paul-Clay (as Clay was then called), was born, they decided to reverse course and take a more hands-off approach.

Their new child, they declared, would parent himself.

The freedom they gave Clay was great when it came to such things as choosing when to go to bed or how many desserts to have. It was not so great when it came to things like, say, trip slips, footwear, or dental care. While he was still living at home, Max-Ernest gave his younger brother as much attention as an ~~overly cerebral~~

---

* IF YOU KNOW THE NAME MAX-ERNEST, YOU KNOW TO KEEP QUIET ABOUT IT. IF THE NAME IS NEW TO YOU, YOU SHOULD KEEP QUIET ABOUT IT ANYWAY. I'M SORRY I CAN'T TELL YOU WHY. JUST TRUST ME ON THIS.

extremely smart and ~~self-absorbed~~ *very busy* person like Max-Ernest was capable of giving. But there was only so much he could do, not being Clay's legal guardian. The Friday night meetings were Max-Ernest's idea. A way of ensuring that their family ship kept sailing.

When Max-Ernest first left for college, he attended a school not very far away, and he always came home on Friday nights. Even after he transferred to a school much farther afield, he kept contributing to the family meetings via weekly postcards. The cards always contained a riddle for Clay to solve ("What travels the world but never leaves its corner? Hint: There's one on this postcard.") or an odd fact for Clay to uncover ("What is the smallest city in the smallest country in the world? Hint: They are one and the same."). Clay didn't always love his brother's riddles and word games (they were usually too silly for Clay, or too difficult, or both); nonetheless, getting a postcard from his brother was the highlight of Clay's week.

Or had been, until the day, almost two years ago now, when that awful card came:

Dear family,
　　You will not hear from me for a while.
　　Do not worry.

　　　　　　　　Love, M-E

Clay looked in vain for hidden clues and secret messages—for a "bad word" that would reveal the note's true meaning—but he didn't find any. As far as he could tell, the message was no more or less than it seemed: a good-bye. The picture on the card was of a rabbit sticking its head out of a top hat, and Clay assumed this meant that Max-Ernest intended to go on the road as a magician, but he had no way of knowing for certain.

Not a single card from Max-Ernest had arrived since, not even on Clay's twelfth birthday.

Most parents, Clay knew, would have made more of an effort to find a missing son. But when he approached his parents about it, they pointed out that Max-Ernest was over eighteen and free to make his own choices.

"Wouldn't you want us to respect your choices?" said his mother. "We expect you to respect ours."

"There's a saying, Clay," said his father. "When you love someone, let them go."

Clay thought his parents were taking that saying too literally, but nothing he said would sway them. For a while, Clay tried to take up the search himself. Alas, Max-Ernest had a deep distrust of technology, and there was no way to contact him electronically that Clay knew of. He did have a physical address for his brother—in Barcelona—and he sent several letters, but they were returned unopened. Next, Clay tried contacting Max-Ernest's friends. They'd all changed their e-mail addresses and phone numbers several times, but finally Clay was able to get a message to Max-Ernest's old friend Cass. She replied through her mother that Clay shouldn't worry, Max-Ernest was fine.

That settled it for Clay. If his brother had cared enough, he would have contacted Clay by now. Obviously, their relationship was no longer very important, if it had ever been.

It was around that time that Clay dropped the *Paul* in *Paul-Clay* and started calling himself simply Clay.* He also stopped being interested in magic and started getting interested in other things, like skateboarding and, more significant for our story, graffiti.

Tonight, as always, Clay had printed a copy of the meeting agenda. It sat on the dinner table in front of him, next to a notebook computer and the frozen pizza he had heated up for himself. At his feet was his skateboard, which he idly kicked back and forth.

---

* HE NEVER TALKED ABOUT IT, BUT I'M GUESSING THE DOUBLE NAME REMINDED HIM TOO MUCH OF MAX-ERNEST'S. INCIDENTALLY, THEIR DOUBLE NAMES CAME FROM THEIR PARENTS' INABILITY TO AGREE ON ANYTHING, A STORY I TELL IN A SERIES OF BOOKS I CAN'T TELL YOU ABOUT.

FRIDAY NIGHT MEETING

1. Clay's act of vandalism—causes (Mom)

2. Clay's act of vandalism—consequences (Dad)

3. Clay's <u>alleged</u> act of vandalism—who really did it? (Clay)

As soon as his father sat down, Clay hit the table with his spoon. It was his turn to chair the family meeting, which in this case was rather like officiating at his own funeral.

"This meeting is now called to order," he said by rote. He looked at the notebook computer propped up on the table next to him. "Mom?"

"Thank you, Clay," said his mother on the computer screen. "First, I want you to know we understand what you've done. The impulse to write on walls is as old as mankind."

Clay's father nodded. "It's a way of saying, *See, world, I am here!* For a boy entering adolescence, this kind of self-expression is very powerful."

"And beautiful. Just think of those wonderful cave paintings at Lascaux!" Clay's mother smiled at her husband. "You remember?"

"How could I forget?" He beamed at the computer, then turned to Clay. "As for *graffiti*, the word

is Italian. First used to describe inscriptions found in the ruins of Pompeii. Another great place to visit!" he added, turning back to his wife. "What is it about volcanoes...?"

Clay's mother blushed on-screen. "Not now, honey!"

Although technically they lived together, Clay's parents could never be in each other's presence for very long without fighting. Thus, they took turns attending the family meeting in person, with one or the other always attending in pixelated form. While this arrangement kept things civil, it had its downside. For reasons Clay could never discern, physical separation always seemed to inspire romantic feelings in his parents.

"Um, guys, can I say something?" asked Clay.

"Of course; you know you can say anything to us," said his father.

"That's why we're here," said his mother (although strictly speaking, they weren't in the same place).

"I tried to tell you guys when I called from school. The graffiti, I—I didn't write it," Clay stammered. "Well, I wrote it—just not on that wall."

Clay did his best to explain, but his parents, perhaps understandably, were very skeptical.

"Clay, you know we aren't here to judge, right?" said his father. "That's not what this is about."

"All we ask is for your honesty," said his mother.

"But I am being honest! I wouldn't do that—it's whacked."

Clay's knee jiggled wildly under the table, sending his skateboard this way and that.

"It's very disappointing that you don't feel you can confide in us," said his father.

"Are you afraid we will withhold love from you if you tell us the truth?" asked his mother.

Clay felt his face reddening. His parents were psychologists, and he hated it when they analyzed his emotions.

"Maybe you'd like to talk about this with another therapist, someone who isn't one of your parents," suggested his father.

"What's the point of talking at all if you're not going to believe me!"

Clay's parents looked at him askance. He had spoken rather loudly.

"Never mind. Just forget it," said Clay through gritted teeth. "It doesn't matter whether I did it anyway."

He took a bite of pizza and chewed furiously.

"What matters, then?" demanded his father.

"That the school thinks I did. And now you have to figure out a punishment."

"Let's not use the word *punishment*," said Clay's father. "Let's use the word *consequence*."

"Whatever—if I don't have one, they're not letting me into seventh grade."

Already, he had been compelled to paint over the graffiti, and he had been suspended for the remaining week of school. However, the school had made it clear that some further action must be taken if Clay was ever going to return.

"All right, Clay, have it your way," said Clay's mother, as if she were indulging him in a meaningless diversion. "What is to be your consequence?"

Clay was very curious—in a morbid sort of way—to hear the answer to this question. His parents had very little experience disciplining him, if any. As Clay would have been the first to admit, this was not because his behavior was especially good (although, I hasten to add, his behavior wasn't especially bad); it was because his parents considered themselves too enlightened for the old-fashioned reward-and-punishment system.

"Well, Clay?" prompted his father.

Clay blinked in disbelief. "You want me to come up with my own punishment?"

"Naturally," said his mother.

"It won't mean anything if we decide for you," said his father.

Clay felt perversely disappointed. Of course, he didn't *want* to be punished, but he'd hoped that for once his parents would act more like normal parents.

"Well..." he said, stalling. "Don't parents usually ground their kids when they do something like write on a wall?"

Clay's mother looked out at him from the computer screen as if he had suggested a trip to Mars. "Should we ground you, Clay? Is that what you want?"

Clay shrugged. "If I wanted you to, wouldn't that kinda defeat the purpose?"

Before anybody could say anything more, the doorbell rang, or more accurately, buzzed. Glad of an excuse to leave the room, Clay leaped up to answer.

CHAPTER
FIVE

A SUMMER CAMP FOR STRUGGLING YOUTH

When Clay opened the door, he saw a large envelope resting on the doorstep. His heart started beating fast; it had to be from his brother. Who else would send mail timed to arrive in the middle of a Friday night meeting?

Clay's mind raced with possibilities as he picked up the envelope. Would Max-Ernest at last tell them where he was? Might he even announce that he was coming home?

But then he saw the return address: Mr. Bailey. No doubt the envelope contained a letter repeating the threat about his not getting to enter seventh grade.

No longer very excited, Clay walked back to the

dining room and emptied the envelope onto the table.

There was no letter, only a stack of summer camp brochures.

A Post-it was attached:

Maybe one of these is right for Clay?
Regards, E. Bailey.

Camp.

Clay had never gone to camp. He'd never even gone on a camping trip. Camp was something that other families did. Like Little League. Or piano lessons. Or family dinner.

Why was Mr. Bailey suggesting camp?

As soon as he started looking closely at the brochures, Clay saw the answer: All the camps were designed for kids with problems of one sort or another. The first offered to "treat mood disorders through music." Which sounded fine except Clay didn't have a mood disorder—or at least not a *diagnosed* mood disorder, agreed his parents—and he didn't play any musical instruments. The next was a high-security facility for violent and "seriously at-risk" youth, with "on-call psychiatric assistance." ("I already have on-call psychiatric assistance," Clay pointed out to his parents. "You guys.") Another offered "rehabilitation through construction"—in other words, Clay thought, slave labor.

The most intriguing brochure featured a photo of a lake backed by a waterfall and, in the far distance, a smoking volcano. A llama grazed in the foreground.

At his mother's request, Clay read the text aloud.

Clay looked up from the brochure. "Animal husbandry? No way am I being some animal's husband."*

"There's no need to joke about it," said Clay's father. "This camp could be exactly what we're looking for."

"Don't tell me you want me to go to this place!" exclaimed Clay. "It's for delinquents."

Clay's mother nodded. "Didn't you say you wanted a consequence?"

"But I've already got summer plans," Clay protested.

"What plans?" asked his father.

---

* In most cases, you will be relieved to hear, animal husbandry has nothing to do with husbands or wives or any kind of marriage at all. Rather, it is the branch of agriculture that deals with livestock, specifically the care and breeding of animals such as cattle, hogs, sheep, and horses.

EARTH RANCH

A SUMMER CAMP FOR STRUGGLING YOUTH

Hike a volcano, feed a llama, cook over an open fire....
Has your child made poor choices? Behaved aggressively or inappropriately? Stolen or defaced other people's property? Refused to listen to reason?

Whether your child has been in trouble with the police or just the school principal, early intervention is the key to future success.

Earth Ranch, a summer camp on rugged and remote Price Island, helps children outgrow problem behaviors and reach their full potential away from the temptations of modern technology. Imagine: a summer with no computers, no television, no video games, not even a cell phone.

Through wilderness survival training, animal husbandry, and simple comradeship, our campers learn to value their environment, their community, and, most important, themselves.

Earth Ranch is a completely self-sustaining ranch and farm; we grow our own food, produce our own energy, and recycle our own waste. We are a model for living responsibly in the twenty-first century.

This is life the way nature intended.

Sign up your child today!

"To go to the skate park. I'm turning thirteen, remember? I'll finally be old enough to go without an adult."

Near the skate park, there was a famously treacherous hill—called Kill Hill by skaters—that Clay and Gideon had vowed to conquer that summer. He didn't feel it was necessary to mention Kill Hill to his parents, however.

"That's not a summer plan," said his mother. "That's a one-hour activity."

"Besides, you're not turning thirteen for weeks," said his father.

Clay seethed as he ate a second slice of the now cold and stringy pizza.

Why would they want to send him to a camp for bad kids, or "struggling youth," as the camp called them? It was one thing for his teacher to think he was a degenerate, but didn't his parents think better of him? Or did they only pretend to be so permissive and accepting? He almost wished he really had been the one to write on Mr. Bailey's wall; it would serve his parents right.

Later, Clay hunted online for some incriminating piece of information about Earth Ranch or Price Island that would convince his parents to let him stay home.

Here is what he learned:

Price Island is a small private island in the Pacific Ocean, approximately eighty miles northwest of Hawaii. The island belongs to the estate of the deceased Wall Street financier Randolph Price and is home to Mount Forge, one of the few privately owned active volcanoes in the world. An eccentric collector of art, books, and other curiosities, Price spent a vast fortune building a palace, which was destroyed in minutes when the volcano erupted. Currently, the island is believed to be uninhabited.

About Earth Ranch itself, Clay could find no information at all. He looked at travel websites, summer camp websites, information-for-parents-of-troubled-kids websites, but nary a mention did he see.

He called his father back into the dining room and called up his mother on his computer. Both his parents had been up late working; neither liked being disturbed.

"Guess what—Earth Ranch is totally off the grid!" he said. "What kind of camp doesn't have a website?"

"An old-fashioned camp," said his father.

"Yeah, too old-fashioned," said Clay. "It probably doesn't have flushing toilets."

"Your father and I have discussed it," said Clay's

mother. "We've decided a consequence isn't such a bad idea after all."

"It's not the graffiti," said his father. "It's your failure to take responsibility."

"There has clearly been a breakdown in our communication," said his mother. "Maybe some time apart will help."

"Great," said Clay, incensed. "You never punish me—sorry, *consequence* me—once in my whole life, and suddenly you're sending me to Alcatraz...on a volcano...with llamas!"

That night, Clay dreamed about the journal. But this time when he looked into the tiny mirror on the front, he didn't see himself; he saw a volcano exploding in flames. Rivers of lava gushed in all directions, until the lava's red glow eclipsed everything else and merged with the journal's red cover.

CHAPTER
SIX

A LOOSE SCREW

I won't tell you how Clay spent his next week—not because he did anything you wouldn't approve of, but because he hardly did anything at all. Except fret about where he would be spending his summer and about whether he'd have a school to return to in the fall.

When the Earth Ranch enrollment packet arrived, it did nothing to assuage Clay's anxiety. Indeed, the brief letter that accompanied the packet raised more questions than it answered. While noting that Clay had applied late and would be enrolling a week after the other campers, the letter said that the camp would make an exception for him because of the "special circumstances" of his case. Furthermore, his entire fee would be covered by the estate of Randolph Price, the camp's founder.

What special circumstances, Clay wondered.

Weren't there kids who were more deserving than he was? Disabled kids, maybe, or poor kids? Kids who were better students? Better athletes? Better artists? Or, if they wanted problem kids, weren't there worse criminals, tougher cases to crack?

What was most peculiar, however, was the packing list—which was quite long, considering everything was supposed to fit in a single backpack. The list included routine items like a water bottle, sunscreen, flashlight, hat, bandanna, socks, and underwear, but also some rather unexpected and even alarming things, such as a gas mask, a life jacket, and a bag of carrot tops. The last item, carrot tops, was underlined, and accompanied by a handwritten notation saying it was very important that the carrot tops be kept handy during Clay's trip to camp.

"You think I'm going to be feeding rabbits, or is it for dusting furniture?" Clay asked his parents at their next family meeting.

"Maybe the carrot tops are for recycling?" suggested his father, whose turn it was to participate via computer screen.

"I think you mean composting," said his mother, now in the room with Clay.

"I think this camp is crazy," said Clay.

Travel instructions were equally specific. In three days' time, a parent was to take him as far as

the seaport, where he was to meet a privately char-
tered seaplane at dock sixteen at precisely 9:12 a.m.
Clay was to be wearing his life jacket and an old pair
of sneakers.

"It's like they're expecting the plane to crash
into the sea!" Clay complained.

Predictably, Clay's parents couldn't agree on
who would take him to the plane. Unpredictably, and
at the last minute, both elected to escort him (in person); and they arrived at the gate to dock sixteen as a
surprisingly normal-looking family of three.

As his parents walked down the ramp to the
dock, Clay lingered, inspecting the various tags
scratched into the gate. Then he jumped onto his
skateboard for one last ride. The ramp wasn't exactly
Kill Hill, but it would have to do for this summer.
(In the Earth Ranch enrollment packet, skateboards
were listed very clearly among forbidden items.) He
sailed down to the dock and sped across the wooden
boards, vibrating like a jackhammer. When he got
close to the end of the dock, he popped the tail of his
board, attaining a last fleeting moment of air, then
skidded to a stop, his face flushed.

He glanced at his parents to see if they were
watching—would they be angry or impressed?—but
their attention was fixed on the object in front of
them. Clay brushed away his disappointment; it
wasn't the first time their attention was elsewhere.

Tethered to the end of the dock was an old sea-plane with two rusty propellers and two ski-like legs. A man with tattooed arms and a long ponytail was attacking one of the plane's propellers with a wrench. Next to him, a fat bulldog lazed in the sun, pink tongue glistening. The man grunted in frustration, then gave up and threw his wrench into the sea.

Clay eyed the plane dubiously. It looked like it would have enough trouble staying afloat on the water, let alone flying in the sky.

"Is this the plane for Price Island?" asked Clay's father.

"Do you see any other planes?" asked the man.

"No boats, either," said Clay's mother. "We thought this dock was closed."

The man grinned. A gold tooth glinted. "That's why I dock here. Much cheaper."

"As in free, you mean," said Clay, smirking. "Is that even... allowed?"

"Clay!" reprimanded his father. "I'm sure he wouldn't dock here without permission."

Clay's mother nodded. "You're going to a camp where they teach kids to respect the rule of law. I hardly think they'd hire a lawbreaker to fly you there!"

The man's smile faded a little bit. "Right you are, ma'am. Even so, maybe we'd better not mention this to the folks at camp, eh?"

The pilot slapped Clay on the shoulder. "You must

be the lucky camper. I'm Skipper." He gave his dog a pat on the head. "This here's my copilot, Gilligan."

The bulldog took a lumbering step toward Clay and drooled all over his hand.

"Hey," said Clay, wiping his hand on his pants.

"What about the propeller?" asked Clay's father. "Is there a problem?"

"Oh, just a couple loose screws..." said Skipper. "Just kiddin'! This plane's sturdier than a tank. Besides, a little rattling builds character, right?"

Clay seized the initiative, pulling his parents aside. "Can I talk to you guys a second?

"Are you really going to make me get on that thing?" he whispered.

"You won't get into seventh grade otherwise, remember?" said his father.

"It won't matter what grade I'm in, if I'm dead!"

"Don't be so dramatic, Clay," said his mother.

Skipper whistled from beside the plane. "All aboard! Last call for Price Island!"

"Fine. Nice knowing you," Clay said to his parents.

Fuming, Clay thrust his skateboard into the hands of his surprised father and headed for the plane. His parents were as crazy as the pilot, he decided. It would be a relief to get away from them.

About to step in, Clay looked at the side of the plane. The letters had chipped away, along with the rest of the paint, but he could just make out a name: *The Tempest.*

"*The Tempest?* Like the play?" he asked, surprised.

"No, like the plane," said Skipper, as if Clay had suggested something idiotic. "It means 'storm.'"

"I know, but it's also the name of this Shakespeare play I was in."

"Oh, is it now?" said Skipper mockingly. "I didn't know I had such a literary traveler on my hands." He turned to his dog. "We'll have to mind our p's and q's, won't we, Gilligan?"

Clay smiled weakly, wishing he hadn't said anything.

Five minutes later, Clay was wishing even more fervently that he had stayed home.

After making several sputtering circles in the water like an oversized bird learning to fly, the plane was finally airborne, but Clay was not convinced it would maintain altitude. The cabin wasn't pressurized or even very well sealed. It was cold and noisy, and Clay, who had inherited a slight fear of heights from his brother, could see bits of blue water through the cracks. He kept picturing the plane plummeting back to earth—and deep into the sea.

His life jacket around his neck, he was squeezed into the back of the plane between his backpack and a large cardboard box addressed to *Jonah P—, c/o*

Earth Ranch, Price Island. At least we're headed to the right place, Clay thought.

Gilligan, the bulldog copilot, occupied the only seat other than Skipper's, which would have been fine except that the dog kept turning his head around and slobbering all over Clay's neck. When Clay pulled away from him, he growled.

Clay tapped Skipper on the shoulder. The pilot pulled his right headphone away from his right ear. "What's that, Shakespeare?"

"Hey, you think your dog could maybe turn back around?" Clay asked, wiping dog saliva off his neck.

"His name is Gilligan."

"Sorry. Do you think you could get Gilligan to turn around?"

"You don't like dogs, huh, Shakespeare?"

"I like dogs; I just don't like slobber. My name is Clay, by the way."*

Skipper pulled his headphones down around

---

* Author's note: *dogs*

As you may have noticed, authors and filmmakers tend to create heroes who love animals—in particular, dogs. The common perception is that a canine companion makes your character more sympathetic. For this reason, I was reluctant to share some of the above lines of dialogue with you. The truth is that Clay hadn't had much experience with dogs. Once, shortly after his brother left home, Clay asked for a dog. But his parents got into such a big fight about what kind of dog to get, who would get it, and who would care for it that he never asked for a dog—or for anything else—ever again.

As for me, I have a cat.

his neck and turned to face Clay, leaving the plane's controls free. The plane dipped slightly, and Clay wondered nervously if it had an autopilot function.

"You think people don't slobber...Shakespeare?" Skipper asked. His bloodshot eyes stared at Clay.

"Sure they do, but—forget it." This was one time, Clay decided, when it was best not to argue.

Thankfully, Skipper turned to face the windshield and put his hands back on the controls. Clay noticed that Skipper's biceps was decorated with a tattoo of a bulldog.

"Cool tattoo," Clay said, trying to be conciliatory. "Looks just like him."

"You mean Gilligan? All dogs look alike to you, don't they?" said the pilot, insulted. "This isn't Gilligan. This is my last dog, Tattoo."

"You mean this is your last tattoo of a dog?"

"No, this is a tattoo of my last dog, Tattoo." The pilot turned around, causing the plane to dip again.

"That was his name? Tattoo?" asked Clay, wishing he'd never brought it up.

"Yeah, you know, like the guy on *Fantasy Island*," said the pilot.

"What's *Fantasy Island*?"

"*Fantasy Island*. The TV show. Who doesn't know *Fantasy Island*?"

"Me."

"And I suppose you don't know *Gilligan's Island*, either, huh, Shakespeare?"*

"Nope."

Skipper groaned in disgust. "You know all these fancy-pants plays and you don't even know a simple TV show? How you going to survive out on Price Island when you don't even know *Gilligan's Island*?!"

"Actually, the play *The Tempest*—it takes place on an island, too."

"Oh, does it now? I guess you don't need TV, then, after all, huh? Shakespeare thought of everything."

That pretty much ended the conversation. The dog continued to drool all over Clay. Clay tried pulling away from him; it didn't work.

"Try scratching his ears," said the pilot after a few minutes. "He likes that."

Sure enough, Gilligan started wagging his tail as soon as Clay started scratching behind his ears. Alas, he didn't stop slobbering.

---

* FANTASY ISLAND AND GILLIGAN'S ISLAND WERE BOTH POPULAR TELEVISION SERIES IN THE 1970S. ON GILLIGAN'S ISLAND THERE WERE SEVEN CASTAWAYS ON A DESERTED ISLAND. MIRACULOUSLY, THEY WERE ALWAYS CLEAN-SHAVEN AND PERFECTLY COIFFED. NONETHELESS, THEY WANTED NOTHING MORE THAN TO GET OFF THE ISLAND AND WERE ALWAYS HOPING FOR RESCUE. ON FANTASY ISLAND THE SITUATION WAS THE OPPOSITE. GUESTS VISITED FANTASY ISLAND FROM ALL OVER THE WORLD, PAYING ASTRONOMICAL FEES TO HAVE THEIR GREATEST WISHES COME TRUE.

Clay woke about two and a half hours later, covered in dog drool.

"There it is. Price Island," said the pilot, pointing out the window. "Your new home away from home."

Clay craned his neck to look. Clouds clustered around the plane, obscuring his view. Ahead, where Skipper had pointed, the clouds were so thick, all Clay could see was a wall of white. Or grayish white.

"I can't see anything."

"No kidding. It's the bloody vog."*

"The what?"

"The *vog*. You really don't know anything about where you're going, do you, Shakespeare?"

"Why, what's to know?"

"Who says there's anything to know," the pilot snapped. "Besides, nothing I tell you is going to do you any good now, is it?"

"Well, what's *vog*?" asked Clay, who was getting increasingly nervous.

---

* *VOG* IS A PORTMANTEAU (PRONOUNCED LIKE *PORT MAN TOE*): A WORD THAT IS MADE BY SQUEEZING TWO WORDS TOGETHER. IN THIS CASE *VOLCANIC* AND *SMOG*. FUNNILY ENOUGH, THE WORD *SMOG* IS ALSO A PORTMANTEAU. IT COMBINES THE WORDS *SMOKE* AND *FOG*. WHICH MAKES *VOG* A DOUBLE PORTMANTEAU. A PORTMANTEAU-TEAU, PERHAPS. *VOG*, BY THE WAY, IS A REAL WORD; I DIDN'T MAKE IT UP. IF YOU DON'T BELIEVE ME, ASK SOMEBODY WHO LIVES ON THE BIG ISLAND OF HAWAII. I PROMISE, THIS PERSON WILL HAVE A LOT TO SAY ABOUT VOG.

"You're so smart, figure it out. Think *v-* word then *-og* word...vuh-og."

"*Vampire dog?*"

"No, vog is volcanic smog." The pilot shook his head. "*Vampire dog?* You really have something against dogs, don't you?"

"No...what are you doing?"

Clay was thrown to the side as the plane entered a steeply banked turn.

"Circling the island so they know we're here."

"But how can they see us?" asked Clay, gripping the seat in front of him.

"They can't. But sometimes they can hear."

Just as the plane tilted so much that its wings were near vertical and Clay thought they were going to drop out of the sky, the vog suddenly cleared. Instead of all white, Clay now saw all black. It took a moment for him to realize he was looking at land and not ocean or outer space. He was torn between terror of the plane falling from the sky and fascination with the forbidding sight below. It looked as though the entire island had been charred in a massive fire. Where was he going, Mordor?*

---

* Mordor, of course, is the home of the dark lord Sauron in J. R. R. Tolkien's *Lord of the Rings*. Clay may not have been familiar with *Fantasy Island*, but he had read his fair share of fantasy literature—before decrying all things magical.

"Why's it all black like that?" he asked when Skipper had at last righted the plane, and Clay's heart rate had returned to normal.

"Lava. That's all lava rock."

"Sheesh. That must have been a gnarly eruption."

In the vast blackness, he could just make out the twists and turns of what must once have been raging rivers of lava headed into the sea.

"What are those white squiggly things?" Clay asked.

"You'll see...."

As they skirted closer to the shore, the white squiggles became letters; they were written on the black rock beach like chalk letters on a blackboard. Clay admired them for a second. Then—

"Wait!" he cried. "It says SOS! Somebody's in trouble!"

"Sorry to disappoint you, Shakespeare, but those letters have been there for years. So whoever it was..." The pilot trailed off.

"What? What happened to them?"

"What makes you think I know?" said the pilot evasively. "Now hold on...."

The plane hit the water with a tremendous splash, like a giant child doing a belly flop.

They taxied for a moment, then Skipper turned off the propellers, and the plane coasted to a stop.

When the windows cleared of spray, Clay glanced toward shore. The black rock beach looked decidedly inhospitable.

"Where's the dock?"

"There isn't any," said Skipper, who was already climbing out of his seat.

"You have a raft or something?" asked Clay, starting to sweat (whether from nervousness or the tropical heat, he couldn't have said).

"A raft? What do you think this is, *The Love Boat*? No, don't tell me, you never heard of *The Love Boat*, either," said the pilot, opening the door.* "You gotta swim, Shakespeare. Or walk. It ain't deep."

Clay felt a rush of warm, thick tropical air as he looked out at the turquoise water.

"What about my backpack?" He gestured to the large backpack beside him—purchased especially for camp and already bursting at the seams.

The pilot shrugged. "It'll dry."

Before Clay could protest, Skipper threw Clay's heavy backpack into the water.

"Hey! It's gonna sink!"

---

* THE LOVE BOAT, AS YOU PROBABLY GUESSED, IS ANOTHER TELEVISION SERIES FROM THE 1970S. IT CHRONICLES THE ADVENTURES OF A CRUISE SHIP CREW, AND AN EVER-CHANGING CAST OF PASSENGERS SEARCHING FOR LOVE.

"So get going. I don't like hanging out here any longer than I have to."

"Why? You make it sound like there's something wrong with this place."

"Just go already, will ya?"

There was no way for Clay to change into his bathing suit; it was in the backpack. Bracing himself, he closed his eyes and jumped out of the plane, fully dressed.

The water was surprisingly warm and, as Skipper had promised, not very deep. Clay's feet hit bottom just as his head was about to go under. When he straightened up, he found that the water was chest-high and as clear as a swimming pool. He could see his sneakers digging into the sand. His backpack was floating nearby, slowly drifting out to sea, shoulder straps and waist belt trailing behind. Clay lunged for it.

As soon as Clay had secured his backpack on his back, Skipper held a large cardboard box out the airplane door. Clay recognized the box that had been taking up half the space on the plane.

"You're supposed to deliver this," the pilot shouted.

"How—?!"

"Hold up your hands!" Skipper tossed the box in Clay's direction. Clay almost fell backward when the box landed in his hands, but somehow he managed to keep it out of the water.

He looked toward the shore; it was a good forty feet away. Getting there without dropping the box was not going to be easy.

It was then that a more serious problem occurred to him: "Hey, Skipper!" he shouted. "There's nobody there."

"You were expecting flowers and coconut drinks?"

With that, Skipper closed the door of the plane.

Cursing to himself and holding the box above his head, Clay started wading as quickly as he could—which was not very quickly—toward dry land.

"Hey, Shakespeare!" Clay turned to see Skipper waving out of an open window.

"Yeah?"

"I should probably warn you...."

"About what?" Clay shouted.

Skipper shouted something in return, but Clay couldn't quite make it out; the propellers were whirring again.

"Did you say, *Beware—you—scary?*"

Skipper shouted again, louder.

"*Beware—the—you—bury?*" Clay repeated.

"Right!"

"So I'm supposed to bury something? Or not bury it?"

But by then the plane was taking off, leaving crashing waves in its wake.

CHAPTER
SEVEN

MAROONED

I f you've ever been shipwrecked on a desert island, then you know how Clay felt. Me, I've never been shipwrecked anywhere. Car-wrecked, yes. Train-wrecked, yes. Shipwrecked, no. (Unless you count the time my cat wrecked that model sailboat I was building out of matchsticks; boy, was I mad about that!) So you'll have to pardon any inaccuracies as I do my best to re-create the scene on the island after Clay waded ashore. Of course, having read about plenty of castaways, I do consider myself something of an expert.*

Clay stood on the black rock beach, drenched

---

* PERHAPS THE MOST FAMOUS LITERARY CASTAWAY IS ROBINSON CRU-SOE, WHO LANDS ON THE ISLAND OF DESPAIR WITH ONLY A FEW ANIMALS FOR COMPANY. HE GOES ON TO BUILD A HOME, FIGHT CANNIBALS, AND INSPIRE COUNTLESS NOVELS AND MOVIES AND REALITY TELEVISION SHOWS. THINK OF WHAT A BRIGHT FUTURE LIES IN FRONT OF CLAY!

from head to toe. His feet sloshed in his shoes whenever he shifted his weight. His backpack sat beside him, leaking seawater. The still-semidry box he was supposed to deliver to camp lay about a yard away, where he'd dropped it in relief when he finally made it to dry land.

But to what land had he made it? Where was he?

In one direction lay an unending expanse of blue; in the other, an unending expanse of black. The lava had demolished everything in its wake. The landscape looked so lifeless, so alien, it could have been a photo taken by a Mars rover.

His eyes landed on a snaking line of white shells. It was the first *S* of the SOS sign he'd spied earlier from the plane, now only a few feet away. The letters were about twenty feet long from top to bottom, and remarkably well preserved, considering they were so old.

It must have taken somebody a long time to collect so many shells, Clay thought. These were letters made by somebody very determined.

Somebody desperate.

Somebody afraid.

A castaway marooned on a tropical island, for example.

Clay felt a wave of panic overtake him. What was he going to do if nobody ever came? Try to make a shelter out of his backpack? Spear fish to eat? Rub two rocks together and build a fire? He knew how to do exactly none of those things. As for drinking water, his water bottle was already half-empty.

When Clay was younger, his brother's best friend, Cass, had been a survivalist. She constantly lectured Clay about disaster preparedness. If only he had paid more attention!

Don't freak, he told himself. Think. You may not be a survivalist, but this isn't the first time you've been on your own.

Clay felt in his pocket for his wallet. It was wet, but still there. The black leather wallet was a gift from his brother—one of the few Clay had kept—and it had a secret compartment. Clay moved his school ID from the secret compartment to the main compartment; that way, if he perished on the sand, the person who discovered his body would be able to identify him.

The sun was getting hotter, and as his clothes dried, he could feel it burning his skin. In a matter of minutes, he went from being wet with seawater to wet with sweat.

A large boulder about twenty feet inland looked like it might offer some shade. It would be a better place to wait, Clay decided. At least he wouldn't get sunstroke.

He hoisted his backpack onto his back, picked up

the cardboard box, and then sloshed across the black rocks in his wet shoes.

As soon as he stepped behind the boulder, Clay let out a cry of surprise.

He wasn't alone after all.

A four-legged animal was standing in the shade of the boulder, drinking from a near-empty bucket of water. The animal was about the size of a pony, and he had the long ears of a rabbit, the long face of a kangaroo, and the long, shaggy brown-and-white fur of a rug in Clay's father's office. The rug, Clay remembered, came from Peru.

Duh, it's a llama, Clay said to himself.

A large bumblebee buzzed around the water bucket, and the llama kept twitching his head, trying to make the bee go away. Clay couldn't tell whether he should approach or whether he'd be shooed away as well.

The llama was wearing a bridle with a rope attached where you might expect to find reins. A greeting card was hanging from his neck:

Hola. ¿Cómo se llama? Yo me llamo Como C. Llama.

During his preschool years, Clay's favorite

cartoon had featured a Spanish-speaking boy naturalist who was always saving animals with his girl cousin, and Clay still knew enough of the language to translate:

Hello. How do you call yourself? I call myself Como C. Llama.

The llama's name was *What is your name?* How cheesy can you get, Clay thought, smiling despite himself.

He flipped over the card. On the other side was a note in English:

Go west, young man. The llama will guide you.

PS-Don't let him eat anything you didn't personally bring with you.

So he had a guide. That was the good news.

The guide was a llama. That was the bad news.

Clay gave the llama a tentative pat on the back of the neck. The llama didn't seem to mind. Then again, he didn't seem to particularly like it, either.

Around the llama's back there was a leather strap that functioned, Clay assumed, like a bridle. Awkwardly, Clay placed the cardboard box on top of the llama and partially secured it with some of the extra string hanging from the animal's neck. The now-empty water bucket he tied above the llama's rump.

"Well, here goes nothing," Clay muttered. The llama had obviously been sent as some kind of test, and there was nothing to do but try.

He tightened the waist belt of his backpack. Then he grabbed the llama's harness and tried to swing himself onto the llama's back, behind the box.

His ears flat back on his head, the llama snorted and jerked away. Clay landed on his backpack, belly up, arms waving, like a beetle in distress.

Before he could recover, the llama spit in his face— a big green wad of chewed grass and llama saliva.

"Yuck! Man, did you have to do that?!"*

As Clay wiped the thick spittle off his cheek, the llama sat down on his back legs, camel-style.

"Great," said Clay, pushing himself up.

When he got to his feet, he grabbed the rope and pulled, but the llama barely blinked.

"C'mon, boy—get up!"

The llama still refused to budge.

Exasperated, Clay sat back down. His backpack fell from his shoulders.

---

* MORAL OF THE STORY: NEVER RIDE A LLAMA. THEY'RE PACK ANIMALS, NOT HORSES. OTHER MORAL OF THE STORY: LLAMAS SPIT. IT'S NOT JUST A MYTH.

"Fail...epic...flippin'...fail."

Whoever had left the llama for him was downright cruel. Somebody who delighted in torture. And he was supposed to spend the summer under this person's care? Forget it. When he got to camp, he was going to call his parents and demand that he go home right away.

Correction: *if* he got to camp.

The greeting card dangled from the llama's furry neck, taunting Clay. *PS—Don't let him eat anything you didn't personally bring with you,* Clay read again.

"What're you supposed to eat, then, my shoes? Oh—I know!"

He started digging in his backpack. Before Clay could pull the carrot tops all the way out, the llama grabbed the entire bunch with his mouth.

"Hey!"

As Clay yanked his hand away, the llama gulped down the carrot tops in one bite.

The llama looked expectantly at Clay.

"Sorry, I don't have any more," said Clay, examining his hand to confirm that he wasn't missing any fingers.*

The llama nudged him.

"I told you. No more carrot tops."

---

* CLAY NEEDN'T HAVE WORRIED; LLAMAS HAVE NO FRONT TEETH.

The llama nudged him again. The card around his neck flipped over.

Hola. ¿Cómo se llama? Yo me llamo Como C. Llama.

"I know, I read that already. Your name is a joke. I get it. Like *como se llama*. It's hilarious. A laugh riot. Total cheese-wizardry."

The llama nudged him again. More like poked him. If you can poke with your mouth.

"What do you want already?" A funny thought crossed Clay's mind. "I'm not answering, am I? You want to know *my* name?"

Well, it couldn't hurt to try.

Sheepishly, he introduced himself. "I'm Clay. *Yo me llamo Clay.*"

The llama nodded his head in a way that almost looked like he was saying hello.

"Um, nice to meet you," said Clay. *"Mucho gusto."*

Wow, Clay thought to himself, five minutes alone on a deserted island and you're already talking to animals! Next thing you'll be having conversations with the rocks.

"Now, stand up. Please. *Por favor.*"

Whether because he understood or (more likely)

because the bumblebee kept buzzing in his ear, the llama rose to his feet.

"*Gracias*," said Clay, relieved. "Now let's go—*ivámonos!*"

He picked up the rope attached to the llama's bridle and held it like a leash, then started walking along the lava field road in a direction he hoped was west. (He knew that the sun always sets in the west, but the sun was too high to say with certainty which way it would set.) The llama followed slowly but willingly behind.

"Wait, you're supposed to be guiding me, Como, remember?" said Clay, stopping to let the llama take the lead. "This *is* the way, right? *Correctamente?* Or, er, *correcto?*"

The llama didn't respond, but he didn't switch directions, either. He just kept going. Clay took this as an affirmative.

The bee circled the llama one last time, then flew away across the lava fields.

The road, which was less a road than a trail, and sometimes hardly even a trail, twisted this way and that, seemingly without rhyme or reason. As far as Clay could tell, they were following the coastline, but they also seemed to be rising. At least, that is what he judged by the tiredness in his legs.

Around them, in every direction, was lava—in ever stranger and more menacing formations. There were lava pits and lava towers and big, looping lava arches. Some lava formations looked like castles. Others looked almost like people, lurching through the lava fields.*

Despite the heat, Clay shivered.

"What happened here, anyway? *¿Qué pasó?*" he asked the llama. "It's like the world was just going about its business and then—*boom!* Huge explosion. Full-on apocalypse. I mean, where are we? *¿Dónde estamos?*" He gestured to his surroundings.

"I know, I know, the real question is, why am I talking in Spanish to a llama?" he said, taking a swig from his water bottle. "*¿Por qué yo hablo español?* What do you care what language I speak? You're a llama!"

A flock of blue birds flew overhead. Parrots.

"Now, those guys—they're the ones who talk, right?"

Clay called out to them. "Hey, parrots! *Hablas español* or *ingles?* Is this the way to Earth Ranch—you know, the camp for bad kids? *Hijos malos.*"

The birds squawked in answer—but in a way

---

* ACTUALLY, THESE WERE NOT PEOPLE BUT LAVA TREES—TREES THAT HAD BEEN COVERED IN LAVA AND INCINERATED BY THE HEAT, LEAVING A HOLLOW LAVA MOLD IN THE SHAPE OF A TREE. A PHENOMENON REMARKABLY SIMILAR TO THE WAY MOLDS FOR BRONZE STATUES ARE TRADITIONALLY MADE, THE SO-CALLED LOST-WAX METHOD.

that sounded nothing like English or Spanish or any other human language. Nonetheless, they were the first living things Clay had encountered on the lava trail.

Cheered, he continued walking.

As the trail began to steepen, the lava ended with unexpected, almost surreal suddenness. Behind, everything was black. Ahead, everything was green. A sea of grass. And in the distance, a forest.

A grayish bush with purplish berries grew on the side of the trail. The llama stopped and was about to have a nibble when Clay remembered his instructions and pulled the llama away. Though small, the berries looked juicy and Clay wanted to try one himself, but he decided it would be unfair to eat what the llama couldn't. Besides, the berry might be poisonous.

He thought of the pilot's cryptic warning: *Beware—the—you—bury.* Could Skipper have meant *berry* and not *bury*? As in, *Beware, don't you eat that berry!?* Or maybe it was a kind of berry—a *you-berry* or *ewe-berry*? Or, maybe the message was just, *Ewww, berries!*

Another large bumblebee buzzed around the bush, irritating the llama. Clay tugged on the llama's leash and kept going.

As the vegetation grew denser and denser, the air turned whiter and whiter. Before he knew it, Clay was ensconced in fog.

Or *vog*, he soon realized.

Like fog, the vog was wet and clammy; like smog, it made his eyes tear and made his throat sore. He got the idea to put his bandanna over his mouth and he breathed more easily for a while, but then the bandanna became so wet, it stuck to his face. He pushed it off.

The trail broadened and merged with a shallow, mossy stream. Following the llama, who was very deft at avoiding stepping in the water, Clay tried to pick and choose his way on the rocks, even though it was difficult to see them in the vog. He gave up and walked in the stream; the water was cold, but it was only ankle deep.

"How much farther, Como? Where are you taking me? *¿A dónde vamos?*"

A minute later—or was it ten minutes? The vog had a way of erasing time—the llama suddenly stopped walking.

He stood stock-still, ears pointed straight ahead.

"What's wrong?" Clay asked. "Do you hear something?"

Then Clay heard it, too: a grunting sound next to the stream.

His heart beating wildly, Clay looked around, but it was impossible to see very much. There were immense trees in every direction, so tall their treetops were obscured by the vog. It was like looking into a maze—or a misty hall of mirrors.

He'd almost decided he'd imagined the sound, when the llama reared back, pulling his leash out of Clay's hand.

Clay heard another *grrunt!!*—this time bigger, deeper, and closer.

Followed by another *grrrrunt!!!*—this time much bigger, much deeper, and much, much closer.

And finally by another...

Grrrrrrrrrrrrunt!!!!!!!!

There was a splash of hooves...and suddenly an enormous muddy hog with long bristly hair and sharp curving tusks was barreling toward him, water spraying in all directions.

Clay tried to jump out of the way, but he tripped and fell, landing on his butt in the shallow stream. Terrified, Clay held his arms over his face to ward off the hog.

Luckily, the hog already had its afternoon meal caught between its teeth. The monstrous animal thundered past without so much as a glance in Clay's direction, frog legs dangling from its mouth.

Eventually, Clay's breathing returned to normal and the llama stopped trembling. They pushed forward, now sticking to dry land.

A mile or two farther (the distance was just as hard to judge as the time), the trail stopped at what appeared to be a root ball as big as a house.

When they came closer, Clay saw that it was a tree, but a tree engulfed in roots. Some roots snaked up the tree trunk; others dangled free, twisting this way and that.*

The main trail turned to the right, bending around this bizarre, inside-out, upside-down tree. But the llama seemed to want to take a smaller foot trail to the left that disappeared in a thicket of ferns.

While Clay debated which way to go, he put down his backpack and stretched. He couldn't remember ever feeling so tired or so sore.

Modestly turning away from the llama, he peed onto one of the enormous tree roots where it met the ground. Other roots swayed above, repeatedly tapping him on the shoulder, as if trying to distract him from what he was doing.

Unnerved, he zipped up and turned back around—and frowned. Was the vog getting thicker? Why couldn't he see the llama?

"Como, where are you? ¿Dónde estás?"

He walked around the tree, calling for the llama.

---

* As Clay would later learn, this roots-y type of tree is known as a banyan tree. A banyan is a fig tree that grows on top of another tree, its seeds germinating in the cracks of its host. This makes it an epiphyte—a plant-on-plant parasite. A monster tree, basically.

There was no response. Then he realized his back-pack was missing as well.

"Hello? Is anybody there?"

He peered nervously into the vog. Was he being stalked by an animal? Was he being hijacked by island natives? In a second, he feared, a net woven from sticky vines would drop down over his head, or he would be hit by an arrow tipped with the venom of a poison dart frog.*

The suspense ended when he heard a sound rico-cheting through the trees.

And no, it was not the sound of an animal pouncing or a net dropping or an arrow flying.

It was the sound of laughter.

---

* ACTUALLY, HIS FEARS WERE MORE GENERAL; I WAS FICTIONALIZING FOR EFFECT.

CHAPTER
EIGHT

THE CREATURE WHO CAME OUT OF THE VOG

Did I scare you?"

As Clay spun around, a short human-shaped figure emerged from the vog. The llama, visible in soft gray silhouette, followed.

"Uh, not too much," said Clay cautiously.

"Oh, shoot. Well, I tried."

Laughing merrily, the newcomer tossed the llama's leash in Clay's direction.

"Thanks," said Clay as he fumblingly caught it.

At first, Clay thought the mysterious creature approaching him was a boy. Or possibly a dwarf. Clay could just make out a newsboy-style cap, suspenders, and a very muddy pair of dungarees.* But as it

---

* I AM TAKING A BIT OF EDITORIAL LICENSE HERE. WHILE CLAY DID IN FACT SEE THE NEWSBOY CAP AND DUNGAREES, HE WOULD HAVE CALLED THEM BY THEIR MORE FAMILIAR, CONTEMPORARY NAMES: I.E., *HAT* AND

came closer, Clay saw that the creature was a girl. A freckle-faced girl with green eyes that seemed to be darting away from him and at the same time daring him to follow.

"You didn't see a backpack, too, by any chance?" he asked.

"You mean this one?"

The backpack landed at Clay's feet.

"Yeah, that one," said Clay.

"And I think you're missing this—"

The girl tossed him his wallet.

"That was in my pants!"

"No kidding," said the girl, grinning. "Pickpocketing is easy. What you should really be impressed by is the way I snuck old Como C. away. First time I've ever stolen an animal. Think I have a future as a cattle rustler?"

"How do you know Como's name? Are you from Earth Ranch?"

"Very astute. Your official greeter, Leira, at your service." The girl bowed in a mocking fashion.

JEANS. I USED THE MORE OLD-FASHIONED WORDS TO GIVE YOU A SENSE OF THE OLD-FASHIONED EFFECT OF THE OUTFIT. ORIGINALLY, INSTEAD OF *SUSPENDERS*, I HAD USED THE RATHER ANTIQUATED TERM *BRACES*, BUT I DECIDED THAT THAT WAS GOING A STEP TOO FAR. YOU MIGHT HAVE GOTTEN CONFUSED AND THOUGHT I MEANT THE KIND OF BRACES YOU WEAR ON YOUR TEETH.

"That's Leira, L-E-I-R-A. Weird name, I know. What can I say? My parents are nerds."*

Clay felt a tremendous surge of relief upon hearing that she was from Earth Ranch. At last, there was evidence that the camp existed and that he might eventually reach it.

Leira pointed to the tree next to them. "By the way, this banyan tree—you just peed all over Old Will. That's bad luck, or maybe good, I'm not sure, but I wouldn't do it again."

"Oh, sorry," said Clay, mortified.

"It's one of the oldest and biggest banyans around. It's like a marker. How you know you've reached Earth Ranch."

Clay looked around. "This is Earth Ranch?"

Leira laughed. "I know, it's kind of weird. There aren't any gates or fences around the camp—just the Wall of Trust. Once you're inside, you're not supposed to go out again, unless it's an emergency or you have special permission."

"Do you have permission now?"

"No, but I still have one foot inside, so I'm only a half criminal," said Leira blithely. "Speaking of criminals, sorry about stealing your stuff."

---

* LEIRA HAPPENS TO BE THE NAME OF A GODDESS IN THAT OLD, FAMOUSLY NERDY ROLE-PLAYING GAME DUNGEONS & DRAGONS. I ASSUME THIS IS WHAT SHE WAS REFERRING TO WHEN SHE SAID HER PARENTS WERE NERDS, BUT I MAY BE WRONG.

Clay shrugged. "No problem." He didn't want to pick a fight with the first person he'd met on the island.

"At least I returned it, right? I always return everything. You know, like those fishermen who throw fish back into the water? They just do it for the thrill?"

"I think that's called catch and release," said Clay.

"Yeah, catch and release, that's it. Anyway, I can't help stealing," Leira explained. "I'm a kleptomaniac."

"You are?" Clay couldn't tell if she was serious.

She nodded. "Everybody at this camp is a maniac of some kind or other. What kind are you?"

"I'm not any kind."

Leira's eyes darkened. He had said the wrong thing.

"You mean you're a think-you're-better-than-the-rest-of-us maniac. An egomaniac."

"That's not what I meant," Clay protested. "I'm not an egomaniac, just boring."

But Leira had already disappeared into the vog.

"Hey—I don't know which way to go!"

Clay tugged on the llama, wanting to run after Leira, but Como wouldn't budge. He collapsed on his hind legs, camel-style, once more.

"*Por favor . . . vámonos,*" Clay pleaded.

A second later, he heard Leira's laugh.

"I almost forgot to give you this," she said. She emerged from the vog—and tossed him a fresh bunch of carrot tops.

"Now follow me, Mr. Not-a-Maniac—"

Then she disappeared again.

CHAPTER
NINE

GUARD BEES

By the time he caught up with her, the vog had started to lift, and Clay discovered that they were descending into a deep green valley. In the center of the valley was a long turquoise lake shaped like a crescent moon. At the far end of the lake, the base of an enormous black mountain disappeared into a ring of billowing clouds. To the left of the mountain, a milk-white waterfall poured out from behind the clouds in an endless frothy stream. The view was beautiful but ominous, like a postcard that had been deliberately smudged.

"That dark mountain—it's the volcano?" he asked as he followed her down the steep trail.

Leira nodded. "Mount Forge. The lake protects us from the lava flows—supposedly."

"And that's camp?"

On the near side of the lake, interspersed with

pine trees and boulders, stood about a dozen structures of assorted sizes and shapes and colors—none of which resembled any buildings Clay had ever seen before.

"It looks like a village," he said. "But like a village designed by someone totally whacked."

"Yeah, that about sums it up." Leira smiled. "C'mon, let's hurry, before the vog comes back."

As if he heard her, the llama strained at his leash, eager to get home. Clay tried to keep up while Leira pointed out the sights.

"Down there is Big Yurt," she said, gesturing in the direction of a large round building. It had mud-brick walls and a woven thatched roof. Hanging by the entryway was a bronze gong that looked large enough to announce an emperor. "That's where we have camp meetings and stuff, and where we eat when it's raining."

Then she pointed to two smaller yurts. They looked just like the larger one, except one was painted with a swirling psychedelic rainbow and the other had a wooden arch in front of its door. "The rainbow one is Art Yurt, which is the arts and crafts studio, duh. The other one is Little Yurt, but we usually call it Sick Yurt, or Puke Yurt. It's the infirmary. Don't go in there unless you have to. The nurse, Cora, I think she's a witch...."

Clay eyed the infirmary with curiosity. It didn't look very witchy, unless you counted the broken wind chimes hanging from the arch. And the giant macramé spiderweb. (Actually, an oversized dream catcher, he would learn later.) The chimes tinkled noisily as they passed.

Next they reached two green, woodsy-looking cabins with dilapidated tin roofs. A small pond occupied the space between them.

"That's your cabin, the younger boys'," said Leira, pointing to the closer of the two. "It's officially named Earth Cabin, which is confusing 'cause this whole place is Earth Ranch. So people just call it the Wormhole. You guys are known as Earthworms, or usually just Worms....The other one is my cabin, the younger girls'. It's called the Pond, and we're known as Muds, or sometimes Frogs....The older girls are up that hill—" She pointed to an A-frame-style cabin that hung precipitously over the hillside just above them. "Their cabin is Falcon's Perch.... And the older boys are behind that rock over there—in Fire Truck. Actually, it's a trailer, not a truck, but it's painted red."

"And what about that teepee?" asked Clay, pointing to a canvas teepee nestled among some trees. "Who stays there?"

"You can see the teepee?" She seemed surprised.

Clay squinted. "Uh, not anymore..." A cloud of vog had just passed over it.

Leira nodded knowingly. "You never see it very long.... It's Over There."

Clay looked around. "Where?"

"No, that's the teepee's name. Over There. It's where the camp director, Eli, lives. It always moves around. So we call it Over There. You know, like, where's the teepee...?"

"It's Over There," finished Clay, although he wasn't sure how or why a teepee would move so often.

"Exactly."

She beckoned Clay forward. "C'mon, Como's getting hungry."

"So, where is everybody else now, anyway?" asked Clay. He had just noticed how quiet it was.

"It's four p.m. That means everybody's in Circle," said Leira. "That's sort of like your daily cabin meeting—slash—group therapy—slash—everybody says what they think about everybody else—slash—somebody always winds up crying hour."

"Sounds fun."

Leira snorted. "Why do you think I volunteered to go find you?"

Leira stopped short just before they reached a rickety wooden gate. Behind the gate, Clay could see two llamas munching on hay, and a chicken running in and out of a big barn painted cobalt blue.

"Okay, stand still and don't panic," said Leira. "They'll sense it if you're scared."

"Who?" asked Clay, his leg already jiggling with anxiety.

"The bees."

She nodded at a dark undulating cloud that appeared to be getting larger and larger.

"It's just that they don't know you and they're very protective," Leira explained. "Kind of like guard bees, you could say."

"Guard bees?" Clay had never heard of such a thing. He could feel sweat trickling down his forehead. The dark cloud—now clearly a swarm of bees—was approaching at an alarming speed.

"Uh-huh." Leira nodded as if this were perfectly normal. "They usually only sting you if they get mad. Just do as I say and you'll be fine...."

As the bees descended on them, the llama snorted and flattened his ears. One bee flew at his nose, taunting him and forcing him to back away. But the others had no interest in the llama—only in Clay. They started circling his head at a dizzying speed.

It was like being inside the eye of a tornado.

"Stop shaking!" said Leira.

"I'm trying! Jeez!"

They were the same large type of bumblebee Clay

had seen earlier, but now there had to have been four or five hundred of them at least.

Slowing down now that he was caught in their spinning vortex, they buzzed around Clay, like miniature spy craft examining a potentially hostile alien spaceship. Five or six bees went so far as to land on his face. They crawled across his forehead, his nose, his ears, his neck, investigating every bump and every pore as if they were looking for the best spot to land a sting. They were fuzzy, hairy creatures, and every touch of their legs and wings tickled the nerve endings in Clay's skin. Certain he was going to cough or sneeze—or scream—Clay held his breath and tried not to move a muscle.

"That's it. You're doing great," said Leira quietly.

She pressed something into his hand.

"Here, take this flower—don't look down!—and slowly hold it up for them, so they know you're a friend."

He held up what turned out to be a big yellow daisy.

At first, the flower had no noticeable impact. Then, one by one, the bees that had been crawling on his face flew over to the daisy. They nibbled on some pollen, then rejoined the swarm.

Finally, responding to some inaudible cue, the bees all rose together in a long, unfurling ribbon and flew back in the direction from whence they'd come.

When the last bee had left, Clay exhaled, gasping for air. He clutched his stomach, afraid he was going to puke, but all that came out were a few dry heaves. He had never felt so relieved in his life.

"See. I told you it would be fine," said Leira. But Clay could tell she'd been almost as nervous as he was.

As they entered the barnyard, the llama broke free of Clay and dropped to the ground. The cardboard box fell off the llama's back and tumbled into a pile of straw. Scared chickens squawked and scattered.

"What's he doing?" Clay asked anxiously as the llama started rolling around in the dirt, legs in the air. "Did he get stung?"

"No, old Como's just giving himself a dust bath," said a tall man in a white beekeeper suit and hat. "Llamas always do that after a walk."

He dropped a bucket to the ground. A large chunk of honeycomb was inside, oozing golden honey. A few bees hovered over it.

"Hope my little flying friends didn't give you a scare." He pulled the mesh veil up over his hat, revealing a bristly mustache and squinty gray eyes. "They get a bit ornery when I harvest," said the beekeeper, indicating the honey.

"Gee, I wonder why," said Leira. "It's not like you're taking their food or anything."

"Leira's a vegan. She doesn't approve," the bee-keeper explained to Clay. "But don't let that stop you from taking a taste."

"Now?" asked Clay, surprised but hungry.

"Go ahead, use your finger."

Clay wiped his finger on his jeans—it was pretty dirty—then dipped it into the honey.

"We call it Golden Lava. Best you've ever had, am I right?"

Clay nodded. It was by far the best honey he'd ever tasted. Like liquid gold with a slightly smoky flavor.

"I'm sorry the director isn't around right this minute to welcome you officially, but I'll try." The man took Clay's still-sticky hand and shook it ceremoniously. "You're Clay. Known hereafter as Worm. I'm Buzz, your counselor. Known hereafter as… Buzz, your counselor. I'm also the camp beekeeper, llama wrangler, and general peacemaker."

Leira rolled her eyes. "I bet the bees think you're really peaceful."

Buzz held up his finger. A bee landed on it. "Perhaps. Perhaps not."

As he looked at the bee, his lips vibrated in a strange, apian fashion.* Then the bee flew off to

---

* APIAN, AS YOU MAY HAVE GATHERED FROM CONTEXT CLUES, DOES NOT MEAN APE-LIKE BUT BEE-LIKE. PERSONALLY, I HAD NO CONTEXT CLUES TO HELP ME WHEN I WAS RACKING MY BRAIN FOR THE WORD. IT TOOK ME

rejoin its peers. If Clay hadn't known better, he would have thought that a message had passed between them.

"Bees are communitarians," said Buzz. "They could teach us a thing or two about how to live in peace with one another." Buzz smiled. "Of course, they also eat their young."

"Right. Well, see ya," Leira said to Clay.

She tossed him his wallet—which she had evidently pickpocketed for a second time—and was gone before he could say good-bye.

"Does she always disappear like that?" Clay asked.

"You mean like somebody just yelled 'fire'?" said Buzz. "Pretty much."

"Well, it's a good thing she found me when she did," said Clay. "A good thing I found the llama, too."

Now that he'd arrived safely at Earth Ranch, Clay was starting to feel angry about the way he was welcomed—or more accurately, *not* welcomed—on the island.

Buzz smiled. "Oh, you found that llama pretty quickly...."

THREE CHOCOLATE-DIPPED HONEYCOMB BARS, TWO HOURS OF CHASING BEES, AND ONE LONG NAP BEFORE IT CAME TO ME IN A FLASH. STILL, A MUCH BETTER OUTCOME THAN WHEN I TRIED TO REMEMBER THE WORD *AVIAN*...

Clay looked at him askance. "How do you know? You've got drones out there, spying?"

"Something like that," said Buzz.*

"Then I was right. The llama was a test." Clay couldn't decide if the idea that he was being watched made him more furious or less.

"Life is a test. The llama was there to help."

"Sure," said Clay, far from satisfied. How could a counselor be so relaxed about endangering the life of a camper? He kept thinking of the SOS on the beach: Was that a kid who never made it to camp? Or, worse, tried to escape from camp?

"Any more questions, Worm?"

Yes, Clay thought. How do I get home?

Clay was on the verge of asking if he could call his parents, but he decided to wait a day. He was tired and sunburned and more than a little afraid of whatever might be coming next, but he had to at least give Earth Ranch a try. As bad as camp might be, it couldn't be as bad as repeating sixth grade.

"Good man," said Buzz, slapping Clay on the shoulder. "C'mon, we're late for Circle. But first you gotta clean up after your llama." He pointed to Como, who had stood up from his dirt bath and was

---

* I'm not sure Clay understood at the time, but I believe Buzz was thinking here not of drone helicopters but rather of the original drones: that is, male bees.

now dropping little brown pellets from his behind onto the ground.

"*My* llama?" echoed Clay.

"Yes, Worm, just like you're *his* human. For as long as you're here." He handed Clay a large rake. "Can't let that fantastic fertilizer go to waste."

"You hear that, Como?" Clay sighed. "We're stuck together. *Nosotros somos...*" He made the together sign with two fingers.

As Clay raked llama poop into a tidy heap, bees circled above like so many tiny sentinels in their black-and-yellow uniforms, and Clay wondered just what it was they were protecting, and from whom.

CHAPTER
TEN

CIRCLE

From the way Circle had been described, Clay expected his new cabinmates to be sitting on the floor with their legs crossed, talking about their feelings. Instead, they were lounging on their bunks with their feet up, talking about...well, Clay couldn't tell, because they stopped talking as soon as he walked in. He suspected they'd been talking about him.

"Cabin, meet Clay," said Buzz. "Clay, meet cabin."

Clay's first impression was that the three other boys in his cabin looked like a rock band—a young and clownish but also somewhat scary rock band. Between the three of them, they had a green Mohawk, a gold-tipped Afro, and one heavily gelled, slicked-back hairdo. Clay felt very dull in comparison—at least hair-wise.

"Well, isn't anybody going to welcome the new Worm?" Buzz prompted.

The boy with the slicked-back hair jumped to his feet and shook Clay's hand. He wore a pair of over-sized eyeglasses that had no lenses and a T-shirt decorated with a picture of a necktie. Clay thought the outfit was supposed to be funny, but he wasn't absolutely sure.

"Welcome to the Wormhole, New Worm," said the boy with the glasses. "We are your Worm-mates. Punk Rock Worm over there is Pablo."

The boy with the Mohawk raised a fist in greeting.

"Lil' Superfly Worm here is Jonah."

The boy with the Afro nodded his head.

"And that leaves yours truly," said the boy with the glasses, pointing to himself. "I'm the Boss Worm, Kwan, which means 'best-looking guy in the room' in Korean, in case you were wondering."

"And it means 'biggest dork in the room' in English," said Jonah.

There were four bunk beds, making eight beds total, but there was only one free bed because Buzz had an entire upper and lower bunk to himself, and the other unused beds were covered with a jumble of dirty laundry and muddy shoes. Clay's bunk, to which he was directed right away, was the top bunk

in the back left corner of the cabin. Since the other campers had chosen their bunks first, Clay figured his was the least desirable, though he wasn't sure why until he sat on the mattress; the springs were popping out, and they jabbed him whenever he moved. The cabin was open-air style, with no glass or screens in the windows, and from Clay's bunk he could peer down to the ground outside. It gave him a slight feeling of vertigo, which he did his best to ignore.

As it turned out, the box that Clay had delivered to camp was a care package for Jonah, who occupied the bunk below Clay. Everyone watched avidly as Jonah opened it. Here was something more interesting than a newcomer in their midst: *food.*

Jonah's eyes lit up when he saw what was inside. "Can I keep it?" he asked Buzz. "Pretty please with, uh, red licorice on top."

Grinning, he pulled out a plastic-wrapped package of skinny red rope familiar to most anyone who's been to a movie theater.

"Go on, poison yourself," said Buzz, who was peeling off his cowboy boots. "But don't think I'll be this lax if you get a cell phone in the mail."

"Thanks, chief," said Jonah, ripping open a package.

"You know what they say, it's more fun to give than to receive," said Kwan.

"Yeah, well, they lied, but have some anyway," said Jonah, tossing licorice ropes around the room.*

As Pablo grabbed his licorice, Clay caught a glimpse of a dark bulky object peeking out from under his sleeping bag. Pablo quickly hid it—whatever it was—and gave Clay a look that plainly meant Clay was not to say anything. Clay looked away, alarmed to find himself keeping secrets so soon.

Jonah dangled another rope of licorice in the air. "For the new guy?"

"Sure, I mean, if there's enough," said Clay awkwardly.

"You kidding?" said Jonah, handing the licorice up to Clay. "There's, like, ten more packages in the box. Plus, my moms'll send more if I ask. They feel all guilty for sending me here."

"So why did they, then?" Clay asked before he could stop himself. It was already clear he wasn't supposed to be too nosy in this group.

"Oh, I got in a little trouble with the neighbors. They said they wouldn't press charges if I came here."

"Go on," said Buzz. "Tell the whole story."

---

* I USE THE WORD *LICORICE* LOOSELY, OF COURSE. IN REALITY, THERE IS NO LICORICE IN RED LICORICE, JUST HIGH-FRUCTOSE CORN SYRUP HARDENED TO A WAXY TEXTURE AND COLORED WITH TOXIC DYES. IN MY NOT-SO-HUMBLE OPINION, RED LICORICE IS THE ONLY THING WORSE THAN WHITE CHOCOLATE. REPEAT AFTER ME: *CHOCOLATE, BROWN. LICORICE, BLACK. ANYTHING ELSE I'M TAKING BACK!*

"How can I? I don't even remember it," said Jonah.

"He's a sleepwalker," explained Kwan. He rolled his eyes back in his head and stuck out his hands zombie-style.

"More like a sleep-driver!" said Pablo. "He drove one of his moms' cars straight into the neighbor's garage."

"Seriously? While you were sleeping?" Clay asked.

"Uh-huh," said Jonah. "And I don't even know how to drive!"

"The other day, he started walking into the lake in the middle of the night, still all snoring and everything," said Pablo. "We just grabbed him and shook him until he woke up."

Kwan nodded. "It's no big deal after a while."

Clay shook his head. "Wow, that's ... crazy."

"What about you, Kwan?" said Buzz. "Can you tell Clay how you wound up here?"

"Sure, I'm not ashamed," said Kwan. "All I did was provide a much-needed service for my peers."

Jonah laughed. "Yeah, you took their money."

"He ran a gambling den in his school bathroom," said Pablo.

"I like to think of it as more of an underground casino in an educational spa," Kwan sniffed.

"You mean like card games and stuff?" Clay asked, looking at Kwan with renewed interest.

He'd never met an underage underground gambler before.

Kwan grinned. "Cards for sure." In a single deft motion, he pulled a deck of cards out of his pocket and started shuffling them like a pro. "But the real action was in the bookie operation."

Clay was a little hazy about what precisely a bookie did, but he nodded as if he understood.*

"Tell him how you got caught," said Jonah to Kwan.

"There was going to be this make-out party at this girl's house, and I got everybody to bet on who would kiss who," said Kwan, fanning the cards in his hand. "I had a full point spread, depending on how popular they were, how pretty, whatever."

He walked over to Clay's bunk and gestured for him to pick a card.

"So what happened?" asked Clay. He took a card, though as you know, he hadn't been a big fan of card tricks since his brother disappeared.

"My class was a bunch of chickens—that's what happened! Nobody kissed anybody," said Kwan, as if

---

* WHEN I WAS YOUNG, I THOUGHT A BOOKIE WAS SOMEBODY WHO READ A LOT OF BOOKS—A BOOKWORM—WHICH IS WHAT I WAS. MY SECOND GUESS WAS THAT A BOOKIE WAS AN AFFECTIONATE TERM FOR A FAVORITE BOOK—LIKE A BLANKIE—AS IN, *THAT BOY PSEUDONYMOUS, HE NEVER LETS HIS LITTLE BOOKIE OUT OF HIS HAND.* I NEVER GUESSED THAT A BOOKIE WAS SOMEBODY THROUGH WHOM PEOPLE MAKE BETS ON HORSE RACES AND BALL GAMES.

he were still offended by his peers' timidity. "Three of clubs, right?"

"Uh-huh," said Clay noncommittally. He knew Kwan had forced the card; his brother had shown him how to do that long ago.

"What? You can do better, New Worm?" Kwan flared.

"No," said Clay, even though he could.

"I didn't think so." Smiling, Kwan took the card back. "Anyway, my position was, there were no winners; therefore the bank keeps the money."

"So everyone got pissed at him and told their parents," said Pablo.

"And now you're here," concluded Clay, relieved that the brief moment of tension had passed.

"And now I'm here," agreed Kwan, throwing his cards to the floor. Kwan looked at Pablo. "Your turn, Pablito."

"I'm an anarchist," Pablo boasted. He pointed to the symbol on his T-shirt. The letter *A* inside a circle.

"It means he doesn't believe in government and rules and stuff," said Jonah.

"I know what it means," said Clay, although this might not have been one hundred percent true.* He

---

* ANARCHISM IS A POLITICAL PHILOSOPHY THAT ADVOCATES "ANTI-AUTHORITARIAN STATELESS SYSTEMS"—SORT OF LIKE CLASSROOMS WITHOUT TEACHERS OR RULES. IT IS THE PREFERRED SCHOOL OF THOUGHT FOR REBELLIOUS TEENAGERS EVERYWHERE.

tried not to look at the mysterious lump in Pablo's sleeping bag.

"Ask him how he got in trouble," said Kwan.

"I didn't get in trouble," said Pablo. "It's just that school is incompatible with my belief system."

"You mean you ditched?" asked Clay.

"I don't *ditch*," Pablo sneered. "I go on strike. I protest school. I defy it."

"Oh...cool," said Clay, impressed but slightly confused.

"Do you know why school was invented?" Pablo demanded. "It was during the British Empire. To turn us all into little cogs in the same big machine."

Kwan rolled his eyes. "No more history lessons, Pablo!" He looked over at Clay. "If you keep shaking your leg like that, nobody's going to be able to sleep tonight."

"Sorry," Clay mumbled, embarrassed. "I do that sometimes."

"Don't listen to him," said Jonah. "Everybody here's got his own freaky habits."

There was silence for a moment. Clay figured it was his turn to talk. "So I guess I should tell you guys why I'm here, right?"

"Oh, don't worry, we know—" said Kwan.

"*Magic sucks!*" they all quoted together.

They laughed as though this were an inside joke.

"Right." Clay forced a smile. How did they know about that?

Buzz shot a warning look around the room. They quieted down immediately.

"Sorry about that," he said to Clay. "Sometimes applications get leaked."

"Dude, what was that all about, anyway?" asked Kwan. "Is Magic the name of a tagger you don't like?"

"Yeah, or like a rival graffiti crew?" suggested Pablo. "Your crew having a war with them?"

"I don't have a crew," said Clay. "Actually, I'm not even a real graffiti artist."

"You mean you're not good?" said Jonah. "Don't hate on yourself, man."

"I mean I didn't write on that wall," said Clay. "I was framed. Somebody copied my journal while I was asleep."

His protestation of innocence was met with laughter.

"So what you're saying is, you're a sleepwalker, too," said Pablo. "You wrote all over your school wall, but you don't remember a minute of it."

"Yeah, that must be it," said Clay sarcastically.

But when he thought about it, the sleepwalking idea gave him pause. It was the best explanation so far for what had happened.

As Circle wound down, Clay looked around at his colorful new cabinmates. They were a jocular bunch, no doubt, but there was a strong current of tension underneath. His instincts told him to be wary, and not just because of the mysterious contraband item under Pablo's sleeping bag. The volcano wasn't the only thing on the island with the potential to erupt.

CHAPTER
ELEVEN

MAGIC ROCKS!

After Circle, Buzz went over the schedule for the summer session.

Although the other boys had already been at camp for a week, they all had questions—especially about the overnight backpacking trip to Mount Forge that they would be taking later in the summer. Apparently, Clay and his fellow Worms would be hiking through lava tubes (whatever they were), traversing live lava flows, and even ascending to the volcano's crater. Clay's arrival on the island sounded like a breeze in comparison.

Before they could go on the trip, they would each have to pass three tests: a swim test, a fire-starting test, and a lava safety test.

"But don't think of them as tests; think of them as rites of passage," said Buzz. "The volcano overnight will be the culmination of the journey that you are taking at Earth Ranch. You will have to trust in your fellow campers. You will have to navigate the hazards of the lava landscape. And because you will be packing no meals, you will have to forage for food, identifying which plants are edible and which are poisonous."

"Oh, man, no more licorice!" Kwan complained.

"Can we hunt?" asked Pablo. He glanced outside the cabin, as if there might be game hiding in the bushes.

"We're here to be at one with nature, not to attack it," said Buzz. "The last thing we need is one of you Worms running around with a spear in his hand."

"Okay, master, sir, we'll all be good boys."

"Pablo..."

"Right," said Pablo, retreating into his bunk. "Got it. No hunting."

"What about that gray bush with purple berries?" Clay asked. "You know, that one that's on the trail on the way here? Is it poisonous?"

Buzz laughed. "Not unless you're allergic to blueberries. Too bad there aren't any growing on top of Mount Forge."

Well, that's one theory out the window, thought Clay. He was pretty sure that *Beware—the—you—bury* did not mean *Beware the blueberry.*

"Don't be fooled by Buzz's Zen beekeeper act," said Jonah as Clay followed him into the shack-like bathroom that night. "He's a total drill sergeant underneath."

"Yeah?"

Jonah nodded vehemently. "He's already bawled out Kwan a couple times, and after Pablo tried to cross the Wall of Trust—I don't know what Buzz said, but Pablo's been wicked scared of him ever since. I think the only reason he hasn't chewed me out yet is that he's afraid of what I'll do to him in my sleep."

"Really?"

"No. I just know how to keep my head down, I guess."

The bathroom lights briefly flickered out, leaving them in darkness. Clay tried not to get nervous.

"It's the generators here," said Jonah when the lights went back on. "They're kinda unreliable.... Just be glad you weren't using the self-composting toilet."

"The what?"

"You'll see."

As far as Clay was concerned, the self-composting toilet was just a hole in the ground with a fancy name, and he wasn't going to squat over it until he absolutely had to. At least it didn't smell. Which was more than he could say for the tap water. He spit it out and put more toothpaste on his toothbrush.

"Ugh—it tastes like rotten eggs," Clay said to Jonah. "Or sulfur, I guess."

"It's from the volcano," said Jonah, his mouth full of toothpaste. "You get used to it."

"I guess there's a lot to get used to around here."

Jonah shrugged. "I don't know, seems like they never really let you get too used to anything at Earth Ranch."

Before Clay could ask Jonah what he meant, an older boy walked into the bathroom.

"That's Flint," Jonah whispered. "He's a junior counselor. From Fire Truck. Ignore him."

Too late.

Flint stepped behind Clay and stared at him in the mirror so that Clay had no choice but to stare back. Flint had black hair, blue eyes, and the muscles of somebody who had started lifting weights at an early age. He looked like Superman's mean-spirited younger brother. Clay disliked him on sight.

"Hey, it's the new kid—welcome to Earth Ranch," said Flint, in the least welcoming voice Clay had ever heard.

"Hi," Clay said curtly. "I'm Clay."

"I know—you're the graffiti artist."

He knows about that, too! Clay thought. Does the whole camp know why I'm here?

"For the record, I didn't do that—" said Clay, turning to face Flint.

"Don't lie," said Flint menacingly. He stepped forward, forcing Clay to back into the sink. "I don't like liars."

"I'm not lying—"

Flint cut him off. "Oh yeah? And I bet you didn't write that, either—"

As Flint spoke, the bathroom lights flickered off and on again. Clay turned back toward the mirror—and froze in disbelief.

MAGIC ROCKS!

As before, the message was written in Clay's bubble letters—only enlarged many times over. But this time the sentiment was reversed. *MAGIC ROCKS!* rather than *MAGIC SUCKS!*

"Look, he's already up to his old tricks," Flint sneered. "Guess you changed your mind about magic, huh, Worm?"

"No!"

Clay tried to move away, but Flint shoved him against the mirror. "What do you think—should

I call your counselor and show him? I wonder how many days you'd be cleaning out the toilet...."

Clay glared at the bigger boy. "I don't know how you did that, but it's not very cool."

Flint laughed. "It's the coolest thing there is. It's magic."

He spit a big loogie onto the mirror. The graffiti started to disappear as soon as the saliva touched it, the saliva sizzling as if it were boiling hot. Flint spit two more times and the graffiti was gone altogether. The mirror looked as dirty and cracked and free of writing as it had looked when Clay first walked into the room.

How did Flint make the writing go away? Baking soda? Hydrochloric acid? Or had it just been an illusion to begin with? Years of practice with Max-Ernest had made Clay fairly skilled at analyzing magic tricks, but he was stumped.

"See you around, Worm!" said Flint on his way out of the bathroom.

"I hope not," muttered Clay.

Flint turned around. "What did you say?"

"Nothing. He didn't say anything," said Jonah quickly.

"I didn't think so," said Flint, disappearing out the door.

Clay turned to Jonah. "What's up with that

guy? How did he even know what my writing looked like?"

"Just stay away from him," Jonah blurted. He looked so shaken, you would have thought he was the one being threatened, not Clay. "Flint is way aggro. A serious pyromaniac. I heard he lit his old school on fire."

"It's true, huh?" said Clay. "Everyone here is a maniac."

"Maybe, but Flint—he's a different level."

Just my luck, Clay thought, my first day at camp and already I have a pyromaniac magician for an enemy. But why? He couldn't have done anything to make Flint angry; they'd never met before. Like so many things recently, it made no sense.

As he exited the bathroom, Clay looked reflexively for his skateboard, but of course it wasn't there. No doubt his father had taken it home, and it was now leaning against one of the graffiti-covered walls of Clay's bedroom. Suddenly, Clay felt an ache in his stomach that had nothing to do with hunger.

Walking back to his cabin, he saw the brightest stars he'd ever seen. He searched for a constellation he might recognize—the Big Dipper, maybe, or Orion—but soon the stars were covered by clouds of vog.

The sky was dark.

CHAPTER
TWELVE

WEEDS

It was still dark when Clay awoke to the sound of the camp gong reverberating in his ears.

He looked sleepily around the cabin and was surprised to see it was empty. Was it later than it looked?

"Five a.m.," announced Buzz, startling Clay. "The others are already at the vegetable garden. You're late, Worm."

Buzz stood outside the door wearing some sort of hooded robe and holding a long spade. He could have been the grim reaper calling Clay to his death instead of his counselor calling him to gardening chores. His mustache only made him look more ominous.

Clay swallowed. "Sorry, I didn't—"

"We weed early, before it gets hot," said Buzz gruffly. "Now get dressed, or you'll be weeding all day."

Clay got to his feet wondering why nobody had

tried to wake him earlier. Did his cabinmates think they'd done him a favor by letting him sleep, or had they set him up for a fall?

"Achoo!"

Alas, Clay never quite recovered from his late start.

As soon as he started weeding, he started wheezing, irritated by the pollen in the air. Sweat and dirt got in his eyes. He itched and scratched until he bled. And those fiercely protective camp bees kept buzzing around Clay's head. It was as if they were threatening him with stings in order to make him work harder. Clay was no insect expert, but he was certain this was not normal bee behavior.

Worst of all, he wasn't making any progress. By the time he got one weed out of the ground, it seemed like there was already a new weed springing up in its place.

"If you don't speed up, you'll be making me lunch for sure," said Leira, when they found themselves weeding adjacent rows.

Their cabins were in competition; whichever cabin finished weeding first would be served lunch by the other. Clay's cabin was responsible for the rows of root vegetables like beets and radishes and carrots, all of which came in a rainbow of colors Clay had never seen before. Leira's cabin, the Pond, had the next set of rows, where the lettuces and spinach and

such grew alongside more exotic fare like fiddlehead ferns and Jerusalem artichokes.

Clay yanked on a weed. It broke at the stem instead of coming out with its roots.

"Try not to tug so hard," said Leira.

Clay found another weed and did as Leira suggested. The weed slipped out of his hand.

Leira laughed. "Maybe you're just not cut out to be a farmer."

"Maybe not," said Clay.

"You don't have to sound so miserable about it," said Leira.

"Sorry." Clay tried to dig out his weed, then gave up.

"Don't apologize."

"Sorr—okay," Clay corrected himself.

"Are you always this cheery?"

Clay shrugged.

"I was teasing," said Leira.

"I know."

"So what's your story, anyway?" Leira asked.

"Story?"

"Yeah, I mean, not *magic sucks*, I know about that—"

Clay shook his head. "Of course you do. Everybody does."

"I mean like where do you come from, what's your sign, do you have any pets?"

"No pets," said Clay.

"Siblings?"

"Brother...well, I *had* a brother."

Leira's brow furrowed under her cap. "You mean he's dead?"

"No," said Clay, attacking another weed. "Disappeared."

"Disappeared?"

"Uh-huh. He just...got sick of us."

Leira waited for him to say more. He didn't.

"You don't have to tell me more if you don't want to..." she said.

"Okay."

"But if you want to..."

Clay gave her a look. "You mean *you* want me to tell you more."

"Well, you have to admit it's pretty interesting— people don't disappear every day!" said Leira defensively. "Besides, what do you want to talk about, the weeds?"

Clay hesitated. He didn't really want to talk about anything, but there was no question Leira was being nice to him—nicer than anyone at camp had been so far. It didn't seem right not to respond.

He told her briefly about the good-bye note from his brother and what had happened afterward.

Leira looked at him, perplexed. "I don't understand. If all he said was you wouldn't hear from him for a while, how do you know he was sick of you?"

"If you knew my parents, you wouldn't ask. And me, I'm just some dumb kid, right?" said Clay, unable to hide his bitterness.

Leira frowned. "Why would somebody have to totally disappear just to get away from his family? He could have just not answered the phone. There must have been another reason. . . . I bet he was in trouble and had no choice."

"Nah, his friend said he was okay," said Clay, thinking of Cass.

"So, maybe they didn't want to raise any alarms," said Leira. "I still think he could be in trouble."

"What kind of trouble?" Clay asked skeptically.

"I don't know. What was he into?"

"Lots of stuff. Magic mostly. He wanted to be a magician."

"Well, there you go!" said Leira enthusiastically. "Magicians always get into trouble. Most of them are thieves."

"How do you know?" It was something Clay might have said himself, but hearing it from someone else irked him for some reason.

"Trust me, I know—" She held out his wallet, which she had apparently pickpocketed sometime in the last few minutes.

"Ha-ha," said Clay, grabbing the wallet from her.

"But seriously," said Leira, "maybe your brother was part of a heist that went wrong."

"You mean you think the police are after him?" Clay tried to picture his brother as a criminal on the lam.

Leira nodded, wide-eyed. "Yeah, or else, like, some bad guy who's mad he didn't get his jewels or whatever? That's why your brother can't communicate! He's being watched!"

"You seem pretty excited about it," said Clay.

Her face fell. "Sorry. I mean, he *is* your brother."

"That's okay," said Clay, even though it wasn't, or not entirely. "But I doubt my brother was in a *heist*. He's too . . . logical. And he's a terrible liar."

Then again, Clay reminded himself, Max-Ernest had hinted more than once that he was involved with dangerous secret activities. Could his absence have been forced on him in some way—even if he wasn't a criminal?

"Anyway, that sucks, him disappearing like that," said Leira. "I don't know what I would do if that happened to my sister. I mean, I hate her half the time. She's this totally annoying know-it-all bookworm. But still—"

"I know, my brother, too," said Clay.

"Your brother, too, what?"

"My brother is a totally annoying know-it-all bookworm, too, but yeah, I miss him . . . sometimes."

It was the first time in a long time that Clay had acknowledged missing his brother. It felt surprisingly... good.

He and Leira looked at each other for a moment. Clay wondered, suddenly, if he had made a friend.

An older girl with long hair and longer legs walked by, carrying a gardening hoe.

"Back to work, Worm!" the girl called out to Clay. "Or you won't just be serving lunch—you'll *be* lunch! And that goes for you, too, Leira. I don't want you messing things up for our cabin!" She pointed her hoe at Leira as if it were a weapon.

"Sheesh. Who was that?" asked Clay after she'd gone.

"Adriana. My counselor," said Leira. "Do yourself a favor and don't get on her bad side."

Clay's Worm-mates had come over to see what the fuss was about.

"You make it sound like she has a good side," said Pablo. "That girl is mean."

"Well, she's got a good-*looking* side, anyway," said Kwan. "Two of them, front and back." He wiggled his eyebrows over his empty eyeglass frames.

"You're gross," said Leira. "Worm."

"Get over it, man," said Jonah. "She ever hears you talk like that, you're toast."

"She's Flint's girlfriend," he added for Clay's benefit.

"Flint wishes," said Leira, snickering.

There was no cafeteria or dining hall at Earth Ranch. There wasn't even a proper kitchen. In the back of Big Yurt, there was a counter on which food could be prepared, as well as bins and cabinets for storing food and food-related items. But there was no stove or oven, no freezer or refrigerator. Occasionally, desperate campers cooked over an open fire or used another natural source of heat, such as a rock that had been sitting in the sun or, if you were willing to walk, one of the nearby steam vents that released heat from the molten lava underneath. Mostly, they ate their food raw.*

Today was an "earth to table" lunch, which meant you had to assemble your own lunch from the ingredients piled on a long table outside Big Yurt. Imagine a salad bar with no condiments and all the vegetables barely out of the ground. The other campers seemed to have very little trouble with this arrangement, whether they were chopping kale or peeling cucumbers. Clay had more experience cook-ing for himself than the average twelve-year-old, but he was used to ingredients that came in packages; his idea of preparing a meal was to press START on the microwave, or if he was really ambitious, to open a

---

* AS IT HAPPENS, THERE ARE MANY PEOPLE WHO CHOOSE TO EAT ONLY RAW FOOD, EVEN WHEN COOKED FOOD IS AVAILABLE. THE PRACTICE IS KNOWN AS *RAW FOODISM*, OR SIMPLY *RAWISM*.

box into a pot of boiling water. As a member of the losing cabin, he was supposed to be helping make the girls' lunches; alas, he couldn't even figure out how to make one for himself.

Not knowing what else to do, Clay put a mango on his plate. Maybe it wasn't a full lunch, but it was his favorite fruit. If only he could figure out how to get the skin off.

The members of Earth Cabin sat at the table farthest from Big Yurt, closest to the edge of the gravel patio. Directly below, shaded by a large cedar tree, was the Earth Ranch dock. A long rope hung from the tree, and as he sat down next to Jonah, Clay watched one of the older boys swing from the rope and jump into the water. It looked like a big drop.

The lake beyond was obscured by vog.

When Clay glanced back down at his lunch plate, his plate was empty. He looked around to see where his mango had fallen.

Leira tossed the mango to him from the opposite side of the table. The other boys laughed.

"Very funny," said Clay.

"Yeah, well, what happened to the lunch you were supposed to make for me?" She gestured to his tablemates. "They all made them for the other girls."

"Sorry," said Clay, looking around to see if any counselors had noticed his lapse.

"No worries. I covered for you. . . . Besides, I'd rather take your money than your food." She held up his wallet.

Clay shook his head. Not again.

"C'mon. Give it back."

He tried to snatch the wallet from her, but she was too fast for him.

"Admit it: I'm good at it," said Leira.

"Stealing? Yes, you're good at it. You're an awesome thief."

"Thanks." Leira handed his wallet back to him. "It's all about controlling your attention. Making sure you're looking over there"—she pointed across the table—"when I'm actually over here."

She held up Clay's wallet again.

He groaned. "Give me a break—"

Grinning, Leira tossed the wallet back to Clay. "Now I'm going to get that lunch you were supposed to get for me, slacker."

"I think somebody has a crush on you," said Kwan as soon as Leira had left. He tossed a carrot at Clay.

"No, she doesn't," said Clay, reddening.

"And maybe you have a crush on her," said Pablo. He took a cue from Kwan and tossed a chunk of cucumber.

"No, I don't," said Clay, fending off the vegetable missiles.

"It's okay, you can have her," said Kwan. "I got all the other ladies lining up already."

"Lining up to do what," said Pablo, "throw water in your face?" He flicked water at Kwan.

A few tables over, Buzz stood up and gave them the *cut it out* signal; there would be no food fights today.

"You may as well admit it," said Jonah to Clay. "There's nothing wrong with having a crush on somebody. My mom says it's normal for kids our age."

"I repeat, I Do Not Have a Crush on Leira," said Clay, who couldn't stand to be the subject of this kind of speculation. "She's nice and all, but she's totally irritating. I swear, if she takes my wallet one more time—"

"Uh—" Jonah pointed.

Clay looked over his shoulder. Leira was standing behind him, her face crimson. She held his wallet in her hand.

"I thought you went to get your lunch..." said Clay nervously. How much had she heard?

"I told you to pay attention. Worm."

Clay couldn't tell whether she meant that he should pay attention to where his wallet was or to what he was saying. Either way, she didn't seem happy about it.

"I'm sorry," he said lamely. "They were bugging me, and I was just—"

"Sure." Leira handed him his wallet and walked away.

Clay thought he should run after her and try again to apologize, but he didn't know what exactly he would say. He felt terrible.

Kwan shrugged. "Told you she had a crush on you."

"Not anymore," said Jonah.

"Now she hates you," agreed Pablo.

Clay was about to reply when he noticed that some of the clouds lingering around the lake had lifted, revealing the ruins of an enormous white stone edifice sitting on a black rock bluff. From where he was sitting, the broken columns and crumbling walls looked like the remains of an ancient temple rising out of the vog.

"What's that?" he asked.

"Price Palace," said Kwan. "You know, the guy whose island this was? Supposedly, it was huge. Just like a palace in Europe or wherever. All marble and gold and stuff. Then—"

He waved his hand, and mimicked the sound of a volcanic explosion.

Clay squinted, trying to imagine a palace where the ruins now stood. "You guys ever check it out?" Clay asked.

The others all looked at one another. Nobody seemed to want to answer.

"He tried," said Jonah finally, pointing to Pablo. Pablo shot Jonah an angry look from under his Mohawk, but he didn't deny it.

"What happened?" asked Clay.

"They always know when you cross the Wall of Trust," said Kwan.

"Who?"

"The bees," said Kwan.

"That's crazy," said Clay.

"Oh, yeah? Explain this—" Pablo pushed up his shirt sleeve. His arm was covered with welts. "That's from when I tried to go to the ruins—those crazy bees kept stinging me until I ran all the way back to camp."

"Whoa," said Clay, horrified.

Pablo nodded. "It's stupid to call it the Wall of Trust if there's no way to cross it, right? Where's the trust in that?"

"What's in the ruins that they don't want you to see?" asked Clay.

"Heck if I know," said Pablo.

"Well, what happened there?" Clay persisted.

"What does it look like?" said Kwan. "The volcano erupted."

"Price was capitalist scum. He leeched money from poor people," said Pablo. "I say, good on old Mount Forge for knocking his place down."

Jonah shook his head. "Don't talk like that,

dude. Say it too many times and the volcano will come for you, too."

"All we know is, somebody died there," said Kwan.

Clay's eyes widened. "In the eruption? Who—Price?"

"A girl," said Jonah. "And now the ruins are haunted."

The others laughed.

"Go ahead and laugh," said Jonah. "But you know that's what people say."

"The only thing that haunts that place is Price's blood money," said Pablo.

"And bees," said Kwan.

As Kwan spoke, the sun shone directly on the ruins, turning them brilliant gold. For a moment, Clay could almost imagine Price Palace in all its former glory.

A girl was buried there, Clay thought. Was that what Skipper's warning *Beware—the—you—bury* was about?

Beware who you bury. Maybe that was the message.

That night, after a dinner that was only slightly more filling than his lunch, Clay walked into his cabin to find Pablo smearing something on his arm with a rag. He almost jumped out of his bunk when he saw Clay.

"Oh, it's you. Man, you freakin' scared me."

"Sorry," said Clay. "Do they hurt?"

"What?"

"The beestings."

"Oh, right," said Pablo, pulling his sleeve down. "Nurse Cora gave me some lotion to put on them."

Clay had the sense there was something more Pablo was going to say—the reason he'd been so scared when Clay walked in maybe? Or maybe he was going to reveal what he'd been hiding under his sleeping bag the day before?—but then the others started coming into the cabin. It was time for bed.

Later, Clay lay on his bunk, sleepless. As he listened to his cabinmates snore, he took stock of his situation. From the moment, almost two weeks earlier, when he found the words *MAGIC SUCKS!* written on his teacher's wall, things had gone from bad to worse:

He'd been wrongly accused and suspended from school.

He'd been sent to a camp for delinquents on a remote volcanic island.

He'd been abandoned with a cryptic warning next to an alarming SOS sign.

He'd been threatened by a wild boar and a swarm of bees.

He'd made an enemy of the scariest guy at camp.

He'd insulted the only person who'd been very nice to him.

He'd failed at the simple task of weeding.

He'd been afraid to use the toilet and he'd hardly eaten a thing.

He was hungry and he wanted to go home.

But even as he started planning how he would approach Buzz, Clay already knew he wouldn't leave. Not yet. It wasn't just that he had to stay at Earth Ranch in order to return to school in the fall. It was something about the place itself. A feeling that there was more to the camp than met the eye. This strange camp with its fast-changing weather and even faster-growing weeds; with its Spanish-speaking llama and bee-speaking counselor; with its now-you-see-it-now-you-don't teepee and its forbidden ruins where a girl had supposedly died. What had Jonah said? *They never let you get too used to anything at Earth Ranch.* Clay couldn't put his finger on it, but he was certain that behind the clouds of vog, all was not as it seemed.

Seeing his own words on Mr. Bailey's wall had been the most bewildering event in Clay's life, but perhaps it had a purpose after all: to lead him to this foreboding but intriguing island. Clay would never have said it out loud—it would have sounded too superstitious—but he was almost convinced that something like fate had brought him to Earth Ranch.

He had a role to play here, he felt sure; he wanted to find out what it was.

CHAPTER
THIRTEEN

FREE TIME

Little by little, Clay began to adapt to camp life.

Within the next four or five days, he learned enough about "cooking" with raw foods to feed himself, and he ceased to be afraid of the self-composting toilet. The bees let him do his chores in peace, and he had no further run-ins with Flint. He even started pulling weeds out at the root. (Unfortunately, he couldn't share the victory with Leira; she still wasn't speaking to him.)

And yet he felt no closer to uncovering the camp's secrets. Indeed, he was almost beginning to feel foolish for thinking that there was anything very mysterious about Earth Ranch at all. Maybe the camp was no more or less than it seemed: a slightly eccentric place where "struggling" kids went to farm and be one with nature.

The thing that made him think otherwise was

Price Palace. Right there, overlooking the camp, were the supposedly haunted ruins of a spectacular mansion, eradicated in a volcanic eruption, a fascinating sight by any measure, and yet the campers seemed afraid to speak about it, and the counselors never mentioned it. It was a conspiracy of silence.

If there were mysteries to be unearthed at Earth Ranch, then they would be found in the ruins.

With all his farm duties to attend to, Clay didn't have an extended period of free time until the end of the week. Even then free time turned out not to mean free time as much as it meant time to walk his llama.

Luckily, a llama walk was just what he had in mind.

In his week at camp, Clay had yet to see the camp beehive. Supposedly, it was in the clearing behind the banana grove, but when Clay looked there for Buzz, Clay saw only a tree. Or what was once a tree. It had been cleaved in two by lightning and now looked like a mismatched pair of blackened towers. Smoke billowed around the tree as if embers still smoldered inside.

Apprehensive, Clay stepped closer. Though long dead, the tree was teeming with life. Hundreds of frenzied bees flew in and out of a dark hole in the base of the tree, while honey oozed like sap out of the burned bark.

Buzz walked toward Clay, holding a smoking branch.

"Don't worry, there's no fire," he said from behind his beekeeper visor. "The smoke calms them. So they don't get too upset with me when I reach for the honey."

"That tree—that's the beehive?" asked Clay, keeping a safe distance from the smoke and the bees alike.

"Yep. We call it the treehive.... Where do you think bees make their hives in the wild?"

He put a dripping piece of honeycomb into a bucket.

"So anyway, would it be cool if I took Como up to the ruins on our walk today?" asked Clay. "I thought it would be fun to check the place out," he added, trying to sound as casual as possible.

Buzz seemed a little put off by Clay's request. "I don't know—this really should be the director's call," he said. "I'm sorry you didn't get here a minute earlier. Then you could have asked Eli yourself."

"Eli was here?" asked Clay, surprised. He'd been at Earth Ranch for seven days and still hadn't laid eyes on the director of the camp.

"Oh, he's always around somewhere," said Buzz vaguely. "He just likes to keep an eye on things in his own way."

He told Clay that as long as he stayed within

view of camp, he could go as far as the old palace gate. "That gate marks the boundary of the Wall of Trust. If you cross it, you may as well not come back."

A bee landed briefly on Clay's arm, as if to emphasize the point. He winced, bracing himself for a sting, but the bee flew away.

"Don't worry," said Clay, relieved. "I'm not actually going into the ruins. I'm just going to look."

He had no intention of crossing the Wall of Trust. The beestings on Pablo's arm were still fresh in his mind.

"Good, because that's the one thing that will get you sent straight home," said Buzz sternly. "And be back in time for Circle. We're having our first fire-starting lesson right afterward—"

An old gravel path connected the camp to the palace. Much of the path was overgrown, and most of the steps broken, but the hike posed no difficulty for the llama, and Clay did his best to follow.

As they zigzagged up the hill, Clay kept looking back and forth between the camp and the ruins. Partly, this was to gauge his progress; partly it was to keep an eye out for bees. At one point, Clay saw Leira standing on the dock in her bathing suit and a bathing cap. He waved to her. She did not wave back, though he was certain she saw him. When is she going to forgive me? he wondered. While he watched,

Leira grabbed onto the rope, swung herself into the lake, and started swimming toward Egg Rock, the large rock jutting out from the water. He remembered that the girls were having their swim test that afternoon. The boys would have theirs the following week.

After twenty minutes or so, the llama stopped, and Clay stepped onto a stone patio built to take advantage of the view of the lake and the volcano beyond. The patio was circled by an elegant marble balustrade that had somehow managed to survive the eruption of Mount Forge intact.

In the middle of the patio, sitting on a rock, was an old bronze statue of a girl reading a book. Years of exposure to the elements had turned parts of the statue turquoise and corroded other parts beyond recognition, but the girl's singular expression remained. Though her eyes were fixed on her book, she seemed to be looking somewhere far, far away.

Clay walked around the statue, studying it from all sides. According to the Worms, a girl had died when Price Palace burned down. Was the statue a memorial to her, maybe?

As clouds of vog started to drift over the lake, Clay tugged on the llama's leash. "C'mon, Como, let's go see what's up with these ruins."

The gate Buzz spoke of—and hence the Wall of Trust itself—stood about twenty feet inland from the patio. The doors of the gate had long ago disappeared, and the gate was now no more than an arch framing Clay's view of the ruins.

Clay glanced around, afraid that at any moment he would be surrounded by a swarm of bees. He didn't see any bees, but just in case, he picked a daisy out of the ground and held it between his fingers the way Leira had instructed him.

To Clay, the ruins still looked more like the remains of an ancient civilization than of some-one's home. A row of columns—a few of them unbro-ken, the others broken off at varying heights—stood alone, no longer holding up anything except the sky. Around them, bits and pieces of wall and roof lay like shards of a giant pot, but most of the ground was cov-ered with lava rock and ash. Evidently, the volcano had made a direct hit on the palace. There was only one wall of any significant size left standing. It was white and unadorned—a perfect spot, Clay couldn't help thinking, for a large graffiti piece.

While mentally writing his name on the wall, he became aware of a buzzing sound: A bee was flying straight at him.

"Aaack!" Clay swatted the bee away, dropping

the protective flower and the llama's leash at the same time.

"Sorry, sorry!" he exclaimed, immediately regretting what he'd done.

He was afraid the bee had flown away to collect recruits, but the bee hadn't left; it had landed on the llama's nose. For a second, nobody moved. Not Clay. Not the bee. Not the llama.

Then, apparently stung, the llama shrieked, reared his head, and bolted. Moving faster than Clay had ever seen him move, he ran through the ruins and disappeared around the hill. The bee disappeared after him.

"Como, come back! *¡Aquí! ¡Aquí!*"

Clay called the llama's name repeatedly, but the llama didn't return.

Panicking, Clay tried to decide what to do. To retrieve the llama, he would have to cross the Wall of Trust, and risk getting expelled from camp. And yet he couldn't just leave the llama; taking care of Como was his primary responsibility, and who knew what kinds of hazards there were on the island for a llama not used to life in the wild.

Clay hesitated, his fingers outstretched, as if there were an invisible electrified fence in front of him.

He looked back at camp. As far as he could tell, nobody was watching. And the bee hadn't come back.

To heck with it, Clay thought. What was the worst that could happen? Just a few days ago, he'd been hoping to go home anyway.

Bracing himself, Clay ran through the gate, and—nothing happened. No alarm rang. No swarm of bees descended. He was in the ruins.

The llama hadn't gone far.

He was grazing next to a round gray stone building that wasn't visible from camp or even from the palace gate. It was a tower, though I hesitate to call such a squat building a tower. About four stories high and equally wide, it had a conical roof covered with red tile. A single row of small square windows snaked around the side of the tower, starting at ground level and rising all the way to the roofline.

The tower looked like no other structure Clay had ever seen, but what was most remarkable about it was that it was completely untouched by fire or lava. Volcanic rocks were everywhere in the vicinity, but they stopped about three feet away from the tower's base, as though the perimeter of the tower had been protected by some invisible force field. In this protected space, wildflowers bloomed.

A few bees hovered among the flowers, but they appeared to take no notice of him; they could have been bees anywhere.

The llama stood a few feet from the front

entrance: two oversized bronze doors that together formed a triangle. Above the tower entrance appeared a cryptic name:

U   BRARY

Why did that name seem so familiar?

When he looked again, Clay could see that the sign had once said PRICE PUBLIC LIBRARY; it was just that most of the letters had fallen away.

Clay smiled sardonically. There was nothing public about this library. The front doors were locked with chains. Most of the windows were boarded up. There were vines covering the walls. It was the most private place he could imagine. Never mind that a private island was an absurd location for a public library to begin with.

In a flash, Clay realized that the library must have been the place the pilot tried to warn him about. That was why the name seemed so familiar.

Not *Beware—the—you—bury,* Clay thought. *Beware—the—U—BRARY.*

Did some unknown danger lurk inside? It was foolhardy, no doubt, but Clay felt a sudden, undeniable desire to find out.

Well, what would you have done? (I would have run back to camp, but I'm assuming you're more adventurous.)

Leaving the llama to graze a moment longer, Clay walked around the library tower, looking for a way in.

He found a small door hidden in a stairwell below ground level, but when he drew closer, he discovered that a large combination lock was built into the door; it was like the door of a safe. It could take years to get the door open. He was almost relieved. In truth, as much as he wanted to see inside the library, he was scared of what he might find.

The sun was shining directly overhead and Clay was beginning to feel hot and dizzy. It was time to go back to camp and drink some water.

"C'mon, Como. *Vámonos.* Maybe we can come back some other time."

As Clay turned away from the library, he happened to glance upward. He froze, his heart pounding.

There was a girl reading in one of the tower windows. Her red hair lit by the sun, she looked as though she were on fire. And yet her face was as pale and serene as snow.

She was pretty, beautiful even, but that wasn't why Clay stood there, rooted to the spot, unable to look away. It was the feeling of déjà vu. He knew he had seen her before, whoever she was, and yet he knew he had not. He'd never seen anyone remotely like her before.

Suddenly, their eyes met. Her mouth opened in

surprise, as if she were as startled to see him as he was to see her.

Clay pointed from himself to the library. *Can you let me in?* he mouthed.

She shook her head vehemently, fear on her face.

Then she disappeared. The tower looked as empty and desolate as it had before.

Clay blinked. Had she been an apparition? An effect of the light?

He considered banging on the door or looking again for a way in. But from far down below he could hear the sound of the gong reverberating across the valley. Free time was over.

Not only that, but wisps of clouds were floating by. The vog had begun to climb up the hillside. Soon visibility would be poor, and getting back to camp would be difficult.

He had no choice. He had to leave.

As he led the llama back down the mountain, Clay realized where he'd seen the girl in the tower before. Or rather why he thought he'd seen her.

The old statue on the patio. The statue of the girl reading. The girl reading in the tower window had worn the same faraway expression.

They could almost have been the same person.

CHAPTER
FOURTEEN

A CAMPFIRE STORY

I'm not sure who first got the idea that you could start a fire by rubbing two sticks together. It is extremely difficult, if not impossible. As you may know if you are a Scout or a forest ranger, a somewhat easier method for starting a fire is to make a hand drill out of a stick. Alas, even this method is difficult unless you've done it many times before. The first time he attempted it, Clay failed to make a spark. Thankfully, so did everyone else in his cabin. He was not alone in his embarrassment.*

The fire pit was situated under a large geodesic dome about halfway between Big Yurt and the lake. They could see the sun setting over the lake as each of them tried over and over to make a flame.

---

* I WOULD EXPLAIN HOW TO START A FIRE USING THE DRILL METHOD, BUT I'M AFRAID NO GOOD WOULD COME OF IT: EITHER YOU WOULD FAIL TO START A FIRE OR, WORSE, YOU WOULD SUCCEED IN STARTING A FIRE.

Eventually, they were sitting under the dome in the dark, like cavemen waiting for the invention of fire. In the center of the fire pit, logs were piled in the shape of a teepee, teasing them with the promise of warmth. Clay felt chilly for the first time since he'd been at camp.

"You're all trying too hard," said Buzz, who was seemingly as impervious to the passage of time as he was to the vagaries of temperature. "You have to let the fire breathe."

"Look at the bright side, this way you don't have to teach us how to put a fire out," said Kwan.

"Can't you just do it for us? I'm freezing," complained Jonah.

"I heard somebody needed a light," said Flint, casually swinging himself under the dome from out of the darkness.

His eyes glinting, Flint stood over the fire pit and snapped his fingers. For a second, sparks flew from his hand as if he were soldering a pipe. Then the logs burst into flame.

Amazed, Clay looked around at the others. They seemed amused more than anything else. It wasn't the first time they'd seen Flint's pyrotechnics.

Buzz's eyes narrowed. "This was supposed to be a teaching moment, Flint, not a fireworks display."

Flint laughed. "Just trying to lend a helping hand."

"I was going to invite you to stay for roasted mush-mallows, but maybe you should just go," said Buzz, visibly irritated.

"Sure, I hate those things anyway." Flint sauntered away, fire crackling behind him.

"I told you he was a pyro," Jonah whispered to Clay.

How did he do it, Clay wondered, watching Flint go. Did he have gunpowder on his fingers? A lighter up his sleeve? For the second time, Clay was stumped by one of Flint's magic tricks. As much as he disliked Flint, Clay couldn't help being impressed by his skill.

The mush-mallows were not mushy marshmallows, as Clay had hoped, but rather mushrooms roasted on sticks, marshmallow-style. Buzz claimed that the mushrooms, which were a very rare species found only on Price Island, had a marshmallow-like sweetness, but to Clay they tasted like dirt. About this one subject, he agreed with Flint. When Buzz wasn't looking, Clay spit his mushroom into his hand and discreetly dropped it to the ground.

While the others roasted more mushrooms, Clay sat on a log, gazing into the campfire, unable to get the mysterious reading girl out of his head. He kept seeing her in the tower window, her red hair seeming to engulf her head in flames.

Who was she? Why was she hiding? What was her secret?

Finally, when he couldn't bear it any longer, Clay pointed in the library's direction. "Hey, what's up with that tower over there—you know, the one past the ruins?" he asked, hoping that his breezy tone would keep Buzz from suspecting that he had crossed the Wall of Trust. "I saw it from a distance when I was walking Como, and I wondered what was inside."

"Ah, the Price Public Library," said Buzz, his expression not giving much away. "One of the world's biggest rare book collections, that's what's inside."

"You ever go in?" Clay asked, trying to hide his eagerness.

Buzz shook his head. "It's outside the Wall of Trust."

"You're a counselor!" said Pablo.

"Nobody is supposed to go in," said Buzz. "Price left strict instructions in his will."

"And nobody's ever tried?" asked Clay.

"Oh, a few have tried," said Buzz, looking hard at Clay. "We moved the Wall of Trust because of what happened."

"Why? What happened?" Clay's leg started to jiggle. Did Buzz know he'd been there? It almost seemed like it.

"A ghost!" joked Kwan. "That's what Jonah thinks."

"Oh, shut up," said Jonah.

"Actually, you're not too far off." Buzz glanced around the group. "You guys want to hear a ghost story?"

"This is a campfire, isn't it?" said Kwan.

"Just make sure there's lots of blood," said Pablo.

"Only a little blood, but lots of gold," said Buzz.

"Like *gold* gold?" asked Kwan. "Or like money?"

"Both," said Buzz. "Do you all know what alchemy is?"

"Kind of like magical chemistry, right?" said Jonah. "Like from the Middle Ages?"

"More or less," said Buzz. "Among other things, the alchemists believed that with the right recipe, they could turn lead into gold."*

He threw a big log onto the fire. It blazed high in the night.

"As the legend goes, Randolph Price was a poor street kid when he stumbled on the lost secrets of the alchemists. Where and how, he never revealed, naturally. But he brought their ancient magic into the modern world. He performed tricks on street corners. Predicted future headlines. Cured sick pets. Turned lead pencils into gold pens."

"That sounds pretty lucrative," said Kwan.

---

* THIS RECIPE, OF COURSE, WAS FOR THE FABLED *PHILOSOPHER'S STONE*, A SUBSTANCE BELIEVED NOT ONLY TO TURN LEAD INTO GOLD BUT TO MAKE PEOPLE IMMORTAL.

"Magicians fake that stuff all the time," said Clay, thinking of Leira and her theory about magicians being thieves. "If he had any gold, it's because he stole it."

"Maybe so. I'm just telling you the story as it was told to me," said Buzz. "When Price was sixteen, he turned his talents to stocks and bonds, and soon he had more money than he knew what to do with. People called him 'the Wizard of Wall Street,' not guessing that he might really be one."

"Wait, so you do think he did magic! Like real magic?" said Kwan.

"Then came the crash of 1929..." said Buzz, ignoring him.

"What crash is that?" asked Jonah. Clay remembered that it was a car crash that had brought Jonah to Earth Ranch.

"Stock market crash." Buzz poked at the fire with a stick. It blazed high again. "Everybody went broke. Except Price. The crash only made him richer. He started traveling the world, buying stuff on the cheap."

"Profiting off the misery of the poor. I knew it!" said Pablo.

"Paintings. Statues. Gold. Silver. He bought everything," said Buzz. "But mostly books. Old books. Rare books. The more books he got, the more he worried they would be taken from him. To keep them safe, he bought his own private island—this island—and he began building a palace for himself and a tower for his books."

"No more books," said Kwan. "I thought this was a ghost story. We want dead hands reaching out of graves."

"I'll see what I can do," said Buzz. "Just when work on the island was about to end, his brother and sister-in-law died in a crash—a real crash, a car crash. I'm sure it was very gory."

"Cool," said Kwan. "Now we're getting somewhere."

"Suddenly, Price had to take care of a three-year-old niece he'd never met. He brought her here, and she grew up with nobody for company but her uncle and thousands of books. You can imagine how lonely she was. It was her idea to make the library public. So there would be visitors on the island. But then Mount Forge erupted and Price Palace caught on fire. The entire place burned down, along with everything in it. Price was in the library at the time, and it was barely touched."

"But the niece was in the palace?" asked Jonah.

Buzz nodded, his eyes seeming to reflect not just the campfire in front of him but also the memory of the burning palace. "She was twelve years old. Price blamed himself—and his magic—for her death. Afterward, he became a hermit, locked up in his library.

Never saw anybody but his caretaker. When he died, he left money for this camp, and strict instructions to keep the library closed. Forever."

"What about the ghost part?" asked Pablo.

"Yeah, has anybody had any mysterious accidents?" asked Kwan. "Or heard spooky sounds at night?"

Buzz shook his head. "Nothing like that. But over the years, three campers have claimed to see a girl in a tower window reading a book."

He looked so serious, nobody said anything for a second.

"What—what does she look like—the girl in the window?" stammered Clay. He'd had an uncomfortable tingling in the back of his neck ever since Buzz first mentioned the niece.

"The descriptions are sketchy," said Buzz. "One camper said her hair was on fire; another that her hair was red with blood."

Clay swallowed. There was no doubt Buzz was talking about the girl he saw.

"So what's the big deal?" asked Pablo. "I mean, why did you have to move the Wall of Trust? Don't tell me you really believe the niece's ghost is haunting the library."

"It doesn't matter what I believe," said Buzz. "It matters what those three campers believe...."

"What do you mean?" asked Clay, his throat dry.

"I don't like using words like *sane* or *insane*," said Buzz, his face solemn in the firelight. "Let's just say that ever since seeing the girl in the tower, all three campers have had a little trouble dealing with what most of us call reality. One of them is now institutionalized. Another hasn't said a word in five years. The third...well, I'm hopeful that the third camper is going to be okay, but I keep a close watch on him."

Clay coughed, avoiding Buzz's eyes. Was this his way of saying he knew Clay had been to the library? Was he, Clay, the third camper? Or was there somebody else at camp who had also seen the girl in the window? Perhaps even somebody else in his cabin?

He looked around at his cabinmates, but he couldn't read anything in their faces except that they were getting very sleepy.

Late that night, Clay was replaying Buzz's ghost story in his mind when his attention was caught by the sound of Jonah murmuring in the bunk below. "Fire...fire..." he seemed to be saying.

Clay leaned over the bunk. Jonah was sitting up, but his eyes were glazed. He didn't look quite awake.

"What's wrong?" Clay whispered. "Do you smell fire or something?"

Jonah didn't answer, just repeated, "Fire...Fire..."

"Jonah, can you hear me?"

There was no response. He was still asleep.

Maybe he was dreaming about the Price Palace fire? Could Jonah be the third camper?

"Jonah, wake up!" Clay whispered a little more loudly.

But Jonah kept staring straight ahead. His expression never changing, he slipped out of his sleeping bag, got to his feet, and headed for the door. The rest of the cabin remained asleep.

Remembering the story about Jonah sleepwalking all the way into the lake, Clay climbed down to the floor and hurried after him. He didn't want to have to fish a sleeping boy out of the water.

Clay stepped out of the cabin just in time to see somebody running away in the dark, and to see the bathroom shack burst into flames—sudden, roaring flames—as if it had been doused in kerosene, then lit with a match.

Clay stared for a second, paralyzed by surprise. Then he saw Jonah, still asleep, walking directly toward the fire.

"Jonah! Fire!" Clay screamed.

He ran and grabbed Jonah, startling him awake.

"Let go of me!" Jonah yelled. "What are you doing?"

"Saving you!"

Jonah looked at him in confusion. "From what?"

"What's going on out there?" Buzz asked, leaning out of the cabin.

"Quick, get a hose or a fire extinguisher!" Clay shouted.

Kwan appeared behind Buzz. "Where's the fire?"

"What do you mean? It's right there—"

Clay turned back to the bathroom hut: The fire had gone out. Completely. There wasn't a wisp of smoke left. Even stranger, there was no evidence that the fire had ever been there. Clay took a step closer. There was nothing burned, nothing charred.

"Jonah, do you know what this is about?" Buzz asked.

"No, I just woke up," said Jonah. "This crazy kook dragged me outside in my sleep!"

"I did not! You were sleepwalking. And you were about to—"

Clay stopped in the middle of his sentence. While he was speaking, Flint had strolled up.

"Maybe you were the one sleepwalking, Worm," he said to Clay.

"I wasn't sleepwalking," said Clay through gritted teeth.

So it had been Flint whose shadow he'd seen running away. Figures, thought Clay.

"Then maybe you saw a reflection of my flashlight and thought it was a fire," said Flint, turning on his flashlight.

"I know what I saw," said Clay. "What're you doing out here, anyway?"

"I went out to take a leak. You got a problem with that, Worm?" Flint stepped right up to Clay and shined his flashlight in Clay's face.

"Leave him alone, Flint. He made a mistake, that's all," said Buzz. "C'mon back inside, Clay."

Confused and embarrassed, Clay followed his counselor back into the cabin—only to find sprinklers raining from the ceiling. Everything—and everyone—was drenched.

Clay pinched his nose. The sulfurous smell of the camp water was almost overpowering.

"We heard you yell 'fire,'" said Pablo, water dripping from his chin. "So we set off the alarm."

"Sorry," Clay muttered.

From the furious looks on the faces of his cabinmates, he could tell he wouldn't be forgiven anytime soon.

As he climbed onto his bunk, a crumpled piece of paper fell out of his pocket onto his wet sleeping bag. He unfolded it and found a short note scrawled inside.

STAY AWAY FROM HER, it read.

CHAPTER
FIFTEEN

THE SWIM TEST

I don't know about you, but I heard a lot of scary stories about summer camp when I was growing up. Snakes in sleeping bags. Underwear raids. Hands put in warm water to make you wet your bed.

Clay had heard those stories, too, and for the next couple of days, he kept looking over his shoulder and checking his sleeping bag, never allowing himself to close his eyes for very long. He knew his cabinmates were sore about getting drenched with water, and he was sure they would take revenge on him in some terrible and humiliating way.

He experienced no retribution, however, except for a few dirty looks, and eventually he stopped worrying about the Worms. His thoughts kept turning back to his strange sighting at the U-BRARY. What was it that he—and three other campers—had seen? If not a ghost, then who or what was the girl in the window—a real girl in hiding? A mass hallucination brought on by the vog? More than anything else, she seemed like a figure from a dream. But then there was the crumpled warning he'd received. Why would somebody want him to stay away from her if she wasn't real?

He assumed the note came from Flint; Clay was almost certain Flint was the mysterious third camper. The pyro-magician, as Clay thought of him, must have created the illusion that the bathroom was burning in order to scare Clay off. Clay told himself to be brave and confront the older boy, but the few times they crossed paths, Clay found himself looking down. Meanwhile, he waited for an opportunity to return to the U-BRARY.

He had to see the girl again. He had to know who she was. Or what.

Three nights after the false fire alarm, Clay awoke to a strange howling sound coming from across the cabin.

He looked over and saw someone—no, some*thing*— sitting up in Pablo's bed. Something with stringy red hair, a lumpy gray face, and a tattered white gown. Clay gasped...then saw that it was just a doll—an ugly ghost doll—lit from below by a flashlight. It looked like a bad Halloween display.

"Very funny, guys," said Clay. "It's the ghost girl from the ruins. I get it."

Scarier than the doll itself was the idea that they thought it would scare him; did that mean they knew he'd been to the library and that he'd seen the ghost?

"You can all stop pretending to sleep now. Pablo, where are you, anyway?"

Nobody moved. Either they were all really asleep or they were doing a good job pretending they were.

Suddenly, Clay started to feel nervous. Maybe the doll wasn't a practical joke by his cabinmates; maybe it was another warning from Flint.

Cautiously, Clay climbed out of his bed. Expecting to find another note, he took a closer look at the doll.

The hair was made from Jonah's red rope licorice, the head was a potato, and the girlie face was drawn with a pen. The doll couldn't have been cruder, but it was frightening-looking nonetheless.

As Clay studied the doll, the howling began again, and—

"Aaack!" Clay screamed, and jumped backward.

—the doll started climbing out of bed. By itself.

About knee-high, the puppet-like creature had a paint-can body, and arms and legs made from rusty pipes and springs—all connected to its potato head by a jumble of wires. It looked like a cross between Mr. Potato Head and the Tin Man—with long red hair and lipstick.

It lurched toward Clay.

"What is that? Somebody, stop it!" Clay yelled, now truly terrified.

The others burst into laughter. They were all awake after all.

Clay exhaled, relieved but deeply embarrassed.

"Dude, you should see your face right now!" said Kwan.

"Okay, very funny, what is that thing?" asked Clay as it teetered and finally fell over just before reaching him.

"That's Pablo's tater-bot," said Jonah. "His potato-robot."

Pablo, who had been crouching in the corner, picked up the tater-bot and set it lumbering in Clay's direction again.

"We're not supposed to have technology here, but they made an exception because Pablo made him all from recycled parts," said Kwan.

"Well, except for the potato," Pablo corrected. "I have to give him a new head every week or he starts to rot. That's where his power comes from."

"His power?" echoed Clay.

"Yeah, haven't you ever made a potato battery? See those wires—they make it all happen," said Pablo, pointing to the curling wires surrounding the tater-bot's head.

"Uh, not really," said Clay.* "Hey—"

The tater-bot was poking him with its extended exhaust-pipe arm.

"He wants to shake your hand."

"Uh, okay." Clay did his best. "Hi."

"His name is Cal, short for Caliban," said Pablo.

Clay looked at Pablo in surprise. "Caliban, like in *The Tempest*?"

"What? You think just 'cause I don't go to school, I don't know Shakespeare?"

"Sorry. It's just—never mind."

The tater-bot backed away from Clay a few paces, as if it were just as insulted as Pablo.

"So, all this time, you've been hiding him under your bed, waiting for the best time to freak me out?" Clay asked.

"Uh-huh. Pretty much," said Pablo, grinning.

Well, here was one question answered: The tater-bot was the mystery object Clay had seen peeking out from Pablo's sleeping bag.

"Look on the bright side," said Kwan. "Now we got you back. We don't have to hate you anymore."

"Well, that's a relief," said Clay.

And it was.

---

* If, like Clay, you have never made a potato battery, you will find instructions in the appendix.

A week later, Clay stood nervously on the dock next to the other Worms. It was time for their swim test.

According to Buzz, who was standing in front of them, their destination, Egg Rock, was exactly one-eighth mile from shore. "A long or short distance, depending on how strong a swimmer you are."

Clay was not a very strong swimmer. He had never been given a single swimming lesson, not by his brother (who swam even less well than he threw) or his parents (who believed Clay should teach himself). Clay could float, but forward motion was a challenge.

Still, it wasn't the prospect of the swim itself that was making him nervous; it was the guy standing on the rock, waving at them. Flint. Supposedly, Flint was a certified lifeguard and was there to ensure that nobody drowned, but based on prior experience, Clay had his doubts about how helpful Flint would be in an emergency.

"Ready, Worms?" asked Buzz. "Go for it. And may the Force be with you."

Clay hung back and went last. It wasn't required, but everyone else had entered the lake via the rope swing, and Clay felt like he had to do so as well. He swung back and forth over the water a few times—to get the hang of it, he told himself—before letting go. The rope dropped him about twelve feet above the water, and he made a big splash as he plunged in feet-first. He was expecting the bottom to be sandy like the ocean; instead, it was squishy and slimy. Gross, in other words. He pushed himself up as fast as he could.

Once he surfaced, he tried to break into a proper crawl stroke, but he had trouble breathing and he kept doing a frog kick rather than keeping his legs straight. After a couple of minutes of flailing around, he settled into a slow and awkward side-stroke. It was a little embarrassing—an old-lady style of swimming—but he tried not to think about what he looked like.

All he had to do was swim to the rock and back.

Ahead, he could hear the first swimmer getting to the rock. It was Kwan, who cheered loudly for himself after climbing to the top. Typical, Clay thought. Then—*splash!*—Kwan jumped back in.

"Took you long enough."

Clay was dizzy and breathing hard by the time he reached Egg Rock. Flint's smirking face stared down at him from behind a pair of dark sunglasses.

"You going to come up or what, Worm?"

Clay looked for a place to climb up, but the rock was covered with moss on all sides. An orange kayak bobbed nearby, tethered from above.

"What's the problem? Can't find a good spot?"

Flint held out his hand to pull Clay out of the water...then yanked his hand away as Clay reached for it. Luckily, Clay was prepared, and he managed to have his mouth closed when he fell back in. If that was all Flint had planned for him, Clay thought, he could handle it.

He swam all the way around the rock until he found a crevice that was relatively moss-free. Mercifully, Flint let him climb up in peace.

The older boy was now lying on a towel that he had managed to transport, dry, across the lake. In his hand was a paperback book with a bright blue cover, also perfectly dry. He looked like he was on vacation, not lifeguard duty. He touched his finger to his sunglasses in mock salute.

"Hate to be the one to tell you this, but maybe you shouldn't try out for the Olympic swim team."

"Thanks for the tip," Clay muttered.

Anxious to get off the rock as fast as possible, Clay waved toward the shore. Buzz gave him a thumbs-up and motioned for him to swim back.

During his time in the water, the younger girls' cabin had joined the boys on the dock. Clay could see Leira, in her trademark hat and suspenders, standing next to the rope swing. When she saw him looking at her, she turned around.

Flint laughed. "Somebody mad at you?"

Clay was inclined to get back into the water

without responding, but instead he looked squarely at Flint. "What do you have against me? What did I do?"

"Who says you did anything?" said Flint. "Maybe I just don't like you."

"This is what I don't understand," said Clay, ready to jump if Flint took a swing at him or threatened him in any way. "Why go through so much hassle just to mess with me?"

"What hassle?"

"That fire thing, for starters. When you made it look like the bathroom caught on fire. What did you use? A projector? A mirror? That kind of magic takes a lot of work."

Clay knew what he was talking about. When he was younger, he and his brother would go to magic shows together, with the express purpose of figuring out how magicians created their illusions. Occasionally, they themselves tried to make things levitate or disappear with the aid of mirrors, not often very successfully.

"And where am I going to get a mirror that size around here?" Flint scoffed.

"But you admit you faked it."

"No."

"So what are you saying? It was a real fire that just vanished?"

"If you knew anything about magic, you wouldn't be asking that," Flint snarled, standing up.

"Fine. I won't ask.... What about the note? Why do you want me to stay away from her?"

"Who?"

"You know who. The girl in the library."

Flint's nostrils flared. "She's mine."

"Why? Did you meet her? Did you talk to her?"

"I don't need to. I saw her."

He glared at Clay.

From the shore came a shrill whistle.

"Get going, Clay!" shouted Buzz through a bullhorn.

"You heard him," said Flint. "Get going."

He took a step toward Clay. His eyes were wild.

Clay meant to stand his ground, but in his anxiety he took an involuntary step backward and slipped on the moss.

Later he would rehearse the fall in his mind, trying to determine whether it had been an accident or whether Flint had tripped him somehow. At the moment, however, the only thing Clay was conscious of was the pain in his ankle and the sound of his skull slamming against rock.

Then...

...blackness...

CHAPTER
SIXTEEN

NURSE CORA

...clink...clank...

...plink...plunk...PLONK...

...cling...clang...cling...

...ding...ding...ding...

...DONG...

...ping...

At first, Clay thought it was his alarm clock, waking him for school. When he opened his eyes, he saw that the sound he was hearing was not his alarm; it was the sound of hundreds of bells and chimes of many sizes and shapes. They hung from the ceiling above him alongside crystals and dream catchers and amulets of all sorts, alternately refracting rainbows and casting shadows around the room.

Somewhere out of sight, a bird shrieked repeatedly—*Caw...Caw...Caw...*—adding another urgent note to the cacophony.

"Good, you're awake. That means you're not dead...yet." A woman looked down at him. She had a face like a shrunken apple, but not unpleasant.

Clay sat up to get a better look. Immediately, he became aware of pain in the back of his head.

"I'm Nurse Cora."

"Hi," Clay said, and started coughing.

Nurse Cora, Clay saw, was very short. Her standing height was approximately the same as his sitting. Beautiful in a munchkin-like way, she had long, thick silver hair that reached nearly to the floor and wrapped around her like a shiny coat. Had she been just a little bit smaller, you might have put her in a box and given her to a child to play with.

Next to her was a tall bamboo birdcage that was home to a parakeet whose shrill shrieks Clay deduced he had been hearing.

"My head hurts," said Clay.

"I'm sorry, you'll have to speak up," said Nurse Cora. "I'm deaf in one ear."

Clay thought she must be deaf in the other ear as

well; there was no way she would be able to tolerate the noise of the bells and the bird otherwise.

"I said, my head hurts."

"There would be something wrong if it didn't," said the nurse matter-of-factly. "You slammed it against a rock and then you almost drowned."

"Drowned?"

"Flint fished you out. Wasn't too happy about it, either, I gather."

Yeah, I'm sure he wasn't, thought Clay.

"Don't worry—you're going to be fine... probably. Sometimes the effects of an injury like yours are delayed. There is always the possibility of a sudden cerebral hemorrhage. Or brain damage, of course," she added sweetly. "Let me get you something to make you feel better."

She walked over to a small table that served as a kind of kitchen with a Bunsen burner and a toaster oven, and she poured from a pitcher of clear liquid with mint leaves and slices of cucumber. Behind her, vials of oils and unguents and jars of herbs filled the shelves alongside many obscure and out-of-date-looking medical textbooks seemingly in every language but English.

"Is that some sort of medicine?"

"The best kind. Water."

Clay sipped. The water was refreshing, he had to admit. The mint counteracted the sulfur taste of the

island's water. It didn't make his head feel any better, however.

"How long have I been here?" He half expected her to say days or even weeks.

"Just about an hour...Well, you seem well enough for me to leave you for a moment. Buzz will want to know right away that you've woken up."

"Um, okay. But could I not have visitors for a while? I think I want to rest."

The nurse studied him. "Very well. But I don't want you going back to sleep—it could be dangerous. I'll be back soon."

The bells tinkled as she left.

Clay got out of bed as soon as the door closed behind her. He was still in his damp bathing suit, but thankfully somebody had brought a pile of clothes for him. It was sitting on a chair beside the bed, next to a stack of books. He waited a moment for his dizziness to subside, then dressed as quickly as he could.

He'd been waiting for days for a chance to revisit the library. This was an opportunity he could not pass up.

In his hurry, Clay bumped into someone as soon as he exited the infirmary.

"Sorry!" he exclaimed. "I didn't—oh, it's you!"

Leira looked him up and down from under the brim of her hat. "So you're okay? I heard you were unconscious, maybe even in a coma."

"Disappointed?"

"A little," Leira admitted. "I thought you would be lying on a stone slab, all bandaged up like a mummy. But I guess this way is better. Now you can apologize to me for what a jerk you were. I wouldn't want you to go to your grave feeling guilty about it."

Clay smiled. "Is that your way of saying you were worried about me?"

Leira smiled back. "Maybe."

"Okay, I apologize," said Clay. "I'm sorry I said that stuff. Even though I didn't think you were listening—I probably shouldn't have said it anyway. I don't think you're annoying; I think you're cool. Well, sometimes annoying, but still—"

"So you won't mind if I steal your wallet again?"

"Well—"

"Check your pocket."

He patted his pocket. Sure enough, his wallet was missing again. "Aargh. You are so annoying! When did you take it?"

She grinned. "Never let a pickpocket bump into you if you can help it."

"I'll remember that.... Now give me my wallet back."

"First tell me where you were going when I bumped into you."

"I wasn't going anywhere, just...getting some fresh air."

Leira laughed. "You are the worst actor in the world."

"Okay, I was going back to my cabin."

She gave him a look. "You'd better do better than that if you want your wallet back."

Clay weighed his options. "Fine. Promise not to tell?"

"No. I don't make promises."

"It doesn't matter—you won't tell anyway. Thieves' honor, or whatever."

"That only applies if you're a thief, too."

"You want me to tell you or not?!"

Clay looked around to make sure they were still unobserved, and then he told her briefly about his llama running away from him and his subsequent discovery of the library. He left out the minor detail of seeing a girl who might or might not have been a ghost.

"So you crossed the Wall of Trust and you didn't get caught?" She whistled, impressed.

Clay nodded. "And now I want to see if there's a way into the library."

"You mean you want to see if the ghost girl is real."

Clay coughed in surprise. "What? How do you know?"

"That's what happened to everybody else who went up there, isn't it?"

"Well, you're not going with me," said Clay, peeved. "We're more likely to get caught if there's two of us."

"Who says I want to go? I'd much rather get credit for telling on you."

Clay gritted his teeth. "You wouldn't!"

Leira rolled her eyes. "Of course not. I guess I'm just not all that interested in seeing a bunch of books."

"Right. I remember. Your sister's the bookworm, not you."

Leira wrinkled her face in confusion. "What sister? I don't have a sister."

"Yes, you do."

"No, I don't. I'm the one who should know, aren't I?"

"When we were weeding, I was talking about my brother, and you said your sister was a bookworm."

Leira laughed. "Okay. Whatever you say. Maybe hitting your head really affected you after all. Because you are definitely imagining things."

Clay shook his head. He wasn't imagining anything. He knew—absolutely, positively—that Leira had mentioned a sister. Which meant that either she was lying then or she was lying now. But why would someone lie about a thing like that? Maybe Leira just really hated her sibling?

"Now listen to me," said Leira. "You got lucky last time. If you don't want to get caught before you go three feet, then you better go the back way, by that old barn."

"What old barn?"

Leira shook her head in disgust. "How were you going to get there if I didn't help you? Did you have any kind of plan at all?"

"Just tell me where to go," said Clay, irritated. "And by the way, what happened to giving me back my wallet?"

Leira giggled, and handed him his wallet. "You are so gullible. It wasn't even in your pants before. I only have it because I found it outside your cabin door."

After giving him directions to the library, Leira told Clay to wait one minute before leaving—if anybody was nearby, she'd warn him—and she slipped out the door.

That was when he noticed that his wallet, still in his hand, felt a little stiffer than he remembered. Curious, he looked inside. In the hidden compartment, he found a laminated card.

PRICE PUBLIC LIBRARY

it said in elegant black letters over a drawing of the
library tower. His name was typed below.

It was a library card.

Somebody wanted him to go back to the U-BRARY.

CHAPTER
SIXTEEN, PART 2

THE BACK WAY

To get to the library via the "back way," Clay had to hike up the trail that had first brought him to Earth Ranch. Then he was to follow the ridge around the camp, making a circle around the ruins.

From the ridge, he could see Pablo and Jonah standing on ladders in the banana grove. They were cutting off clumps of bananas and tossing them down to Kwan.* Clay experienced a pang of guilt; he

---

* Now here's some information that is sure to come in handy: A bunch of bananas is called a "hand," the word *banana* itself coming from an Arab word for finger, *banan*. While we're talking bananology (what, that's not a word?), I should note that the correct term for a bunch of banana trees is not banana *grove* but banana *plantation*. Still, *grove* is the word that Clay and others at Earth Ranch used, and it's the word I'm going to use in this book.

should be helping. Of course, he had almost drowned today. Shouldn't he get a get-out-of-banana-picking-free pass? He kept going.

After a few minutes, the trail dipped down to a small creek and passed through a forest of ferns so tall, Clay could walk under them without crouching. The vog was dense here, and Clay had trouble seeing where he was going. Feathery fern fronds tickled his face, and he slipped a few times in the mud.

At first he thought it was just the ferns making him jumpy, but soon he became convinced that he was being watched.

And/or followed.

"Leira, I know you're out there," he said loudly.

There was no answer.

"C'mon. Just walk with me. This is stupid."

Still no answer. Maybe it wasn't Leira. Maybe it was Flint, who wanted to keep Clay from seeing the ghost girl again. But then why wait—why not accost Clay now? He kept hiking.

The real question was how the library card had made its way into his wallet. If Leira was telling the truth and she'd really found his wallet lying outside his cabin, then anybody might have slipped the card in. But who? And why?

Perhaps the ghost girl had escaped the library, planted the card in his wallet, and was now escorting him back to her cold stone tower home? Clay glanced around for a second, as if she might float by or appear out of thin air. Then he laughed at himself for even entertaining the possibility.

Leira had said it should take about twenty minutes to reach the barn, but he had now been hiking for almost an hour. He was beginning to think he might have taken a wrong turn, when he saw a gray wooden structure with a moss-covered roof. According to Leira, the barn was the oldest building on the island, and indeed it appeared to be on the verge of collapse. That is, if the surrounding jungle didn't overtake it first.

As he drew closer, Clay was startled by the sound of barks coming from inside the barn—startled and scared, because the barn's door was hanging off its hinges. Whatever stray dog lurked inside could jump out at any second. The barking grew louder, but the dog never appeared. Clay hurried past, not taking his eyes off the barn door.

From there Clay pushed his way through a thicket of bushes, just as Leira had instructed, and he came right up on the back of the U-BRARY.

For a second time, the bees did not bother him. They buzzed around the library tower without paying him any notice. Clay was beginning to think that Pablo had exaggerated their vigilance. Either that or they

had decided to let Clay enter their domain unmo-
lested. Was it possible they wanted him to visit the
library? The thought was reassuring and unnerving
at the same time.

Without really thinking about it, Clay had
assumed he would find the red-haired girl in the
window again, and he felt a sharp pang of disappointment when he didn't see her. He tried to brush
away the feeling. What had he expected—that she
would be waiting for him with balloons and a welcome sign? He would just have to work harder to find
her this time, that was all.

Ginning up his courage, he knocked on the front
doors of the library. He was greeted by silence.

He knocked on the side door in the stairwell.
Silence again.

He knocked on one of the boarded-up windows.
More silence.

Then he walked around the library tower looking for vines to climb, windows to pry open, secret
doors to enter.

The library was a fortress.

Still determined to get inside, Clay returned to
the side door in the stairwell. He rotated the alpha-
betical combination lock built into the door, putting
his ear to the dial and listening for clicks and ticks
like a safecracker in a movie. On the first rotation,
he heard nothing, but after he slowed down for the

second rotation he was rewarded by a clicking sound at the letter *P*.

P for *Price*!? Could it be that easy?

He turned the dial the other way. Sure enough, there was a click when he got to *R*.

Excited, he turned the dial again, listening for the click when he got to *I*, but he heard nothing. He tried several more times, unwilling to give up, but eventually he had to concede that *PRICE* was not the combination. He tried a few other letters—*PRA* for *PRAY*? *PRE* for *PRESENT*?—with no luck.

In reality, he had no idea what he was doing. Word games were his brother's specialty, not his.*

Feeling like a fool, he walked back up the stairs. When he turned around for a last look, he noticed for the first time the words carved into the stone above the stairwell:

> *I'll break my staff,*
> *Bury it certain fathoms in the earth,*
> *And, deeper than did ever plummet sound,*
> *I'll drown my book.*

The Tempest! Yet again!

Those were Prospero's words. The words that had

---

* WORD GAMES? I KNOW CLAY'S BROTHER AS WELL AS I KNOW MYSELF, AND HIS SPECIALTY IS NOT WORD GAMES; IT'S BIRD NAMES.

made Clay clench his fists on stage weeks before. The words that were the basis for Mr. Bailey's confounding essay question. The words that led Clay to Price Island, and ultimately to this very place.

Then it struck him: The combination wasn't *PRICE*; it was *PROSPERO*.

CHAPTER
SEVENTEEN

INSIDE

*B*eware the U-BRARY.

The pilot's words reverberated in the back of Clay's mind, making his palms sweat as he pushed on the stubborn library door. Clay had the feeling that the door hadn't been opened for years, and for a moment he wondered why he should be opening it now. Nobody was making him enter the library. He would only get in trouble for it—or go mad, like the others. This was needless bravery.

Before he could change his mind—*crrrreak!*—the rusty hinges finally gave way, and Clay fell forward into the cool, quiet interior.

As soon as he was inside, he saw why the door was so heavy: It was hidden behind a bookshelf laden with thick leather-bound tomes. Clay tried to leave the door ajar, but it swung shut as soon as he let go. So much for his escape route!

Clay brushed cobwebs off his shirt as his eyes adjusted to the dim and dusty light. He was standing on a sort of endless balcony that spiraled around the interior of the tower like a corkscrew. As it went upward, the balcony became narrower and narrower, hugging the walls more and more closely, ultimately coming to a point just before reaching the ceiling. There it met a large round skylight covered with decades of dirt and bird droppings. At the same time, the balcony grew wider and wider as it traveled downward, creating the illusion that it was spinning beneath his feet. From where Clay stood, the library appeared to sink deep underground—like the rabbit hole in *Alice in Wonderland*. Exactly how far, Clay couldn't tell, because a massive indoor banyan tree was blocking his view. He estimated that the base of the tree was several stories below ground level, making the library at least twice as large as it had looked from the outside.

If only he'd had his skateboard. The library balcony would have made an awesome skating ramp. It was a crime that it remained unused.*

There was a thumping sound. Clay stiffened. It was footsteps. Or maybe something falling. From down

---

* JUST TO BE CLEAR, I AM EXPRESSING CLAY'S OPINION HERE, NOT MY OWN.

below. Or maybe it came from above. He couldn't tell. The circular walls created an odd, oscillating echo effect.

"Hello?" His voice came out in a whisper.

"Hello, is anybody here?" he tried again.

There was no response. Only the strange echo.

Clay waited a moment, his legs jiggling. As far as he could tell, he was alone. There were no more sounds. No signs of life other than the occasional spider sitting in wait or dropping from the ceiling to spin another web.

Walk, he told himself. Move. Go.

There was almost too much to look at.

The dark mahogany bookshelves that lined the walls of the library were full to overflowing, not just with books but with all manner of curiosities and art objects. Not to mention, books that were curiosities or art objects in and of themselves.

As Clay walked slowly and cautiously upward, he passed treasures large and small: elaborately painted vases from China and Greece. Antique microscopes, telescopes, and gyroscopes, and other relics of the scientific revolution. Fossils, corals, and shells from the seven seas. There were crystals and meteorites and a collection of volcanic rocks culled, according to their labels, not just from Price Island but from volcanoes the world over.

On one wall, stone tablets etched with obscure

cuneiform symbols were propped up on steel shelves. Another wall was covered with framed papyrus pages decorated with Egyptian hieroglyphs. Still another wall was devoted entirely to a collection of miniature books housed in miniature libraries that were decorated with miniature artwork, miniature desks, and miniature globes.

Everything was meticulously organized and labeled with identifying characteristics and call numbers. Even the nonliterary artifacts seemed to have been adapted to the Dewey decimal system.* Clay had the feeling that if he moved anything an inch, somebody would notice. But of course the library's owner was long dead. For all Clay knew, he was the first living person to enter the library in decades. It was like walking through an enormous tomb full of books—enough books to last an eternity, if you happened to be a ghost-in-residence.

---

* THE DEWEY DECIMAL IS THE WORLD'S MOST WIDELY USED LIBRARY CLASSIFICATION SYSTEM. (TRY TO NAME ANOTHER ONE—I DARE YOU.) FIRST PUBLISHED IN 1876, IT WAS DEVELOPED BY LIBRARIAN MELVIL DEWEY. (NOT TO BE CONFUSED WITH JOHN DEWEY, THE PROGRESSIVE EDUCATOR, OR EVEN DEWEY OF THE TV SHOW MALCOLM IN THE MIDDLE. AND DEFINITELY NOT TO BE CONFUSED WITH THE ANIMATED DUCK OF THE TRIO HUEY, DEWEY, AND LOUIE.) THE DEWEY DECIMAL SYSTEM USES THREE-DIGIT NUMERALS TO REPRESENT TEN MAIN CLASSES OF SUBJECTS, WITH DECIMALS EXPANDING TO REPRESENT MORE DETAIL. WHILE THE SYSTEM CONTINUALLY EVOLVES, SOME SPOTS REMAIN UNASSIGNED. OR SO THEY SAY. WE CAN ONLY IMAGINE WHAT TERRIBLE SECRETS ARE PLACED IN THOSE UNASSIGNED SPOTS. MY FAVORITE DECIMAL: 000—IT STANDS FOR "GENERALITIES." SECOND-FAVORITE: 135—"DREAMS AND MYSTERIES."

Clay stopped at the library's locked front doors. Directly across from them was a long desk that looked not unlike the checkout desk at Clay's local library. Nearby was a bank of wooden cabinets, composed of small, alphabetically labeled drawers—several hundred of them, Clay guessed. This bank of cabinets, by the way, is called a *card catalog*. (A card catalog contains cards identifying all the books in a library; once upon a time, every library had one.) The Price Public Library was set up to be a fully functioning lending library, although it seemed unlikely that Price would ever have lent any of his books; most of them looked much too rare and valuable.

Clay noticed that one of the drawers in the card catalog had been left open. A card was sticking out conspicuously from the others:

Price, Randolph A. 1901–1985
Memoirs (incomplete)

Clay thought about the library card in his wallet. Had the card catalog intentionally been left open for him by the same mysterious benefactor?

Clay couldn't have said what made him aware of her presence—a faint stirring of the air?—but he turned around and there she was, standing before him. The red-haired, pale-cheeked mystery girl from the library window.

Her hair was pulled back in a ponytail, and she was wearing a navy polka-dot dress, white socks, and shiny black shoes of the type (although Clay didn't know it) known as Mary Janes. She may not have looked like a ghost, or not like what you expect a ghost to look like, but she certainly didn't look like she was part of the modern world. If anything, she looked like a girl from the 1950s on her way to a sock hop.

He sensed that she was very afraid. It could have been the dimness of the light, but it seemed to Clay that fear was draining the color from her face.

He wanted to tell her that she had no reason to fear him—that he meant no harm. But before he could say anything, she put her finger to her lips. At once, he realized it wasn't him she was afraid of. Silently, she moved behind the checkout desk and motioned for him to follow.

As he crouched down next to her, he thought he could feel her cool breath on his shoulder. He wanted to touch her, to confirm she was real, but he didn't dare. She sat very still but trembling slightly, alert to danger like a deer in the presence of a hunter. Lumbering footsteps echoed around them.

Clay caught only a few brief glimpses of the man passing by, but they were enough to paint a picture: Dark rubbery coat. Stained overalls. Big leather work gloves. Protective goggles. Lumpy, blotchy, scabby bald scalp. There was no way to tell how old the man was. Nor could Clay tell how tall he was; he was too stooped over. Judging from his limping gait, he had been injured in some way. And yet he projected strength. His muscles bulged defiantly, unwilling to hide under his coat.

He held an old brass torch in his hand. As Clay watched, the man stopped, tapped the canister, and pressed on the nozzle, testing the flame. Clay couldn't help imagining him using the torch as a weapon to ward off unwanted intruders.

Seemingly satisfied, the man limped away, heading into the depths of the library.

For a few moments, the red-haired girl remained hidden behind the desk with her finger to her lips. Finally, she stood, her dress grazing his shoulder. At least her clothes are real, he thought.

"You must leave right now," she whispered urgently.

"Why? Who are you? Who was that man?" Clay whispered back.

"That man is my uncle, and he is the only person allowed in the library. Nobody else. Not even me...officially. There's no saying what he'll do if he sees you."

"Don't I have a second at least? It looked like he was going to fix something."

"He has a workshop in the boiler room. Sometimes he's in there for hours, but sometimes only minutes—" She looked stricken.

"Isn't there somewhere we can hide? I have to talk to you. Please." Clay felt as though he were being let in on the first real secret of his life. He couldn't leave without knowing more.

The girl hesitated. It seemed to Clay that part of her wanted him to stay.

"All right. In there." She pointed to a door.

She led him into a large underground room that looked something like a laboratory with a long counter, a sink as big as a bathtub, and jars and jars of solvents and glue. Shelves were piled with papers and cardboards of varying weights, as well as leather and thread. It was a room for restoring and repairing books, but it looked like it had not been used in years.

The girl hovered nervously while Clay inspected the shelves. There was an awkward silence.

Clay didn't know where to start. "I'm Clay, I go to the camp."

"Camp?"

"You know, Earth Ranch. Right down the hill."

"Oh, yes, the camp," she said vaguely. Clay had the impression that she'd never heard of it, which was close to impossible, given that Earth Ranch was the only other habitation on the island.

"What's your name?" he asked.

"Mira. Pleased to make your acquaintance, I'm sure."

Clay laughed. "Pleased to make your acquaintance, I'm sure," he repeated.

"Are you mocking me?"

"No, of course not," he said hastily. He didn't want to offend her. He was sure she would run away at the slightest provocation. "So, what are you doing here? I mean, do you live on the island or what?"

"I summer on the island...well, in the library," said Mira, no longer whispering, but still with hesitation in her voice.

"Summer?" Clay had never heard the word used as a verb before.

"Yes, I spend summers here."

"What about the rest of the year?"

"Oh. I...I go to boarding school," she said, as though she'd almost forgotten.

Mira explained that she was an orphan; her uncle Ben was her only surviving relative.

"The problem is, nobody can know I'm here because nobody's supposed to enter the library except him; he's the caretaker. It's in Mr. Price's will."

"So you have to stay inside?"

"That's right."

"You know, people think you're a ghost," said Clay, studying her. "The ghost of Price's niece."

"Golly! Imagine that!" She seemed amused by the idea. It was the first time he'd seen her smile.

"She lived here with her uncle, too. That's kind of a big coincidence, isn't it?"

"Yes, I suppose it is.... Hey, do you think I'm her ghost and I just don't know it?" Mira giggled. "Boo!"

Clay forced a laugh, though for some reason he didn't think her idea was so funny.

"Well, if you're not a ghost, what do you do here all day? Seems kind of...boring."

"Oh, there's tons to do! Read, for one. I just adore books! Positively adore them," exclaimed Mira, forgetting her nervousness in her enthusiasm. "And if I'm ever tired of reading, I can always watch a picture show. There's a projector here and everything. I absolutely adore the cinema, almost as much as books. Don't you? I'm practically a cinema fanatic! What's your favorite motion picture?"

"Of all time? I don't know. I used to be really into *Star Trek*. Not so much the movies, though. Mostly the TV show...you know, the old-school one," he added to make sure he didn't sound too uncool.

"*Star Trek*? Is that about Hollywood stars?" she asked hopefully. "Where are they going on a trek to?"

"No." Clay laughed, incredulous. Who didn't know *Star Trek*? "It's science fiction. You know, spaceships and stuff?"

"Oh," said Mira, disappointed. "Well, I'm going to be a big Hollywood star someday. Katharine Hepburn is my idol."

"Who's that?"

Now Mira looked incredulous. "Do you live under a rock? She's only the greatest actress in the world! *Bringing Up Baby? The Philadelphia Story?*"

Clay shook his head. "Sorry, never heard of her."

"Well, I just think she's the bee's knees. She's a very modern woman. Can you believe she only ever wears pants?"

"So?"

"Maybe it doesn't mean anything to you—you're a boy. But imagine if you had to wear skirts every day. It makes it so hard to ride a bike or a horse. It's so unfair!"

"So wear pants, then," said Clay.

"Easy for you to say! Uncle Ben doesn't approve." Mira pouted. "But when I get older, I'm going to be just like Red—that's what Cary Grant calls Katharine Hepburn. She has red hair, just like mine. You wouldn't know it from her films, of course. They're in black and white."

"They must be really old."

"True art never gets old." Mira sniffed.

"How old are you, anyway?"

"What a question to ask a lady!"

Clay was now certain Mira was the oddest girl

he'd ever met. She seemed to be locked in some kind of time capsule—as if she had stepped out of one of the old movies she loved so much. At the same time, there was something dream-like about her; when he was with her, the rest of the world seemed to fall away.

"Have you ever seen *Citizen Kane?*" asked Mira. "Uncle Ben made me watch it. He thinks it's the best film of all time, but it gave me the creeps."

"I know what you mean," said Clay. "My brother likes it, too, but I think it's boring."*

"We agree on something, then. Maybe we can be pals after all. Deal?"

"Deal," said Clay.

They smiled at each other.

Clay was just thinking how glad he was that he had forced his way into the library, when the door opened. They were caught.

Correction: Clay was caught.

Mira slunk out of sight.

---

* COINCIDENTALLY OR NOT, *CITIZEN KANE*, THE FILM CLASSIC BY ORSON WELLES, IS ABOUT A WEALTHY MAN, NOT UNLIKE RANDOLPH PRICE, WHO COLLECTS TREASURES FROM AROUND THE WORLD, ONLY TO DRIVE HIMSELF TO DESPAIR WHILE BUILDING A PALACE TO HOUSE THEM.

CHAPTER
EIGHTEEN

THE CUSTODIAN

You—boy! What are you doing here?"

Uncle Ben was still wearing his goggles and gloves, but he was no longer carrying a torch; he was pointing a finger in Clay's direction.

Clay took a step forward, a small step, to show he wasn't afraid. Which was ridiculous, because of course he was afraid. Very afraid.

"Hi, I'm from the camp. I'm a guest of your niece," he anxiously explained. "I mean, not that she invited me. She didn't—I just kind of, um, let myself in." He didn't want to get her in trouble.

"Niece? I don't have a niece," Uncle Ben growled, in a voice that sounded like the revving of an outboard motor.

"Well, whatever you call her, the girl in the library, then," said Clay.

Uncle Ben glared. "The only girl in this library

died almost seventy years ago. Is this your idea of a joke?"

Clay glanced at Mira, who was suddenly visible again, tiptoeing out of the room. She nodded vehemently, signaling that Clay should play along. Then she slipped out the door.

"Uh, you're right, I'm sorry," said Clay, remembering that officially Mira wasn't supposed to be there, either. "The other campers say there's a ghost girl haunting the library, and...I guess the joke wasn't very funny."

"No. It wasn't."

Clay kept expecting Uncle Ben to wink, but he didn't. He was so stone-faced it was as though Mira didn't exist and never had.

"Now, I'm asking you one more time: How did you get in here?" barked Uncle Ben. "Answer me, boy, before I throw you out on your ear!"

"Um, I got in through the side door. I recognized the quote."

"Huh," Uncle Ben grunted suspiciously. "Not many boys your age read Shakespeare."

"*The Tempest* is my favorite Shakespeare play." Clay didn't mention that it was the only one he knew.

"I see," said Uncle Ben. "It was the master's favorite, too."

"The master?"

"Mr. Price. I believe he related to the story."

"Because it's about a man on an island...with his books...and his daughter?" asked Clay, putting it together for the first time. "Price was with his niece, but I guess other than that..."

Uncle Ben unclasped a key ring from his pants and motioned for Clay to follow him out of the room.

"Well, you got in, you saw it, now go," he said as he limped toward the library's front doors. They were locked from the inside with a heavy iron chain. "That's what you came for, right? Bragging rights?" He started unlocking the padlock on the door. "Or were you planning on taking something? I warn you, you won't get far on this island."

"I swear, I wasn't going to take anything. I just wanted to look," said Clay.

"So you say." The padlock now hanging loose, Uncle Ben started to open the door.

"Hey, is there any chance—could you show me a book?" Clay asked, stalling. "I mean, since I'm inside anyway? The library looks awesome."

He knew he should leave, but he had noticed again the open drawer in the card catalog. He couldn't get over the feeling that somebody had left that card sticking out as a message for him.

"I was kinda hoping to see Mr. Price's memoir," he said. "He sounds like a real interesting guy."

"Name one reason I should let you." Uncle Ben

removed his goggles and stared hard at Clay. His eyes were gray-blue and bloodshot.

"Um, because I have this?" said Clay impulsively. He pulled his wallet out of his pocket and handed his Price Public Library card to Uncle Ben.

"Well, well..." Now Uncle Ben looked like he was the one seeing a ghost. "Where did this come from?"

"Uh, somebody at the camp gave it to me," said Clay.

Uncle Ben appeared to debate something with himself.

"All right," he said abruptly.

As Clay watched, Uncle Ben pocketed the library card. Clay knew better than to ask for it back.

"But remember, this visit never happened. If even one camper knocks on my door saying he heard you were here, I'm coming for you—"

"Don't worry, I can keep my mouth shut," said Clay.

"Good. I'll show you that book you asked about, but first I will show you the library," said the old man. "The library is Mr. Price's real memoir."

The tour was surprisingly formal. Apparently, Uncle Ben had decided that if he was going to show Clay the library, he was going to do it right.

"The master was very particular about how his books were handled," he began. "You have to be very careful with the spines."

To demonstrate how to treat a rare book properly, Uncle Ben opened a book on one of the velvet V-shaped "cradles" that were found at convenient spots throughout the library.

"Go ahead—flip through the pages," he said. "A bit of finger grease is good, the master always said. Helps preserve the paper."

The book Uncle Ben had chosen had a very ordinary-looking brown leather cover. The interior, however, was extraordinary, at least to Clay's eyes. Paging through, Clay saw brooding black-and-white drawings of angels and monsters, and brilliant full-color illustrations of golden suns and silver moons. But what struck him most was the lettering. In some cases, single letters took up entire pages and were decorated with intricate three-dimensional designs, all hand-drawn—graffiti art from hundreds of years ago.

"What is this book?" he asked.

"Oh, just one of our illuminated manuscripts," said Uncle Ben, the ghost of a smile on his lips. "Would you like to see some others?"

"Heck, yeah," said Clay, who was suddenly much more interested in old books than he ever imagined he'd be.*

---

* IN THE PAST, CLAY HAD BEEN AN AVID READER, ESPECIALLY OF FANTASY BOOKS. BUT AT A CERTAIN POINT HE DECIDED FANTASY BOOKS WERE SILLY AND FAKE—YES, THIS WAS AT THE SAME TIME HE DECIDED MAGIC WAS SILLY AND FAKE—AND HE HAD READ FAR FEWER BOOKS SINCE.

Under Uncle Ben's guidance, Clay inspected enormous maps of long-gone countries, and manuscripts by long-forgotten authors. He unfurled ancient parchment scrolls, some as simply designed as a rolling pin, others with handles as ornate as the hilt of a royal sword.

Besides the illuminated manuscripts Uncle Ben had promised, Clay got to see an actual Gutenberg Bible and an early Shakespeare folio, as well as first editions of *Robinson Crusoe*, *Treasure Island*, and *The Wonderful Wizard of Oz*.

"Have you noticed anything about the way the library is laid out?" asked Uncle Ben.

"Uh, the books get newer as you walk up, and older as you go down?" Clay guessed.

"Yes, that is exactly how the master envisioned it," said Uncle Ben, pleased. " 'To walk the length of the balcony will be to see the history of books unfold'—those were his very words."

He pointed around the library. "Down there you see the scroll of the ancient world being replaced by the codex—that is, by the bound book of today. There you see how calfskin was replaced by paper from trees. And over there are the incunabula—the first books printed after the invention of movable type."

MAYBE I SHOULDN'T SPEAK FOR HIM, BUT I THINK HE MISSED READING MORE THAN HE REALIZED.

"Am I really the first one to see all this stuff in years and years?" said Clay, who was still trying to get Uncle Ben to admit Mira's existence. "It's too bad. You're an awesome librarian."

"Oh, I'm no librarian!" Uncle Ben shook his head as if the idea were totally outlandish. "I have no training, no formal education.... Everything I know, the master taught me. He even taught me to read, if you can believe it. I was just a wild island boy until I met him.... Oh no, I'm just the custodian here. A caretaker, nothing more."

He sighed, surveying his domain. "It's a losing battle, though. Guess what is the single most dangerous place to keep a book, historically? A library."

"You're joking, right?"

The custodian shook his head. "Just think of Alexandria... Pompeii.... Every great library burns down eventually."

"Isn't this building fireproof?" said Clay, thinking of the mysterious lava-free ring around the exterior of the library.

"Oh, I doubt we'll be so lucky next time," said Uncle Ben mournfully. "Of course, the most valuable books are housed in a special vault that the master built." He nodded to the base of the banyan tree at the bottom of the library.

"What could be more valuable than a Shakespeare, what do you call it, folio?" asked Clay.

"I don't know for sure—the access code died with Mr. Price—but some say there are grimoires in there."

"Grimoires?"

"Magic books."

"You mean books *about* magic or books that *are* magic?" asked Clay.

"Maybe both." The custodian's eyes twinkled—as much as bulging bloodshot eyes can twinkle.*

The tour ended in Randolph Price's office. It was small, considering the size of the library, not to mention his vast wealth. But it was lavish enough, with antique chairs upholstered in red velvet and gold-framed paintings of men and women with enormous ruffled collars.

"The master barely left this office after his niece died," said Uncle Ben, his hand on an old library globe that showed the world as it was two hundred years ago.

Clay looked at the coffee cup and cigar butts on the desk. "And now you work in here?"

"What? Never!" said Uncle Ben, horrified. "Those are the master's things."

---

* A GRIMOIRE IS A MAGICAL TEXTBOOK. USUALLY MANUALS ON HOW TO CREATE MAGICAL OBJECTS AND PERFORM SPELLS, THEY ARE ALSO SAID TO BE IMBUED WITH MAGIC THEMSELVES. CURIOUSLY, THE WORD GRIMOIRE IS ETYMOLOGICALLY RELATED TO THE WORD GRAMMAR. SO THE NEXT TIME YOUR LANGUAGE ARTS TEACHER OFFERS TO GIVE YOU A GRAMMAR LESSON, DON'T BE SO QUICK TO SAY NO; A COVERT MAGIC LESSON MAY FOLLOW.

"You mean they've been here since he died?"

"Of course," said Uncle Ben stiffly. "I wouldn't dare touch them."

Clay nodded, trying not to show how creepy he thought this was.

"Is there a picture of his niece around?" Clay asked. He figured if they kept talking about her, eventually Uncle Ben would have to get around to the subject of his own niece.

Uncle Ben shook his head. "The master couldn't bear to be reminded of Mira after she died."

"Wait, who?" Clay asked, confused. "You mean Mira was the name of *Price's* niece?"

Uncle Ben's eyes narrowed. "I thought you knew about her."

"Yeah, I did. I just—"

Clay's mind raced. What did it mean? If Mira was the name of Price's niece, what was the library girl's name? Also Mira? That seemed unlikely, to say the least.

"What did Mira look like?" he managed to ask.

"I never met her. They say she was very beautiful, with long red hair."

"Red hair?"

"Yes, and ivory skin, the master said."

The custodian was describing the girl in the library! Could the ghost girl actually be a ghost? Clay found himself wondering.

Or was he going crazy, like everyone else who'd seen her?

"Is something the matter?"

"Uh, no. I just...hurt my head today." In fact, his head was starting to throb again.

"That's what happens when you break into buildings.... The only personal item the master kept after the fire was his journal." Uncle Ben pointed to a glass box on the desk. THE MEMOIRS OF RANDOLPH PRICE, read the brass plaque. "That's what you wanted to see, isn't it?"

Clay glanced at the journal inside. Why did it look so familiar?

With a start, he realized it looked exactly like the journal Mr. Bailey had given him, the journal that had gotten Clay into so much trouble. Price's journal had a rust-red cover with a triangular mirror inset in the leather—just like Clay's had. It even had the same ink-splat stain! Or was this just another sign that his mind was playing tricks on him?

"Can—can I take it out?" Clay stammered.

"Sorry, it's private."

"Please. I'd really like to see it."

The custodian was adamant. "The master didn't want anyone coming into this library. Imagine how he felt about his journal. I've never even looked at it myself."

"You don't understand. I think it's mine."

"The journal?"

Clay nodded. "I know it sounds crazy—"

"Are you pulling my leg? That journal has been in that case for fifty years."

"But it has an ink stain, just like mine—"

"So? There are ink stains everywhere." The custodian pointed to an ink stain on his shirtsleeve as proof.

"Please—"

"No! I shouldn't have let you stay in the first place. The master would never have approved," said Uncle Ben, agitated. The loquacious librarian was gone; the churlish custodian had returned. "Now get out before I report you to the director of your camp!"

He practically pushed Clay out of the office.

On the way out, his head throbbing with pain, Clay looked up at the highest tower window. There she was again. The red-haired girl in the polka-dot dress who might or might not be named Mira. She raised her hand, parting her fingers slightly, then receded into the darkness of the library.

CHAPTER
NINETEEN

THE JOURNAL

Clay's mind was a jumble of thoughts as he made his way back to camp through the vog.

Among the things bothering him: the way Mira had parted her fingers in the window as he was leaving. He could have sworn she was giving him the *Star Trek* Vulcan hand salute. But if she was, why had she pretended never to have heard of *Star Trek*? Was there a normal, modern girl hidden inside her, waiting to get out?

And then there was the uncle, claiming not to know who she was, then describing her exactly. None of it added up.

An odd idea occurred to Clay: The girl and her uncle—if he really was her uncle—could it be that they were deliberately conspiring to make him think she was the ghost of Price's niece?

Yes, Clay was suddenly sure of it. That was why Uncle Ben pretended she wasn't there; he was trying to make Clay think Mira was visible only to Clay. And that was why she used those old-fashioned expressions and talked about that old actress Clay had never heard of; the girl herself was acting. She was pretending to be a girl from seventy years ago!

But why would they want him to think she was a ghost? Maybe they thought a ghost would scare away the camp kids. That was the only explanation Clay could think of. But it was hardly a satisfying one—

Clay didn't know what to expect when he got back to camp. It was more than three hours since he'd left, and it was likely that everyone would be on red alert, searching for him, the errant camper with the head injury. Then again, maybe Nurse Cora had never signaled that he'd gone. She seemed like somebody who heard only what she wanted to hear and saw only what she wanted to see.

The camp was quiet, in any event. The vog was so thick that Clay could see no more than ten feet ahead. He had never been so grateful for the cover it provided.

As he reached Big Yurt, Clay glanced back in the direction he'd come from—and was astonished to see the director's teepee hovering about two feet in the air. At least, that's what he thought he saw. He blinked and the teepee was sitting on the ground. He blinked again and it was gone, lost in the vog.

He rubbed his aching head. Whether it was an effect of the injury or of meeting Mira, something was making him imagine things that weren't there. What he needed was to lie down and stop thinking so much.

Thankfully, his cabin was empty.

By the time he climbed into his bunk, Clay was so tired—and his head was in so much pain—that he almost didn't see it waiting for him.

The red journal on his white pillow.

His first reaction was panic and confusion. He looked around wildly to make sure nobody was watching, then he thrust the journal under his pillow as if it were evidence of a crime.

Mira must have absconded with it when her uncle wasn't looking, he concluded when he started thinking rationally. Somehow she'd managed to run it down to camp ahead of Clay. Perhaps she knew a shortcut.

Unless it was someone else who had stolen it for him? Maybe that same secret benefactor who'd left the library card in his wallet?

He was just pulling out the journal for a second, calmer look, when somebody entered the cabin.

"Clay, there you are!" It was Buzz, his expression all concern. "How's your head?"

"Uh, it's okay. I couldn't rest in the infirmary," said Clay, slipping the journal back under his pillow. "Too noisy."

Buzz smiled. "I know what you mean. That bird always seems to have something really urgent to say."

"Sorry, guess I should have told somebody I was leaving."

"Well, I've got bad news for you," said Buzz, causing Clay's heart to skip a beat. Had Buzz already heard about the stolen journal? "Your rest is over. Everybody's about to come in for Circle."

"Oh, right. What's the topic for today?" Clay asked, relieved.

"Honesty. With ourselves and with others," said Buzz, staring Clay down. Clay gulped, but Buzz didn't say anything further until Circle started.

Clay didn't dare look at the journal again until close to midnight, when he was sure his counselor and his cabinmates were all asleep.

Tense with excitement, Clay turned on his flashlight and shined it on the journal's cover. The ink-splat was just as he remembered: star-shaped but smeared. If you squinted, it looked almost like a shooting star. How had his journal landed under glass in a library on an island thousands of miles away from where he lived?

In a week full of mysteries, this was perhaps the biggest mystery Clay had confronted yet.

No. As soon as Clay opened the journal, where he expected to see the words *MAGIC SUCKS!*, he instead saw a date and the title

The Memoirs of Randolph Price

followed by pages of handwriting—neat, careful handwriting—that looked nothing like Clay's own. There was no mystery after all; the journal wasn't his. It was just a coincidence that the journal covers looked so similar. Clay was disappointed and relieved at the same time.

He sighed and started reading. Maybe he would learn more about the original Mira, or more about the library the pilot had warned him about weeks ago.

Soon, Clay was sitting up in bed, mouth agape. *MATH STINKS!* the memoir began:

> I was a mischievous miscreant of twelve when my math teacher caught me writing those words on his wall. For me, it was the last straw. In short order, I was sent away to a dreaded reform school in a faraway city.

What misery! The Ian G. Grantland School for the Moral Improvement of Wayward Boys was a grim, gray place with scary teachers and even scarier students. My classmates included an underage bookie, an anarchist, and a sleepwalker who got into trouble every night trying to knock down his neighbors' doors. And those were just the boys in my room!

A bookie, an anarchist, and a sleepwalker? Clay thought immediately of Kwan, Pablo, and Jonah. The parallel with his cabinmates couldn't have been more obvious. Never mind that MATH STINKS! sounded so much like MAGIC SUCKS! . . .

He continued to read with increasing disbelief.

I spent most of my time hiding in the school library, where I read morning 'til night. I liked adventure stories best, stories like TREASURE ISLAND and ROBINSON CRUSOE, that always seemed to wind up with their hero stranded on a desert island.

The librarian was an old bald man with bulging eyeballs and a nasty temper, but he took a liking to me for some reason.

One day, he handed me a tattered copy of a play by William Shakespeare, THE TEMPEST.

"Think of it as another desert island adventure," he said.

It took me a few attempts before I could make sense of Shakespeare's flowery language. His THEES and THOUS and WHATNOTs. But I found that if I read it aloud, I understood it better.

The other kids had a lot of fun at my expense—they all called me Shakespeare— but I kept at it until I almost had the play memorized. There was something about the story that struck a chord. I guess I wanted to be like Prospero the magician, to control my enemies like puppets.

Clay held his pounding head in his hands, trying to organize his wildly careening thoughts. The librarian—he sounded just like Uncle Ben. And here was *The Tempest* again, too?

Clay's reflections were interrupted by murmuring from the bunk below. He looked over the edge of his bunk to see Jonah, apparently still asleep, sitting up in bed, talking to himself.

"My spirits... in a dream... bound up..."

Clay listened, marveling. He could only make out some of the words, but he was pretty sure he recognized them. They weren't taken directly from Price's journal, but they might as well have been.

Clay reached down and gave Jonah a shake. "That was a line from *The Tempest*," Clay whispered. "Did you know I was reading about *The Tempest* right now? Is that why—?"

His eyes still closed, Jonah mumbled something to the effect of, "Huh? What the heck are you talking about?" Then he fell back, snoring, onto his pillow.

Even more unsettled, Clay went back to reading:

It was when I finally returned THE TEMPEST to the library that I found the red leather book that had been hidden behind it. The very book that you, Dear Reader, are holding now.

Inside, the book was blank—strange, seeing as it was so old. It would be my journal, I decided.

But that night, when I opened it again, I had a surprise. The book was full of

writing! Had some secret chemical acted on the ink? Was the writing revealed by the light of the moon? I couldn't figure it out.

On the title page it said,

THE BOOK OF PROSPERO

HEREIN LIES THE LOST KNOWLEDGE OF THE MAGES OF THE PAST.

At first, I couldn't make heads or tails of what was written inside. It seemed to be a scientific textbook, or a book of recipes, or a book of poems, I couldn't tell which.

But I was a stubborn boy, and I liked a challenge. After studying the book for several sleepless nights, I determined that the science wasn't science but alchemy, the science of the occult. Likewise, the recipes weren't recipes so much as potions. And the poems weren't poems so much as spells.

It was, in sum, a book of magic, a grimoire, like Prospero's book in THE TEMPEST.

*Who had written it? As far as I could
tell, a magician from the eighteenth
or nineteenth century. He called himself
Prospero to disguise his identity.*

*I had no way of knowing it then, but his
book would bring me great wealth. And
great grief—*

Clay looked up in frustration.

The memoir ended there, when it had seemingly only just begun. As if something had prevented the author from writing more.

Or, Clay thought bitterly, as if he had decided to torture his "Dear Reader."

That Dear Reader being Clay.

He had no idea what to think. On one level, Price's memoir was about Price. On another level, it was about Clay. As if it had been written yesterday.

But why would someone fake a journal to make it resemble Clay's life?

Unless the journal was genuine and it was Clay's life that was being made to resemble the journal? That idea was even more difficult to fathom.

And then there was Jonah reciting Shakespeare in his sleep. How did he fit in?

It was the kind of puzzle that his brother would have loved. Clay tried to think of what

Max-Ernest would do. What was that Sherlock Holmes quote he always talked about? Something like, *When you have eliminated the possible, the impossible must be true.**

Clay scrutinized the handwriting in the journal, trying to ascertain whether it was new or old. The writing looked authentic, but he knew there were people who could fake that sort of thing.

Like Price, Clay was stubborn and liked a challenge. And yet he had to admit there was no way he was going to figure this one out tonight. It had been a long day, and his head hurt. He stowed the journal under his pillow, closed his eyes, and tried—tried—to sleep.

---

* ACTUALLY, IT'S THE *IMPROBABLE* THAT MUST BE TRUE, NOT THE IMPOSSIBLE. IN *THE SIGN OF FOUR*, SHERLOCK HOLMES QUOTES HIMSELF FOR WATSON'S EDIFICATION: "HOW OFTEN HAVE I SAID TO YOU THAT WHEN YOU HAVE ELIMINATED THE IMPOSSIBLE, WHATEVER REMAINS, *HOWEVER IMPROBABLE*, MUST BE THE TRUTH?"

CHAPTER
TWENTY

TWICE STOLEN

C lay woke very early, with that anxious feeling you have when you don't remember ever falling asleep. Sitting up in his bunk, he gazed at the clouds of vog that were drifting by his cabin.

Sleep had done nothing to illuminate the mystery of Price's memoir.

Who had left it on his pillow? he wondered again. Was this unknown person trying to help him, or was he trying to make Clay feel even crazier?

Clay leaned over his bunk.

"Jonah!" he whispered. "Tell me the truth—were you really sleeping last night?"

"Huh? What? I'm still sleeping now."

"What about the line from *The Tempest*?"

"The line from what?" asked Jonah, sitting up.

"You were reciting Shakespeare in your sleep. Or your pretend sleep."

Jonah scratched his head. "Shakespeare? I think you have me confused with Caliban." He pointed at the tater-bot, which was sitting motionless next to Pablo's bed. No longer made up as a ghost girl, the tater-bot had a new potato head and a painted-on mustache that looked suspiciously like Buzz's.

"Oh, come on. I read Price's journal," said Clay. "About the kids at the reform school. And the boys that just happen to be exactly like you guys. Including the sleepwalker. It's like they might as well have just named him Jonah."

"Dude, I have no idea what you're talking about," said Jonah grumpily. "Or why you had to wake me up."

"I'm telling you, it's all in the journal!"

"What journal? Show me—"

Clay hesitated for a moment, then thought, why not? There was nothing to lose. Maybe the sight of the journal would get Jonah to fess up and tell him what the heck was happening. On the other hand, maybe Jonah was telling the truth, and he was an unwitting participant in whatever it was that was taking place. In that case, the journal was about to open Jonah's eyes.

"Okay, I'll show you," said Clay.

But when he reached under his pillow for the journal, he couldn't find anything; the journal was gone!

"What are you guys going on about?" asked their counselor, climbing out of his bunk. "What time is it?"

"I dunno...early," said Clay, frantically feeling around his sleeping bag.

One thing was certain: He had to find the journal and return it to the library as soon as possible. The last thing he needed was for Uncle Ben to come roaring through camp, accusing him of robbery.

When Clay realized the journal had been stolen out from under him, a certain person came instantly to mind—a certain thief-type person—but he didn't see her until well after breakfast.

Clay was in the barnyard, feeding the llamas, when Leira walked by in her newsboy cap and suspenders. He dropped a bale of hay to the ground, tossed a carrot top to Como, and ran up to the edge of the split-wood rail that kept the llamas from running away—most of the time.

"Yo, Leira!" he called out. "Come here a sec!"

She ran up. "Well, did you get in? Did you see the ghost girl?" she whispered excitedly.

He nodded.

Her eyes widened. "You did?"

"That's not what I wanted to talk to you about, though," he said in a low voice.

"Wait. But how—"

"Never mind right now," said Clay. "Do you have it?"

"Do I have what?"

"The journal. Where is it?"

"What journal?" she asked.

"The red leather journal that was under my pillow. Don't tell me you don't know what I'm talking about." Clay stared at her.

"Why would I have your journal?"

"I don't know. Why do you steal my wallet all the time? Why did you steal my backpack and my llama?" Clay stared at her some more.

Leira squirmed under his gaze. "That's different."

"It is?" Clay's big eyes bored into her. His staring powers were in full effect.

"Yes. Totally," said Leira. "And stop staring at me!"

"Well, tell me this: What do you know about what was written in the journal?"

"Why would I know anything about it?"

"I don't know. Everybody knows everything at this camp."

"Boy, are you paranoid," Leira scoffed.

"You would be, too, if you were me!"

As quickly as he could, Clay told her about the library and about finding the journal on his pillow.

"Okay, I agree, that sounds...bizarre," said Leira. "But what are you saying? You really think somebody forged an old journal about you, then locked it in a forbidden library?"

"Uh-huh."

"And then somebody stole the journal from the library to give to you?"

"Uh-huh."

"And then after all that, somebody else stole it from your bed?"

"Uh-huh. Unless it was the same person, which seems..."

"Doubtful? Yeah, it does," said Leira. "Why would anybody do any of this?"

"I don't know," Clay admitted. "To mess with me?"

"To mess with you, right," said Leira, unconvinced. "You know what I think?"

"What? That I'm crazy?" said Clay.

Leira grinned. "That it takes a thief to catch a thief."

"Meaning?"

"That you need my help, duh."

Leira took off her cap and bowed. "Leira, master thief, at your service."

Clay did a double take. "Whoa, wait a second. Have you always had red hair?"

"No, I dyed it today," she said, rolling her eyes. "Yes, I've always had red hair."

How could he not have noticed that she had hair

the exact same color as Mira's? Clay thought back and realized he'd never seen Leira without a hat.

It wasn't just the hair, though. Despite their polar-opposite styles, he saw for the first time that Leira and Mira looked remarkably similar.

"Has anybody ever told you that you look like her?" he asked.

"Who?"

"The ghost girl."

"Really?" Leira laughed. "Maybe I am her and I just don't know it."

Clay blanched. "That's just what she said!"

"Oh, come on, I was just joking," said Leira. "This whole thing has really freaked you out, huh?"

She turned to the llama, who'd stepped up to them, obviously wanting another carrot top. "You better talk some sense into this guy, Como," she said. "He's going loco."

While Clay stood there, trying to sort out his thoughts, the llama nipped the remaining carrot top from his hand.

CHAPTER
TWENTY-ONE

FIRE CABIN

Over the next few days, Clay kept expecting Uncle Ben to show up at any moment, demanding Clay return the journal, but he never did. Either the custodian hadn't noticed the theft or, more likely, he was biding his time, waiting for the right moment to strike.

Meanwhile, Leira was excited to try solving a crime for once rather than perpetrating one. She insisted on meeting daily with Clay to discuss the Case of the Missing Journal, as she called it. There were all kinds of questions to consider. Who wrote the journal? Who would want Clay to read it, and who wouldn't? But of course the most urgent was, who took the journal from Clay's bunk?

At Leira's suggestion, they wrote lists of everyone at camp, starting with the boys in Clay's cabin, and weighed each person's potential as a suspect. For example,

PABLO

PRO – HAS GUTS, HAD OPPORTUNITY TO TAKE JOURNAL
CON – NO MOTIVE

or,

KWAN

PRO – MISCHIEF-MAKER, HAD OPPORTUNITY
CON – TOO LOUD? NOT STEALTHY?

The only person they approached directly was Jonah. They figured Clay had already spoken to him about the journal, so there was little to lose, but they swore him to secrecy anyway. Jonah claimed innocence; he knew nothing about the journal, he said, nor did he have any idea who'd taken it. But Clay was never wholly convinced. Not that he suspected that Jonah had done anything truly terrible. It was just that there was something fishy about Jonah's nocturnal Shakespearean rambling, not to mention the night when he led Clay outside to see the bathroom shack on fire.

Although they considered all possibilities, Clay

and Leira agreed that by far the most likely culprit was Flint. He had already shown a willingness to torture Clay, as well as a fierce interest in the ghost girl, Mira. If anybody had the journal squirreled away, he did. Naturally, there was no question of asking him; they would just have to steal it back.

They took turns staking out Flint's trailer cabin, Fire Truck, watching for a safe time to enter. Each of them had to feign running for the bathroom more than once. Frustratingly, their camp schedules didn't allow for extended stakeout periods, and days passed without there being a good opportunity for a break-in.

Late one afternoon, Leira entered Clay's cabin just as Circle was ending.

"You have to come with me—now!" she whispered, and dragged Clay outside without explanation.

Finally, Flint's cabin was empty.

"Okay, you go in," said Clay when they reached the door. "I'll knock twice if somebody's coming."

"No, you go in; I'll stand guard," said Leira.

"But you're the expert thief!" Clay protested.

"Yeah, but you're the boy, and it's a boys' cabin!"

"Older boys' cabin," said Clay. "And it's a trailer."

"Same difference," said Leira. "Besides, if I get caught taking anything, I'm dead. My parents will *kill* me."

"Doesn't stop you from taking my wallet every five minutes," Clay pointed out.

"Only because I know you won't tell. Please—"

"Fine, I'll do it," said Clay, not wanting to lose any more precious time.

"Make it fast," said Leira. "Dinner starts in five minutes, and if we're not there, somebody will definitely notice."

On the inside, Flint's cabin, Fire Truck, was a mess. Clay figured this was because the older boys' counselor, Eli, who also happened to be the camp director—he of the mysterious moving teepee—was never around to make them clean it up.

Clay thought he could tell which bed was Flint's. It was the choicest one, the one next to the window, apart from the others. Sticking out from underneath was a shiny red metal trunk covered with stickers. It looked like something that might have once belonged on a real fire truck, not just a fire-truck-red trailer.

Clay felt under Flint's pillow, but the journal wasn't there. He lifted up the mattress, but the journal wasn't under the mattress, either.

He had no choice but to look in the trunk. If he didn't find the missing journal, at least he might clear up the mystery of how Flint did his pyro-maniacal magic tricks.

The trunk was heavy and screeched loudly when he pulled it out.

"What was that?" Leira asked from outside.

"Nothing."

"Well, don't do it again. I could hear you all the way out here!"

The trunk wasn't locked—maybe because it contained no magic supplies, only dirty laundry. Feeling a little guilty—and more than a little disgusted—Clay rifled through the trunk. At the bottom, he thought he felt what he was looking for. But what he pulled out was not a red leather journal; it was a bright blue paperback. The one Clay saw Flint reading on top of Egg Rock.

Clay could see the title now. Of all things, Flint was reading *The Tempest*!

Why did everything keep coming back to that play? It was like *The Tempest* was the answer to some cosmic riddle, but he didn't know what that cosmic riddle was.

Clay flipped through the paperback. It looked like Flint had read it more than once. Clay noticed that he had written *Mira!* next to a line belonging to Miranda, the magician's daughter.

"Leira? What are you doing here?"

It was Flint. Right outside the door. Clay replaced the book as quickly as he could.

"Nothing..." said Leira. *"I just, uh, had a question for you."*

"Yeah, what? I'm in a hurry," said Flint.

Clay managed to close the trunk without making any noise, but he was terrified to slide it back under Flint's bed; it would almost certainly screech again. Should he run or hide, he wondered.

"Um, is dinner tonight outside or inside?" asked Leira.

"Outside. You waited just to ask me that?"

"Uh—uh..." Leira stammered. *"I just thought you'd know."*

"That's the lamest excuse for talking to somebody I've ever heard." Flint laughed, as cocky and rude as ever.

"As if I'd ever want to talk to you!" Leira spit out. Clay could imagine how furious she must have looked. He was almost amused.

"Don't worry. You'll get over it," said Flint. *"When little girls have crushes on older boys, it doesn't mean anything."*

Yeah, kinda like you having a crush on a ghost, Clay thought.

"You're disgusting!" said Leira.

"Whatever you say," said Flint. *"Now can you maybe let me in?"*

"Wait. I have another question," said Leira, stalling. *"Um, what time is dinner?"*

Just then, somebody rang the gong. And rang it again. And again. Three times.

"Sounds like dinner is now," said Flint. *"Lates."*

Clay took advantage of the ringing gong to push Flint's trunk into place. Then he scrambled up onto Flint's bed and shimmied out the open window, more certain than ever that Flint was guilty—but of what, Clay didn't know.

Contrary to Flint's assertion, dinner that night was not outside; it was inside Big Yurt.

As everyone ate vegan cashew nut cheese and sun-dried potato chips, Jonah pulled something out from under the table—his last package of red licorice—and started passing ropes around the table.

"What, he doesn't get one?" asked Pablo. He pointed to the tater-bot, which was propped up at the table next to him and was now sporting a Mohawk to match Pablo's.

"He can eat potato chips," said Jonah.

"He's made from a potato!" Pablo protested. "You want him to be a cannibal?"

Kwan laughed. "Well, his name's Caliban, isn't it?"

"So what's the deal with *The Tempest*, anyway?" asked Clay, still thinking about the paperback he discovered in Flint's trunk.

"You mean, why did I name him Caliban? Because he's my little cannibal monster," said Pablo. "Aren't you, Cali-boy?"

He gave the robot a poke, and it shook its arms in an arguably monstrous fashion.

"No, I get that," said Clay. "I mean why is everybody all about *The Tempest* here? I saw Flint reading it and also—" He was about to mention the references to *The Tempest* in Price's journal but stopped himself. "And also the plane to get here, Skipper's plane, it was called *The Tempest*."

Pablo shrugged. "Means 'storm,' doesn't it? Seems like a normal name for a seaplane to me. And Flint—the play's about magic, and Flint's into magic, right?"

"Clay hates Flint," Jonah volunteered. "Hates magic, too."

"We know—*magic sucks!*" said Kwan, grinning. "So, how much do you really hate magic, Clay? Like, if I did a magic trick, right now, what would you do? 'Cause I've got some mad magic skills."

"Do what you want," said Clay. "It's a free country."

"That's what you think," scoffed Pablo.

"Okay, we've got licorice rope, right? So I'm going to do a rope trick," said Kwan.

With a wolfish grin, he grabbed the rope of licorice out of Clay's hand and shoved it into his mouth.

"Now, that's real magic, folks," he said, chewing.

His teeth were so red, he could have been a vampire.

Clay forced a smile. "Nice."

Kwan stopped. "You can do a real rope trick?"

Clay shrugged. "My brother taught me a few, but I probably forgot.... Rope tricks are pretty cheese-wiz-y, anyway."

"Prove it," said Kwan, holding up a rope of licorice for Clay.

Clay shook his head. "No way."

"C'mon, bro, you know we're not going to let you out of it now," said Pablo.

"Yeah, give us magic or we give you the worst, most epic wedgie in summer camp history," said Kwan.

"Give the guy a break," said Jonah. "He doesn't like magic. So what."

"It's okay, I'll do the trick," said Clay, feeling foolish for giving in so easily. But why not? What was the big deal, really? He couldn't stay mad at magic forever.

"All right, that's more like it," said Kwan, handing Clay the licorice. "Amaze us, Fellow Worm."

Standing up, Clay dangled the licorice rope in the air, as his brother had taught him years before.

"Okay, let's see.... Gentlemen, I have in my hand an ordinary rope," he said haltingly. "Just, uh, forget the fact that it's red and rubbery and made of sugar."

As the Worms watched, Clay tied the two ends of the licorice into a square knot.

"I will now cut the rope with my special magic scissors—"

Holding the licorice with two hands, he bit the licorice in half with his teeth. The others laughed.

"As you see, there are now two pieces of rope. But as a master magician, I have the power to heal all," he said, just the way his brother used to.

"Now, who has a bad word for me? I mean, a magic word!" he corrected himself, blushing.

"Oh, we have lots of bad words," said Pablo. "What about—"

(Please. Did you really think I was going to repeat Pablo's word here? You know better than that.)

"I was thinking of *abracadabra*," said Clay. "But sure, any word works if you say it right, right?"

Clay panicked, thinking he'd forgotten how to do the trick. But when he pulled on the square knot, it loosened and the licorice rope dropped from his hand—in a single unbroken piece.*

"And there you have it, gentlemen, the licorice is as good as new."

---

* IF YOU CARE TO TRY THIS TRICK YOURSELF, THERE ARE INSTRUCTIONS IN THE APPENDIX. DON'T TELL ANYONE, BUT IT'S NOT TERRIBLY DIFFICULT.

Clay bowed his head as his dining companions—as well as a few people from neighboring tables—clapped and whistled enthusiastically.

"Very nice!" "Bravo!" "Way to go!"

Even Caliban jumped up and down, clapping.

Clay flushed, remembering the way he'd felt as a child of five when he mastered the trick for the first time. His brother took the rope out of his hand afterward, checking and double-checking to see that Clay had really done it correctly. "How 'bout that?" Max-Ernest had said, the way he did when he was happy. And Clay had grinned, squinting his eyes, the way he did when *he* was happy.

Seven years later, Clay was grinning and squinting in the same way when he saw Kwan's face light up with astonishment.

"Where did that guy come from?" asked Kwan, his eyes looking at a spot behind Clay's back. "Nobody ever comes here."

"Nobody even lives here," agreed Jonah. "I mean except us."

"I dunno," said Pablo. "There are caves all over this island, right? Who knows who lives in them."

"Yeah, like, maybe this guy hasn't spoken to anybody in thirty years," said Kwan.

"Right, and he's like a caveman or Tarzan or something," said Jonah. "Gotta admit, he kinda looks like it."

Clay didn't want to turn around. He had a suspicion he knew who it was. "Is he a bald older guy?"

Jonah nodded. "Why, you know him?"

"Sorta bulging eyes? Muscles?" Clay persisted.

"Just tell us who he is," said Kwan.

"He's the custodian at the library—you know, Price's library," said Clay, figuring it was only a matter of seconds before they heard anyway. There could be only one reason Uncle Ben had shown up at camp.

"How do you know?" asked Pablo.

Clay didn't say anything. He didn't have to.

"No way—you got in!?" exclaimed Pablo. "The bees didn't get you?"

Before Clay could answer, the newcomer thundered at the assembled campers. "Where's the director? I demand to speak to the director of this camp!"

Clay finally turned and sneaked a peek. It was the custodian, all right. His goggles were off, but he still looked bug-eyed.

Buzz rushed up to him. "Sorry, sir, Eli's not here. Can I help you with something?"

"One of your campers is a thief!" said the custodian, his voice still booming.

His heart thumping in his chest, Clay considered his options. There were none. It was no use running. Where would he go?

He looked around. Uncle Ben caught his eye.

"Him! There's that little lying criminal!" He shook his fist at Clay.

Girding himself, Clay walked toward the custodian and Buzz. Though he'd been waiting for this moment for a week, it was no less scary now that it was happening.

"This boy broke into my library and I—I gave him a tour, sucker that I am," said Uncle Ben to Buzz, still loud enough for the whole camp to hear. "And how does this ungrateful delinquent return the favor? By taking the most irreplaceable book in the library— *The Memoirs of Randolph Price!*"

He lunged at Clay. Buzz had to hold him back.

"Clay, is this true? Did you take this book?"

"Uh. No. I mean, I don't have it..." Clay stumbled.

"But you did break into the library? You admit that?"

Clay hesitated, then nodded.

"Yeah, but I don't know where the journal is," he said truthfully.

"That's a bunch of bull!" said the custodian.

"You crossed the Wall of Trust," said Buzz to Clay. "Which means you betrayed all of our trust, not just his."

"Yeah, I guess I did," said Clay.

"You guess?"

"No, I mean I did that, yes."

"Well, it's all over, then," said Buzz evenly, looking into Clay's eyes.

Clay swallowed. "What do you mean, *it?*"

"Camp, what else would I mean?" said Buzz, his face not giving anything away. "You broke the rules. You're out."

"Just like that?" Clay couldn't quite believe it. Even though he had been warned repeatedly.

"Yep. Just like that. You're going home, Clay."

It was only the second time Buzz had called him Clay and not Worm since they'd met. The message was clear: He was no longer one of them.

"It's what you wanted, isn't it?" said Buzz. "Why else would you cross the Wall of Trust."

"I don't know," said Clay bleakly.

It may have been what he'd wanted once, but now he was only conscious of a crushing sense of loss.

CHAPTER
TWENTY-TWO

THE NEXT MORNING

It only took a few minutes for Clay to throw all of his belongings into his backpack. Soon he would be home and it would be as if Earth Ranch had never happened. He was already worried about the ramifications. He had been kicked out of school, then kicked out of camp. It was almost certain he wouldn't be allowed to return to his school for seventh grade.

He extracted a last dirty T-shirt from behind his bunk and stuffed it into his backpack.

His cabinmates watched respectfully from their bunks. Now that they had learned about the library break-in, they looked on Clay with newfound esteem. "He crossed the Wall and came back to tell the tale." Kwan shook his head. "Who knew the dude had it in him?"

"Let's just hope he doesn't go insane like those other three guys," said Jonah, not letting on that he'd already known about Clay's library visit. "That would suck."

"What sucks is him getting kicked out," said Pablo. "Cali and I were just beginning to like him. I mean kinda. Right, little dude?" The tater-bot nodded its potato head.

"Gee thanks," said Clay. "That's the sweetest thing I've ever heard." His tone might have been sarcastic, but he meant what he said. Now that he was being sent home, he finally felt like he was making friends.

"Anytime," said Pablo. "You know, you could always beg Buzz to let you stay. It worked for me."

"But you didn't actually cross the Wall," Kwan pointed out. "You just got a lot of beestings."

"Buzz said it was over," said Clay, closing his backpack. "You know, like it's all over, not just camp, but whatever else is going on here...or was going on."

"What else is going on?" asked Kwan. "Besides the fact that we all secretly plotted to get you booted from camp, and now we're feeling guilty about it."

Clay forced a smile. "Right. That's pretty much what I meant."

"He thinks there's a conspiracy," volunteered Jonah. "It has to do with the journal that got stolen from the library."

"Oh yeah? Tell us more," said Kwan. "Pablo loves conspiracy theories. Have you heard him talk about the stuff they put in school lunches?"

Clay hesitated. "You guys really don't know anything about the journal?" He still thought it was possible—barely—that one of them might be in on it.

Kwan and Pablo shook their heads. "Why would we?" said Kwan.

Clay stared at them for a second. Either they really didn't know anything, or they were really good actors.

"Forget it," he said. "I'm just going crazy."

What was the point? There were essentially two possibilities: Either he truly was going crazy, or there was some elaborate game that somebody had been playing with him as a pawn. And if there had been a game, it was now over. The book was closed even if the story wasn't finished.

"Hey, I think your ride is here," said Jonah, pointing upward.

Cocking his head, Clay could hear the distinctive sound of propellers coming from high above. Skipper's plane was circling the island.

It was time to go home.

Clay had assumed he would be hiking down to the black lava beach right away to meet the plane. But when Clay stopped by the corral to say good-bye to Como, Buzz spotted him and told him that Skipper would be making some deliveries to camp first. Clay wouldn't be leaving until the afternoon.

Clay went back to his cabin to wait while the other Worms went to collect eggs in the chicken coop. He almost wanted to join them, even though it most likely meant getting pecked by a hen. Anything was better than sitting around, wondering how he had gone from being expelled from school to being expelled from camp.

After he had been waiting in the cabin for what seemed like hours but was probably more like twenty minutes, Leira entered. "Package for you."

She handed him a cardboard box, not unlike the one Clay himself had delivered when he first arrived at Earth Ranch. Only this time, his name, not Jonah's, was on the box.

"Funny timing, huh?" Leira said, seeing his expression. "Right before you leave."

"It's not just the timing," said Clay. "It would be weird even if I was staying. My parents aren't really the care package types."

Leira shrugged. "Maybe they missed you. Stranger things have happened.... Well, are you going to open it or what?"

Clay shrugged. Without much enthusiasm, he

ripped open the box with a pencil and pulled out a few crumpled pieces of newspaper.

Clay blinked, not believing his eyes. "What the—?"

"Is that what I think it is?" asked Leira.

Inside the box was an envelope—and a familiar red leather journal.

"I don't think so. I mean, I don't think it's the missing journal; I think it's *my* journal."

"Huh? I'm confused."

"Remember, there were two? This is the one from my school play, the one my teacher gave me. The one that got me into trouble in the first place...."

Clay cracked open the journal—just to confirm that it was his, and not by some wild chance, Price's. Sure enough, there they were on the first page, those two fateful words—*MAGIC SUCKS!*

Clay opened the envelope and pulled out a note.

"It's not from my parents," he said, fighting a small feeling of disappointment. "It's from my teacher."

He showed it to her.

Dear Clay,

Your friend Gideon has confessed. He says he was the one who wrote on my wall at school. A prank that got out of hand. I'm sorry I doubted you. You are welcome to return for seventh grade.

Please accept the journal back with my apologies.

Warm regards,
E. Bailey

P.S. I hope you stick it out at Earth Ranch anyway. I think the camp may surprise you.

While Leira read the note, Clay looked at it for a second time. Was it possible that there was such a simple explanation for the writing on Mr. Bailey's wall?

"Nice friends you have," joked Leira. "If they aren't stealing your wallet, they're setting you up."

"Actually, Gideon's a pretty decent guy . . . usually," said Clay, perplexed. "I don't get it, him doing something like that."

"You must have really pissed him off."

"I can't think of anything I did. I mean, he's always pushing me to do a big graffiti piece, but it's not like he gets all mad when I don't." He studied the journal in his hand as if it might hold the answer.

"Maybe he's just jealous of you."

Clay laughed. "Yeah, sure."

"Why's that so funny?"

"Well, like, why would anybody be jealous of me?"

"I don't know. Maybe because you're so cool."

"I am?" Clay couldn't have been more surprised if she'd told him he was covered with green stripes.

Leira nodded. "Yeah, you have this thing. This, like, toughness or something. It can be a little intimidating, actually."

"Huh. Really?" said Clay, blushing. "Thanks, I guess?"

"You're welcome," said Leira matter-of-factly. "By the way, you're also cute."

"Cute?!" Clay sputtered. "Now I know you're lying."

He remembered the Worms saying Leira had a crush on him. Could it be true? The thought was alarming.

"No, I'm not. I mean, that's not my opinion. That's objective information."

"I have the most messed-up hair in the universe. I'm short. I have crooked teeth. My clothes are always wrong...."

"Trust me, you're cute. Even Adriana thinks so. She said you were like a little wild animal she wanted to tame and make into her pet."

"Ugh! And, ugh! I don't want to be anybody's pet."

"I know," agreed Leira. "You're too cool for that. You see what I mean?"

"Not really," said Clay. "I think I'm just going to pretend we never had this conversation."

"Suit yourself. So, you gonna return the journal to the library or what?"

"Well, it came from home, so I wouldn't really be returning it, strictly speaking."

"Right. I forgot for a second."

"But I guess Uncle Ben doesn't have to know that, does he?" Clay ruminated. "He said he never opened the journal. Maybe he wouldn't even notice the difference...."

"See what a criminal you've turned into!" Leira laughed, then quickly turned sober. "Anyway, I gotta go. It's been, uh, nice knowing you and all that stuff. If I don't see you ever again ... well, bye."

She gave Clay a quick embarrassed hug, and hurried out the door.

"Yeah, bye," he said to her departing back.

Clay checked for his wallet. It was still there, which made him sad. He probably wouldn't ever be able to look at his wallet again without thinking about Leira stealing it.

He would miss her.

CHAPTER
TWENTY-THREE

LOCKED OUT

Clay found Buzz standing by the fire pit under the dome, talking to the other Worms. Or rather, talking to *the* Worms, since Clay was no longer one of them. When Buzz saw Clay, he gave him the one-minute sign and kept lecturing as if he were teaching in an outdoor classroom.

One minute turned to ten as Buzz talked about lava and lava safety. While Clay waited impatiently, Buzz told the Worms about how lava is formed, how it erupts, and how it solidifies. He also told them how to walk around it (when you could) and over it (when you had to).

"Walk over lava? No prob," joked Kwan. "I played 'hot lava' all the time when I was little."

"Me too," said Jonah. "But back then the lava was cracks in the sidewalk. Here the lava is...lava."

"Lava is never just lava," said Buzz. "It's molten rock, yes, but it's also liquid fire. It's the blood of our planet."

"That's deep, man," said Pablo.

"I don't think it's the blood," said Kwan. "I think it's the pus. It's like volcanoes are zits, and when you squeeze them, lava comes out."

"Nice image," said Jonah. "Thanks for putting it in my mind."

That night at sundown, the entire camp would be taking a lava walk together, Buzz told them. "Well, not all of you," he said with a glance in Clay's direction, that felt to Clay like a slap.

"It's an annual tradition—a rite of passage for the newer campers, and a way of honoring this place for the older campers," said Buzz. "It's also the kickoff for your volcano overnight, which, as you know, starts first thing the next morning. Again, for most of you."

Clay gritted his teeth. Why did Buzz have to keep harping on the fact that he was no longer part of the group?

"So no lava safety test?" Pablo asked.

"Think of the lava walk as your safety test—an unconventional one." Buzz smiled. "You know those hot lava games you played when you were kids? Those aren't just games. They build your imagination, your agility, your leadership ability, your trust in your peers. The same is true for a lava walk now. You will have to be mindful at all times tonight; otherwise you'll burn your feet or worse....Now scoot, all of you—

"So what can I do for you, Clay?" he asked formally, after the others had left.

"I found the book—it fell down behind my bunk," Clay said. Which for all he knew was true. He held up the journal, but Buzz didn't take it. "I know I messed up big-time, but is there any way—I mean, could you give me a second chance?"

Buzz looked him up and down, as if assessing his sincerity. Clay held his breath as he waited for the verdict.

"I'm glad you're taking responsibility for your actions, but let's take one thing at a time," said Buzz neutrally. "First, go give the book back. The plane's not leaving until the afternoon, anyway."

"You want me to take it to the library?" said Clay, surprised. "That's past the Wall of Trust!"

"You can cross any wall you like—you're not a camper anymore," Buzz reminded him. "But take Como with you. He needs a walk."

With no need for subterfuge, Clay was free to take the most direct route, and he and Como made their way up the hill to the ruins in record time.

As they came in view of the library, however, Clay began to get nervous.

"What's Uncle Ben going to do if he discovers that the journal *no es* Price's?" he asked aloud, half to Como, half to himself. "*Sí, sí,* I'll play dumb, like I don't know what's supposed to be written inside, but let's face it: There's a pretty good chance he won't believe me anyway. And that guy has serious anger issues."

Ignoring his human companion, Como continued walking toward the library. Clay rushed to catch up.

When they got there, the library looked more shut down and unassailable than ever. Clay looked upward, hoping to see Mira, but all the windows were dark. Clay didn't want to aggravate the situation by breaking in for a second time, so he tried knocking on the front doors. Alas, nobody answered.

Next he tried the side door. But as soon as he started turning the dial on the lock, he could tell that the combination had been changed. It wasn't *PROSPERO* any longer. It didn't even start with *P*. The custodian had made sure that Clay wouldn't be able to enter ever again.

"What are we supposed to do, leave the journal on the doorstep?" he muttered to the llama. "It could be days before he picks it up."

There was a metal slot next to the front doors that Clay hadn't noticed before. BOOK RETURN, it said, just like at a real public library, though most likely the slot had never been used. Clay held the journal in his hand for a second longer, feeling oddly reluctant to let go, then deposited it in the slot. He could hear it thud on the other side.

He was about to retrace his steps and return to camp, when Como abruptly turned in the other direction—the direction of the old barn. The llama stood still, his ears pointing straight ahead. Clay knew by now that forward ears meant the llama was listening to something he deemed unusual or dangerous.

A second later, Clay heard it: barking.

And then: banging.

Clay was almost as scared of facing the barking dog as he was of facing the custodian. Even so, he decided to investigate.

"I know, it sounds *muy peligroso*," he said to Como. "But maybe the custodian is in there. Or maybe even Mira."

The barking and banging got louder as they made their way through the bushes toward the barn. Cautiously, Clay pushed forward and peeked his head out of the bushes. The barn door was opening and closing over and over again in the wind. Inside, the dog barked madly in time to the banging door.

Suddenly, the wind stopped and the door stopped, and the barking stopped, too.

"Come on, let's go see what's going on," said Clay, more confidently than he felt. *"¡Ándale! ¡Vámonos!"* He tugged on the llama's leash, but the llama wouldn't move.

Now his ears were flat back on his head, which roughly translated as *You're crazy if you think I'm going into that scary old barn, and if you keep pulling me, I'll spit on you.* Or however you say that in Spanish.

"Fine, you wait here," said Clay, figuring it was best to keep the llama away from the other four-legged animal inside. He looped the llama's leash around a tree branch and then, feeling very uneasy, he forced himself to walk over to the barn.

The door was barely hanging on to the old rusty hinges. It swung open with a touch.

Grrrr.

Before Clay could step inside, the dog jumped in front of him, growling. Clay jumped back. The dog stood barely a foot away, straining on his leash. Clay had no doubt that the dog would sink his teeth in Clay's leg if he took another step.

"Hi there, nice doggy..."

It was a bulldog. Clay was almost certain he recognized the dog as Skipper's drooling copilot. What was that dog's name? *Tattoo?* No, that was the other one. *Gillian?* No, *Gilligan.* That was it. Of course, Skipper had jeered at him for thinking all dogs looked alike. Maybe he couldn't trust his own judgment on the subject. Besides, why would the pilot have left his dog here in the barn, so far from camp?

Still, it couldn't help to try saying his name.

"Hey, Gilligan," said Clay. "How's it going?"

The dog continued to regard him suspiciously, but he stopped growling. Encouraged, Clay stepped forward. "Okay, I'm going to scratch your ear now. You like that, right?"

Slowly, he reached his hand toward the dog's head. So far so good. He reached farther and proceeded to scratch, just the way Skipper had suggested weeks ago. Soon the dog was sitting down and wagging his tail contentedly. A long string of drool connected him to Clay's arm.

It was Gilligan; it had to be. How and why the pilot had left him there, Clay couldn't guess.

Inside, the barn was not a barn, or it wasn't being used as a barn, anyway. Sometime, long, long ago, it had been converted into an office. There were desks and bookshelves and file cabinets—most decayed nearly to the point of being unrecognizable, and all of them covered with dirt and leaves and animal droppings. It looked as though nobody had stepped inside for years.

In the center of the room, illuminated by a dusty shaft of light, was a large, hulking dark object. Made of iron, it had a table-style base and stood about six feet high. A heavy disk attached to a long lever was suspended above the table surface, ready to squash anything unlucky enough to lie below it.

In his nervous state, Clay mistook this mysterious machine for some kind of medieval torture device. But when he looked underneath the big disk, he didn't find a place to bind a prisoner's hands or head; he found a rack full of wooden blocks, each bearing a raised letter.

Clay looked at the blocks with curiosity. They were similar to a baby's alphabet blocks, but smaller; and rather than being multicolored, the letters were covered with black ink.*

It wasn't a torture device; it was a printing press.

What was the last thing printed on the press? Clay wondered. A poster? A page from a book? Like everything else in the barn, the typographic blocks were covered with a thick layer of dust, and it was very difficult to read them—all the more so because the letters, each about an inch long, were backward, as if he were looking in a mirror. It took Clay a moment to figure out why: The letters had to be backward in order to print forward.

As he examined the press, the dog started

---

* These baby blocks are more commonly known as *movable type*, which is exactly what it sounds like: a system of movable (and luckily *removable*—helps to keep things secret) pieces that are used in printing. The invention of movable type made producing previously written books infinitely easier. Alas, there is more to writing a book than moving letters around. One also has to choose the words that the letters create; that's the part that always stumps me.

barking again and the door started banging again. The wind had picked back up. A breeze made its way into the barn, disturbing the dust on the letters, and—*bang!*—the disk slammed down on the plate below. Clay jumped, startled.

When Clay lifted the disk again, three blocks in the center of the plate were left totally dust-free, as if they had been deliberately cleaned and placed there just moments earlier. For a second, Clay didn't recognize the letters. They looked like designs or symbols of some sort: two squiggles on either side of a circle. But when he read the letters backward, they resolved themselves into that familiar distress signal:

CHAPTER
TWENTY-FOUR

THE LAVA WALK

C lay half ran, half walked all the way back to camp, to the annoyance of Como, who sometimes preferred to pick his steps carefully on a downhill slope.

He couldn't make sense of what he'd seen. Although, he had to admit, there was something almost supernatural-seeming about the way the sudden wind had revealed the SOS, his rational mind told him that the wind's appearance was an accident of timing. Very likely, he would have discovered the SOS, wind or no wind. On the other hand, the placement of those three letters in the exact center of the rack—that could hardly be an accident, could it? He felt sure that somebody had left him a message.

"But who? *Quién?*" he asked Como. "*Mira,* right? There's nobody else around here except for Uncle Ben, and, I mean, can you imagine him leaving an SOS? No, amigo, you cannot." He laughed at the thought of the angry old bear of a man asking for help.

"What? You think Mira is really a ghost and she was in there with us? Very funny," Clay continued. "But seriously, do you think Mira is in trouble? Does she want our help? What are we supposed to do? I can't even get into the library anymore. And she's stuck inside with her creepy uncle! Remember how scared of him she was?"

Distraught, he decided that all he could do was return to camp, find Buzz, and beg to stay. If Mira truly needed Clay's help, he would be of no use to her at home.

As it turned out, Clay didn't have to beg.

When Clay found him, Buzz was assembling campers and staff around the dome in preparation for the lava walk. Before Clay could say anything, Buzz pointed him toward where he was supposed to be.

"Over there, Worm. And make sure you have your flashlight."

Clay felt a surge of relief at being called Worm once more. "Okay, cool," he said.

He scurried over to join his cabinmates and happily accepted their fist bumps and high fives. And yet he couldn't help thinking that his counselor had let him back in pretty fast, considering he'd made such a point of ostracizing Clay earlier. Had it all been for show? Had Buzz never really planned on sending him home?

It was yet another unanswerable question to add to the list.

Grouped loosely by cabin, the campers proceeded up a trail that took off from the west side of the lake. Their destination: the island's westernmost lava field, Plume Canyon.

It was only a two-mile hike, but it was slow going on the jungle trail, and by the time they reached Plume Canyon, it was getting dark. There were just a few glowing streaks of red left in the sky, uncannily mirrored by the glowing trickles of lava on the ground. Illuminated by the lava, smoke and steam rose out of fissures in the rocks, some places in steady streams or "plumes," some places in intermittent puffs.* In the background, Mount Forge loomed, dark and menacing.

As Clay and his Worm-mates settled on a spot where they could all stand without fear of stepping in hot lava, they saw Flint emerging from the jungle. He was shirtless and smeared with mud. On his back, he carried the bloody carcass of a large hairy animal;

---

* THE AREA WAS CALLED PLUME CANYON, YOU WILL OBSERVE, NOT BECAUSE IT WAS FULL OF BIRD FEATHERS BUT BECAUSE OF THE MANY PLUMES OF SMOKE.

he held one leg in each of his hands, while the head rested gruesomely on his shoulder. Beside Flint was Adriana, the counselor for the Pond, also covered with mud and blood, and holding a long spear in her hand.

Clay stared at the wild boar hanging down Flint's back. "One of those guys almost killed me my first day on the island."

Kwan nodded. "They're all over the island. Descended from Price's pigs."*

"How do you know?" asked Jonah. "You hunted one?"

"Sure, tons of times," Kwan boasted.

"Don't believe him," said Pablo.

"I saw one when I was walking to camp," said Clay. "Those guys are fast."

"And mean," said Kwan.

"And ugly," said Pablo.

Flint lifted the boar high in the air, then dropped the boar to the ground. The older boys from Flint's cabin cheered and beat their chests. "The hunters return!" "Meat!" "Meat!" "Meat!"

Shushing them, Adriana pulled a big bundle of

---

* KWAN IS CORRECT. ESCAPED PIGS, WHETHER RAISED FOR FOOD OR AS "PETS," WILL REVERT TO A WILD STATE IN A MATTER OF MONTHS. THAT DOESN'T MEAN THAT ONLY THEIR DESCENDANTS GROW UP WILD; THE ESCAPEE ITSELF BEGINS TO GROW HAIR AND TUSKS. AND WATCH OUT, BECAUSE FERAL PIGS NOT ONLY HAVE RAZOR-SHARP TUSKS BUT ALSO RUN FAST (THIRTY MILES PER HOUR!), SWIM WELL, HAVE KEEN HEARING AND SENSE OF SMELL—AND THEY'LL EAT ALMOST ANYTHING.

banana leaves out of her rucksack. Together, she and Flint wrapped the boar with the leaves until only its tusks and tail were visible. Somebody handed Flint a shovel, and he started digging into a nearby lava pool. He dumped shovelfuls of molten lava on top of the boar until it was covered by a mound of lava sludge. Almost immediately, the lava started to blacken and harden.

Clay winced, unable to stop picturing himself in the pig's place.

Buzz stood in front of the smoking mound. "Thank you, Adriana, Flint."

Adriana made a small bow. Flint saluted with a finger.

Buzz turned to the rest of the camp, assembled in front of him. "Before commencing, can we observe five minutes of silence? Starting now—"

The silence that ensued was absolute. There was no wind, no bird or animal cry, no stifled laughter or coughing.

As the red faded from the sky, the pools of lava glowed brighter, and the lava seemed magically to absorb the light of the dying sunset. Stars appeared in the blackness above, and Clay had the feeling that he was floating through space, standing on top of a burning comet.

After their five minutes of silence, Buzz and Flint and the other counselors began to arrange the campers strategically around the lava field, creating a human trail that wound around the glowing lava hot spots. When everybody was in place, the counselors began to hum. The sound came from low in their throats, like a yoga *om*. Soon the entire camp was humming, infusing the lava field with an unexpected sense of electricity.

One by one, campers were asked to close their eyes. They walked the lava trail, navigating by sound alone. Whenever somebody came dangerously close to a steam vent or a pool of lava, the nearest person started humming louder in warning.

As Clay walked blind through the lava field, his emotional state kept changing: from disorientation to terror to resignation to giddiness. Maybe in some ways it was similar to the imaginary lava walks of childhood, but the fact that it was real made all the difference. One false step and you knew your foot would be incinerated. And yet you couldn't be too cautious, or you'd never move. There was no choice but to let go of your fear.

After the campers finished, it was the counselors' turn. Flint went last, but he didn't follow the course everyone else took. He threw off his shoes and socks, uttered a strange word Clay had never heard, and then calmly walked across a snaking stream of lava—just like a swami walking across hot coals in an

old circus sideshow. When he reached dry land, he turned and raised his arms in victory.

Clay rubbed his eyes while people applauded. He was getting used to seeing Flint perform astonishing magic tricks, but walking barefoot on molten rock was something else altogether. The other Worms, Clay noted, were staring, slack-jawed, at the teen magician. At last, Flint had done something that shocked them, too.

"Awesome," said Pablo.

"You'll never catch *me* doing that," said Kwan.

A moment later, Buzz and Flint stood over the roasting boar. The lava mound was now completely black, a rock shell.

"Thank you, mighty beast, for the gift of your life," said Buzz solemnly.

He turned to the volcano behind them. "And thank you, mighty mountain, for the gift of your lava. May you protect these young men and women as they journey forth tomorrow into your fiery domain."

Flint raised a hammer in the air—and brought it down on the smoking lava shell. The shell cracked open, revealing the roasted boar. The banana leaves had turned to soot, and the boar's skin was black and crispy.

Buzz started slicing off chunks of the lava-cooked pork and offering them around. This was the first meat Clay had encountered since he had arrived on the island, and his mouth watered at the smell. There were no plates or utensils; Clay ate with his hands, like everyone else. Ravenous, he tore into the pork with his teeth, the juices dripping everywhere, eating and eating until the combination of acrid smoke and gamey meat started to sicken him.

When he had had his fill, Clay watched his fellow campers continuing to gorge on wild pig, their faces lit by the glow of the lava. They looked like members of some lost tribe of cannibals. How many of these people were privy to all the secrets of Earth Ranch, he wondered. Who among them knew the answers to the mysteries that haunted him?

Afraid he was going to throw up, Clay moved away from the smoke and found himself face-to-face with Nurse Cora. She looked at him with concern from beneath her floor-length silver hair. "Are you feeling sick?"

"Huh?" asked Clay.

"Are you feeling sick, Cora asked," said Buzz, who was standing next to Cora.

"Sick...Cora...asked..." Clay repeated, uncertain why the words sounded so strange to him, as though he'd heard them in a dream.

"Right," said Buzz. "Are you sick?"

Sick...Cora...asked...Sick...Cora...asked...

"Clay?"

"I'm fine," said Clay, pushing away from the nurse and his counselor.

"Watch out!" Pablo grabbed Clay's arm and pointed to a hole in the ground that Clay had been about to step into. Steam rose out of it in a steady stream, a sign of volcanic activity below.

"Thanks," said Clay, pulling away from him.

Clay felt off balance, and his one cogent thought was that he should sit down. He scanned his surroundings for a good perch, but he was distracted by the sight of Leira, wearing a baseball hat, standing over a lava pit that was below and to the left of Clay. In the light of the lava, her hair, face, and baseball hat looked like shades of the same fiery color, as if he were viewing her through the lens of an infrared camera.

Whether it was due to his dizziness or to the odd angle, Clay found himself reading the name on her hat as *ARIEL* before he read it as *LEIRA*. Leira was Ariel backward. Ariel the tree spirit. Ariel, who casts spells on everyone. Ariel from *The Tempest*.

"Can't I ever get away from that freakin' play?" Clay muttered to himself. "Wait a second—"

He stood up straighter. Now he knew why the questions from Cora and Buzz had unnerved him.... What he was hearing in his head wasn't *Sick Cora asked*, it was *Sycorax*—the name of the witch in *The Tempest*! Hadn't Leira said Nurse Cora was a witch?

How could he have not seen it earlier? Half the names around him were names from *The Tempest*. It wasn't only Mira—Miranda—who had been playing a part; it was Leira and Nurse Cora, too. Who knows, Clay thought wildly, they could all be acting. All the counselors and all the campers. Maybe that was why Flint had been reading *The Tempest*—the whole camp was performing together in a Shakespeare production!

It was a crazy idea, but was it possible that everyone had been playing a part? For all these weeks? While Clay ate and drank with them, and fought with them and befriended them? That they'd all been acting while he alone had actually been . . . living?

If so, what was Flint's part? One of the bad guys, obviously. Maybe Sebastian, the other treacherous brother in the play? Unless Flint was Antonio, the villainous part Clay had played at school?*

Clay was making himself dizzier and dizzier thinking about it.

---

* Inspired by Antonio, Sebastian plots to kill his older brother, Alonso, the King of Naples, just as Antonio has plotted against *his* older brother, Prospero, the Duke of Milan. In the end, of course, their plots fail. I must admit, younger brothers do not come off very well in *The Tempest*.

His head swam with question after question. He figured his best chance of getting his questions answered lay with Leira. But by the time he started walking toward her, she—and her telltale hat—were gone.

CHAPTER
TWENTY-FIVE

ACTORS

As soon as Clay got away from the lava feast, the air became clearer and so did his mind. He told himself to think rationally. What were the chances that an entire camp's worth of people were secretly putting on a play that only he didn't know about?

The similarity of the names Leira and Cora to names in *The Tempest* could easily be coincidental, he reasoned. As for everyone else, it was difficult to determine what roles they might be playing. In most cases, the characters at camp didn't match Shakespeare's characters—at least not that he could see. To recast his camp experience as a production of *The Tempest*, you really had to force it.

By the time he was back on the shore of the lava lake, Clay had fully convinced himself that he had an overactive imagination.

That was when he saw Leira again.

She was standing behind a tree, deep in conversation with somebody whose face was hidden in shadow. Leira put her arm around this other person and whispered in his or her ear. Clay watched, surprised; he couldn't think of anybody at camp with whom Leira was that close. He felt something a lot like jealousy.

He was about to tap Leira on the shoulder, when the moon rose over the lake and he saw the face of Leira's companion.

Mira.

Clay stared at her, flabbergasted.

The ghost girl of the library was now wearing shorts and a T-shirt, just like a normal girl of the modern world.

"What are you doing here?" he asked, rushing up to her. "Do you guys know each other?"

"Shh!" Alarmed, Leira put her finger to her lips.

Clay could tell that Mira was surprised to see him, but she recovered quickly.

"What do you mean? How would I know her?" she whispered. "You silly goose!" she added in her typical old-fashioned way.

He looked from one girl to the other. Now that Mira was dressed in contemporary clothes, the resemblance was even more striking. "Wait, you're sisters,

aren't you?!" said Clay, the implications just beginning to dawn on him. "Admit it, you're sisters and you're in it together, this whole thing, whatever it is."

"Keep your voice down," said Leira. "How could we be sisters? We've never even met before."

"Then why are you here, Mira, or whatever your real name is?" Clay demanded.

"I came to find you," said Mira. "Leira was the first person I saw. She said you went to the library. Didn't you see my message?"

"What message?"

"The SOS. I think...I'm in danger, and I...I need your help."

"Yeah, sure you do," said Clay, his anger at the deception growing. "How do you expect me to believe anything either of you says?"

Leira frowned, insulted. "Are you saying we're liars?"

"Yes, and you can stop now, because I figured it out," said Clay, his conviction getting stronger by the minute. "I thought I was insane before, but now I know it's true. I don't know why, but you guys are playing parts from *The Tempest*. You, Mira, you're Miranda, the magician's daughter. And you, Leira, you're Ariel, the tree spirit...."

"What's *The Tempest*?" asked Leira.

"It's a play by William Shakespeare. You've

heard of him, I hope," answered Mira haughtily. "As for you, Clay, you must be mad."

"Oh, come on, you guys, just admit it already," said Clay, exasperated. "I know you're sisters. Remember, Leira, when you said you had a bookworm sister? That was obviously Mira. I can't believe I didn't see it sooner."

The girls looked at each other, communicating silently.

"Okay, you're right," said Leira quietly. "That was a big mess-up when I said that—man, did Buzz yell at me—but yeah, she *is* my sister and she *is* a bookworm."

"I am *so* not a bookworm," said Mira in a voice that suddenly sounded *so* not at all old-fashioned.

Leira gave her a look.

"Fine, maybe I am, whatever. But we're both actresses. And that's the main thing right now."

"Aspiring actresses," Leira corrected.

"Well, anyway, acting is what got us into this whole crazy situation," said Mira.

"What crazy situation? Can someone please tell me what's going on?" Clay pleaded.

"To be honest, we're not totally sure," said Leira.

"We thought Earth Ranch was a theater camp. When we got here, they told us we were doing experimental 'life theater' based on *The Tempest.*"

"'An immersive theater experience,' they called it," said Mira.

Leira nodded. "It seemed really exciting and cool at first, but now it's getting kind of…"

"Creepy," said Mira, finishing her sister's sentence. Leira looked around nervously, making sure nobody was within earshot. "If they find out we talked to you like this, we'll get in serious, serious trouble. We're never supposed to break character, especially with you."

"They call you the 'unwitting cast member,'" said Mira.

"Right," said Leira. "Or the 'audience of one.'"

"So it's not just you—everyone here is putting on a play? Just for me? Why?" asked Clay, stunned. Thinking it was one thing; hearing it said aloud was another.

The girls shrugged.

"Actually, we have no idea what they're doing," said Mira.

"We think the idea of theater camp was just an excuse to get us to the island," said Leira. "We don't think it's really about *The Tempest* at all. The play is like a front, a cover-up for something else."

"You mean that's what you think," said Mira.

"You said yourself you were scared," said Leira.

"I said I was creeped out. Wouldn't you be if you had to spend all your time in that library with Ben?"

"What does everybody else think?" asked Clay.

"We don't know—we're not allowed to talk about anything with anybody," said Leira. "Not even each other."

"So you're not supposed to be here right now?" Clay asked Mira, looking around to make sure they were still unobserved.

Mira shook her head. "At least she gets to have pretend conversations with people." She pointed to her sister. "I just sit around by myself all day."

"So if it's not a play, then what do you guys think is really happening?" asked Clay.

"I think Earth Ranch is like a cult," said Leira.

"What do you mean a cult?"

"Like some weird religion or something. I'm afraid they're going to sacrifice my sister, throw her into a volcano—"

"I told her that was totally crazy," Mira interrupted.

"You saw them tonight," said Leira. "That lava walk was not normal. Tell her."

"Oh, come on, nobody's going to sacrifice anybody," said Mira. "That doesn't happen in real life."

"This isn't real life—that's the point," said Leira.

Clay looked at Mira. "If you don't think you're going to be sacrificed, why did you leave that SOS?"

"Actually, that was part of the play—you're supposed to get all worried about me," said Mira apologetically. "But it's true I've been freaked. Uncle Ben is completely out of his mind. He doesn't talk to me all day, like I'm really a ghost. Then he locks me up at night, like he's afraid I'm going to run off or something—"

"See," said Leira. "Next thing you know, they're going to be fattening you up and roasting you like that pig!"

"Thanks for the reassuring words," said Mira.

"What about just leaving?" asked Clay.

"There's no way off the island," said Leira. "Except the plane that Uncle Ben flies."

"So he is the pilot—I knew it!" said Clay. "That's why his dog was in the barn."

"Oh, yeah, he plays two parts. I forgot you didn't know," said Mira. "He's a pretty good actor, actually."

"Why don't you ask to stay in your sister's cabin?" said Clay.

Mira shook her head. "I don't want to set off any alarms."

Leira nodded. "We have to investigate more first, find out what's really going on."

"But the volcano overnight starts tomorrow," Clay protested.

"Right, and we have to go on it," said Leira firmly.

"But that means Mira could be locked up for days!"

"Clay, is that you?" It was Jonah, walking along the lake.

"Uh-oh—I better get out of here," said Mira, disappearing into the shadows.

Leira followed, slinking away just as Jonah walked up to Clay, his mouth agape.

"Where did that girl come from?" Jonah asked.

"You mean Leira?"

Jonah shook his head. "The other one."

"Oh, so you admit you saw Mira? You're not going to pretend I was talking to a ghost?" asked Clay.

"Ghost? Was that the girl from the library?"

"Yeah. But that's not really where she's from. As you know."

"What do you mean? I've never seen her before in my life. I've never seen a girl like her anywhere," said Jonah reverently. "I think...I think I'm in love."

Clay appraised Jonah. He was acting very strangely. "Oh, I get it. You play Ferdinand, right?"

Jonah looked blank. "Huh?"

"In *The Tempest*, you fall in love with Miranda at first sight," said Clay. "Although, it does seem a little late in the play for you to be falling for her now..."

"What are you talking about? Who's Ferdinand?"

"Oh, come on. You even said his line in your sleep. Leira told me everything. You're better than the guy who played Ferdinand at my school, I'll give you that."

His face pale in the moonlight, Jonah grabbed Clay's arm and squeezed tight. "Just shut up, dude, right now, or you'll mess things up big-time," he whispered. "It's dangerous to talk like that."

"Please, just tell me what's going on," said Clay, thrilled and slightly unnerved that Jonah had finally admitted that something was up. "It's more than just *The Tempest*—I know that much."

Jonah looked around nervously. "Later. After lights-out. Just trust me: It's better to play along."

Jonah gave him another warning squeeze, then ran off into the night.

By prearrangement, the Worms met at midnight in the middle of the banana grove, where there was little chance of being overheard.

It was dark under the banana trees, and Clay, who was standing a little apart from the others by choice, could barely see their faces.

"Well, are you going to tell me what's going on?" he said angrily. "I thought we were friends, and now it turns out you're all actors?"

"We are your friends!" said Jonah. "We weren't really acting...much."

"Seriously, dude. Don't be mad at us," said Kwan. "The only part that was a script was the stuff about the ruins."

Jonah nodded. "That was our main job. To make you wonder about it being haunted or whatever. To get you there."

"Well, you did a good job on that, all right," said Clay bitterly.

"It's not like we felt good about it," said Pablo. "We didn't like lying."

Clay shook his head in disgust. "So that makes it okay?"

"They told us you'd have fun," said Kwan. "They said you wouldn't want us to ruin the surprise or whatever."

"We never thought it would go on so long or get so... weird," said Jonah.

"What about your personalities?" asked Clay. "Was that from the script? Who even are you guys?"

"No, no, it's not like that," said Pablo. "We're us. I swear."

"Or like versions of us," said Kwan.

"What does that mean?" asked Clay.

"Ourselves, but more so, that's what they told us to be," said Jonah.

Clay looked at him skeptically. "You're telling me you really sleepwalk?"

"Uh-huh. I mean, sometimes," Jonah amended.

"Yeah, I was faking it that night to get you to go see the bathroom on fire. I admit that. But that story about my neighbor's garage—that was true. All the stories about why we got sent to camp are true."

Clay turned to Pablo. "And you're really...uh, an anarchist?"

"You know it," said Pablo. "All my ideas are one hundred percent my own—not that I believe in ownership."

Clay looked at Kwan. "And you—I know you're really a gambler, 'cause I saw what you do with those cards."

Kwan grinned. "I give myself away, huh?"

Their story was pretty much the same as Leira's and Mira's. The only difference was that they weren't expecting a theater camp—just a run-of-the-mill bad-kid camp. When they arrived at Earth Ranch, they were told they would be doing "performance therapy" based on a Shakespeare play.

Although they didn't necessarily think the camp was a cult, they agreed with Leira that there was something strange and possibly sinister going on.

"I mean, c'mon, those bees," said Pablo. "That's just not right."

"So they really stung you?" asked Clay.

"Well, no, that was special-effects makeup," Pablo admitted sheepishly. "Remember when you caught me rubbing my arm? I was taking it off."

Just then a cloud of vog passed over the moon, and it was momentarily pitch-black in the banana grove. There was a tremendous rustling from the trees, and the Worms collectively held their breath. Had they been found out? But when the moon shone again, they saw a flock of parrots flying out of the trees, banana peels dangling from their beaks.

"Go on, Pablo, tell Clay your theory," said Kwan after the last of the parrots had flown away.

"Pablo thinks it's one of those *Lord of the Flies/Survivor*-type things," said Jonah.

Clay laughed. "You mean they're going to let us all kill each other?"

"No, I think they're going to sell us—to rich guys," said Pablo earnestly. "So on the overnight they can hunt us down for sport."

Clay tried to process this. "You have evidence?"

"'Course he doesn't," said Kwan, laughing. "It's totally ridiculous."

"Think about it," said Pablo. "Who cares about us? We're the bad kids, remember? Expendable."

"If they're just going to kill us, why go through all *The Tempest* stuff, then?" said Clay. "That's whacked."

Kwan and Jonah nodded in agreement. "Totally whacked."

"Anyway, I gotta admit, you guys are amazing actors," said Clay, thinking about the elaborate charade that had just ended. "I don't think anybody else could have pulled this thing off. So props to you for that."

The others grinned. Kwan gave a small bow.

"I didn't say I liked it!" Clay laughed.

"But you forgive us?" asked Jonah.

Clay looked at his cabinmates. They looked back with puppy eyes.

"We're still your cabin, New Worm," said Kwan.

Pablo nodded. "We've got your back."

"Yeah, whatever," said Clay. He figured he had no choice but to let it go. "The question is, what do we do next?"

They all looked at one another. Nobody had an answer.

CHAPTER
TWENTY-SIX

THE HIKE

In the end, they did nothing. Which is to say, they decided to go on the overnight exactly as if nothing had changed.

"We're already trapped on the island," Jonah pointed out. "They're in control of us, whether we go or not. What's the difference?"

At least on the overnight there was a chance that the purpose of their camp would be revealed.

As it turned out, the person who wasn't going was Buzz. He had to "hold down the fort," he said. It was a welcome surprise, and made them feel more optimistic about the trip, until they discovered who would be taking their counselor's place as their leader: Flint.

Everyone assembled by the lake before embarking.

Strapped to his backpack, each hiker had a volcano "surfboard"—a rough-hewn piece of wood with rope loops to hold your feet; basically, a homemade snowboard. The boards were heavy, but the ride down the volcano was the big reward at the end of the hike; nobody wanted to leave his board behind.

The girls, who would be hiking separately under the direction of Adriana, left first. They would meet again at the campsite that evening.

The hikers started by following the same trail off the lake that they had taken the night before, but instead of turning into Plume Canyon, they kept climbing until they were looking down on the site of the previous night's lava walk and feast. Plume Canyon looked smaller from this height, and the lava pools less spectacular. Where before there had been steady plumes of smoke rising from the fissures in the ground, thin wisps now rose like the dying smoke of so many abandoned campfires.

"Just be glad you guys can see," said Flint to the hikers as they took in the bleak view. "Sometimes the vog is so bad up here, I can't see my hand."

After several hours they reached a wide river that seemed mysteriously to end about fifty yards to their right. Clay guessed—correctly—that there was a waterfall below, the very waterfall that could be seen from camp on a clear day. A narrow rope bridge connected one side of the river to the other.

"Just so you know, the current's pretty strong

down there," warned Flint. "You fall in, the water's gonna want to send you down to the falls."

"Watch out," whispered Pablo. "This is a perfect spot for them to get a clean shot at us."

The other Worms rolled their eyes. "Sorry to disappoint you," said Kwan, "but nobody's trying to take us out."

Nonetheless, they were all a bit nervous as they walked single file on the swaying bridge, holding the rope rails to steady themselves.

Flint made it across first.

As if he were reading their minds, he held up a knife to the rope supports. "This way I can get rid of you all at once!"

Flint laughed, pocketing his knife. "I was just joking, you pathetic losers!"

The hike was strenuous, but worse than his sore muscles were the pangs of hunger that had started afflicting Clay around lunchtime. Each camper had been allocated one handful of trail mix. Any other food, they would have to forage.

As they hiked, Clay and his cabinmates started talking about their favorite meals, one-upping each other with descriptions of lobsters and cheeseburgers and everything in between. It all sounded great to Clay. Even a typical Earth Ranch kale salad now seemed irresistibly delicious.

They were still lost in food-fantasy land when they reached a dark gaping hole in the mountainside. Flint entered without stopping.

"C'mon, Worms, it's a big wormhole—this should be right up your alley!"

It wasn't a big wormhole, of course; it was a lava tube, a tunnel formed by a river of lava so forceful that it had carved its way through the mountain.

Holding their flashlights in front of them, the campers walked through the tunnel single file. The tunnel had rippled black rock walls that widened and narrowed over and over again, as if a giant hand were squeezing it, forcing the kids sometimes to crouch, sometimes to crawl. Clay, whose head kept hitting the ceiling, couldn't help imagining getting trapped inside by another volcanic eruption. Just as the claustrophobia was about to become unbearable, he saw sunlight reflecting in a puddle of water. In all, it took about twelve minutes to walk from one end of the tunnel to the other, but it seemed much longer.

When they came out, they were standing at the base of Mount Forge. From where they stood in a small rocky ravine, the blackened mountain looked impossible to climb. The slope was steep, but worse than that, it was perfectly smooth. This side of the volcano, the south side, was covered entirely in ash. It was the side that they would be surfing down, Flint explained. To climb to the top, they would first hike to the north side of the volcano.

The girls had laid their sleeping bags by a steaming pool with a yellowish-greenish cast—a hot spring, although not one that anybody wanted to swim in. The boys laid their bags on the other side of the water so that they were separated much the way their cabins were back at camp. The water was smelly and sulfurous, but according to Flint and Adriana, Vulcan Springs, as it was known, provided the best campsite in the vicinity.

At some point during the summer session, everyone had actually learned to start a fire, and soon there was a fire tall enough to reflect in the murky hot springs. Clay half expected Flint and Adriana to return with another pig to roast, but no such luck.

Still, there were several edible plants growing nearby, and the kids foraged with varying degrees of success.

"Isn't this great?" said Leira, sitting down with the boys for dinner.

"Sure, if you like eating weeds," said Clay.

"Try this—it's a nettle," she said, handing Clay a thorny leaf.

"Looks more like needles to me."

"I brought the main course," said Pablo, standing over them with a closed fist.

"What, you got some of Jonah's licorice stashed away, I hope?" asked Kwan.

"No. I've got something way more nutritious." Pablo opened his palm and revealed a handful of iridescent green beetles. "Lots of protein in these critters."

"Gross," said Leira. "Bug Killer."

"Yeah, I think I'll pass, too," said Jonah.

"You're missing out," said Pablo, popping a beetle into his mouth and chewing with an audible crunch. "Most of the world eats bugs. It's just us squeamish Westerners who think we're too good for them."

The plan was to make it to the top of Mount Forge by sunrise. Which meant waking at four a.m. Which meant going to sleep early.

Clay tried to fall asleep along with the others, but he tossed and turned in his tight sleeping bag for what seemed like hours. Unable to keep his eyes closed, he watched the ominous clouds of vog float across the night sky.

Where was Flint leading them? Were they in danger? Would the real purpose of Earth Ranch be revealed here by the volcano?

He kept having the feeling there was something he was forgetting. Some key piece of information.

As he drifted off to sleep he remembered what it was: his birthday. It was tomorrow.

CHAPTER
TWENTY–SEVEN

THE CRATER

O w." "Ouch." "Aw, man."

Flint woke everyone with a kick. There were many groans and cries of protest, but in a few minutes the campers were packed up. They were to leave most of their things to be picked up on the way back.

Clay was the last of the Worms to get out of his sleeping bag.

"Hurry up," said Jonah. "You know Flint would be happy to leave you behind."

The others were all heading toward their final ascent in the darkness, flashlights in hand and volcano boards strapped to their backs.

The plan was to make it to the top in time to watch the sunrise from the lip of the crater. But it was slow going. Most of the volcano was covered with ash, even on the north side of the mountain.

The hikers had to pick their way among rocks and patches of harder ground. At times they would come upon an unexpected precipice or other dead end, and they would have to switch course.

There wasn't much talking. Everyone was too tired. And too spread apart despite the fact that they'd been told to stay close together. It was a long and steep hike in the dark. At times, Clay could see none of his fellow hikers; and then flashlights would appear like fireflies darting back and forth up the mountain. As they progressed, one after another hiker stopped to rest or tie a shoe or have a swig of water. The volcano seemed to be wearing everyone down. Clay kept trudging forward and eventually found himself passing everyone but Flint, who was leading the way.

After about an hour and a half, Clay noticed that his feet were getting cold. He looked down and was surprised to find that he was hiking in snow. His sneakers were wet through to his toes. In fact, he was cold all over. Like the other campers, he wore only a sweatshirt for warmth; nobody had brought winter gear to the tropical island.

A glimmer of dawn lit the horizon, and the sky was starting to turn from black to gray, but visibility was still spotty; clouds of vog kept blowing by. Clay put his bandanna around his mouth to ward off the chill as well as the vog as best he could.

The first sun rays touched him just before he reached the top. The wind had picked up, and now he could see all the way to the ocean. He almost thought he could see the black beach on which he had landed weeks ago. To his far right were the smooth ashy slopes of the south side of the volcano—where they would be "surfing" later that morning.

It wasn't necessarily where he would have expected to celebrate his birthday, but all in all, not a bad spot to turn thirteen.

He turned, looking for Leira or one of the Worms to share the moment with.

There was no one there.

"Hey, is anybody around? Can anybody hear me?" he called out. "Yo, dudes! Answer me!"

His voice was lost in the wind.

He figured he must be far ahead of the others. Unless they had passed him in the dark? Either way, he would see them at the top.

The last twenty feet or so, he was walking on ice. His feet kept slipping and he fell more than once, scraping himself on the ice and ash. His hands felt raw and he could feel his knee bleeding beneath his jeans. It would have been impossible to get to the top were it not for a few rocks jutting out from the mountain. These gave him just enough of a hold to pull himself up.

The top of the volcano was much bigger and flatter than it had looked from below, not quite the size of a soccer field. Hard icy snow covered most of the ground, except where plumes of smoke or bubbles of lava melted it. On the far side, the ground dropped off into sky. On the side where Clay stood, little jagged peaks stuck out where the mountaintop had broken away. The volcano had literally blown its lid.

The crater was in the middle. A perfect circle, except in a few places where the edges had collapsed. Clay had imagined he would see red, bubbling molten magma inside the crater. Instead, there was water. The surface of the water was perfectly smooth, and as Clay looked at it, it turned from inky black to a silvery mirror—like a giant mood ring reflecting the changing colors of the sky.*

He walked to the edge and saw himself looking up from the water with his big searching eyes. His face was smudged; his clothes were torn; his hair, wilder than ever. His wooden volcano surfboard slid forward slightly and stuck out over his head; it looked like something dark and predatory about to

* MOOD RINGS WERE A BIG FAD IN THE 1970S, AN ERA WHEN A PERSON'S FEELINGS WERE CONSIDERED OF PARAMOUNT IMPORTANCE. SUPPOSEDLY, THE RINGS CHANGED COLOR ACCORDING TO THE EMOTIONS OF THE WEARER. IN REALITY, OF COURSE, THEY MOSTLY MEASURED HOW SWEATY YOUR FINGER WAS.

overtake him—a floating shark, perhaps, or a stealth aircraft.

And then there was someone else standing by his side. Flint.

Clay turned to face the older boy. "Where is everybody?"

Flint shrugged. "Slow, I guess."

Flint held something in his hand. It was a small, crudely made rag doll, with red yarn hair and a polka-dot handkerchief dress. It looked like a voodoo doll, at once harmless and frightening.

Clay felt sick to his stomach. "Is that supposed to be Mira?"

"I made it in the Art Yurt," said Flint. "Do you like it?"

"What are you doing with it?"

Staring at Clay with his icy blue eyes, Flint stepped closer to the edge of the crater. He dangled the doll by a string tied to its leg.

Clay watched, incredulous. "You're dropping it into the crater?"

Not saying anything, Flint carefully lowered the doll headfirst into the crater.

"Is this your way of saying you're done with her?" asked Clay hopefully.

"It's my way of saying she's done," said Flint.

Clay remembered Leira's prediction that her

sister would be sacrificed in a volcano. It appeared to be happening—but as a strange and disturbing puppet show.

"Is this part of the play?" Clay asked.

"There's no play," said Flint. "There never was a play."

"What, then?"

Flint smiled. "A magic show?"

Then he pronounced that strange word in the language Clay didn't recognize.

The doll had almost hit its target. The silvery water rose upward to meet it, as if pulled by an invisible gravitational force, then fell back down with a loud splash. As ripples spread outward, Clay thought he saw Mira's face reflected briefly in the water. Then the water disappeared, replaced by roiling, churning, glowing lava. Clay tried to comprehend what he was seeing, but he couldn't. It was spectacular and terrifying and absolutely magical.

"You still think magic sucks?" asked Flint snidely.

Now the doll was almost submerged. As lava bubbled and spurted around it, the doll's hair caught on fire, and Flint yanked on the string. He pulled the burning doll out of the crater like a fish.

"Wait 'til you see what comes next."

He swung the doll back and forth. Its hair

burned unnaturally bright, more like a flare gun than flaming cotton.

"Price was a great magician, but he was a coward," said Flint, the fire passing in and out of his eyes. "What's the life of one girl compared to the power of fire? Price had everything within his grasp, and he gave it up because of his silly guilt."

"What do you mean? Where are you going with that thing?" Clay still couldn't tell what Flint was up to or how serious he was.

"Where do you think? The volcano wants to be fed, and I will feed it," said Flint. "She will burn, and I will have the volcano's magic."

"This isn't real," said Clay. "You're just saying lines. You're not really going to kill anybody."

"Maybe that's what Buzz and Eli think," said Flint scornfully. "But deep down they know what needs to be done, and I'm doing it."

Holding the doll aloft like a torch, Flint ran to the far side of the volcano.

"Don't try to stop me," he called over his shoulder, "or you and everyone else will burn, too!"

With that parting sally, he grabbed his volcano board off his back, tossed it over the edge, and jumped after it.

Clay stood on top of the volcano for a moment, too stunned to move.

If Flint was to be believed, Mira was about to burn to death. But where? How?

The library, thought Clay. He's headed to the library. He's going to light it on fire. Flint was rewriting Randolph Price's story to his own liking.

And then Clay stepped into action.

CHAPTER
TWENTY-EIGHT

VOLCANO SURFING

There was a twelve- to fourteen-foot drop. Then snow. Then ash. And ash. And more ash. All the way down the mountain.

Normally, Clay would have spent some time standing on the edge, before getting the courage to jump. He didn't have the worst case of vertigo in the world. But he didn't *not* get vertigo, either.

This time, he didn't hesitate. He tossed his board into the snow below, gulped, then jumped right after it the way Flint had.

The snow went on for about thirty yards.

Clay had only snowboarded once—on a school trip that got cut short when a classmate broke her arm. He slid around, unable to catch an edge with the handmade wooden board, and almost started spinning uncontrollably. But then he righted himself, willing his skateboarder legs to adjust to the wheel-less ride across the ice crystals.

Far below, he could see Flint surfing the ash. Gray clouds billowed in his wake as he effortlessly carved his way down the mountain. Flint was going so fast, he would make it to their base camp in minutes.

And then...

"#Ɛ*%!!!"

Watching Flint, Clay failed to prepare for the transition to dry land and did a face-plant in the ash. It wasn't as soft as it looked, but as far as he could tell, he didn't break anything. He just got scratched up. And got a lot of ash in his mouth and eyes...and nose... and ears. His pockets were full of ash, too.

By the time he wiped himself off and stood shakily to his feet, he couldn't see Flint anymore. Just a few clouds dissipating at the bottom of the mountain.

He put his bandanna back around his face, slipped his feet under the rope loops of his board, then started wiggling back and forth until he was moving down the ash slope.

The ash was slower than the snow, allowing Clay

to get used to the feel of it. Soon he was making long arcing turns, ash spraying behind him. The slope was smooth and steep and very, very long.

He was so lost in his mission that at first it almost didn't register. And then it did. He was surfing a volcano.

Who needed Kill Hill? This was awesome.

The campsite was empty. Only Clay's backpack remained. There was no indication that anyone else had ever been there.

Clay threw his shredded board to the ground and put his backpack on. He looked for signs of what direction Flint had taken, but he couldn't find any. He would have to retrace their steps back to Earth Ranch.

When he got to the mouth of the lava tube, he realized he no longer had his flashlight. It must have fallen out somewhere on the mountain. While he debated what to do, he saw a curl of smoke coming out of the lava tube. He ran inside.

At first, it was so dark, he couldn't see. And he had to walk slowly with his arms outstretched, navigating by feel, coughing from the smoke. But soon there was a glimmer of light ahead. Flint? It went in and out of view, but Clay kept pushing forward in the dark. He hit his head, scraped his shoulder, tripped and fell. More than once he worried he would die there in that tunnel, a present-day casualty of a volcanic eruption that occurred long ago. But somehow he made it all the way to the end.

When he came out on the other side, he thought he saw the burning doll again in the distance. He ran toward it, only to find that Flint had made a fire next to a tree. The fire was small, just a few twigs and leaves, but there was a good possibility it would spread and cause a forest fire if left unattended. Clay covered the fire with dirt and stamped on it until it was out.

There was another fire about a quarter mile down the trail. And then another. And another. Flint had left a trail of fires behind him, like signposts leading the way. Clay snuffed them out as he went along, cursing to himself about how much time it was taking.

Between fires he ran to make up the time. What had been a seven-hour hike going up took no more than two hours going back.

When Clay could finally see the library, Flint was standing in the doorway, as if he'd been waiting for him. He waved to Clay with the burning doll.

"Cool—you made it," Flint shouted. "Now I'll have an audience for my biggest fire ever!"

"Stop! Don't do this!" Clay shouted back.

Without responding, Flint disappeared into the

library. The door closed behind him. It seemed he was going to burn down the library from within.

Clay was about to try to run in after Flint when he noticed it: The ring of flowers that had circled the building was gone, replaced by hot molten rock.

A lava moat was guarding the library.

Clay stared in horror. There was nothing he could do. Part of him, most of him, had believed it was all a charade. But the lava said otherwise.

He looked up to the top of the tower. Mira was back in her window. The last time he'd seen her there, she had tried to shoo him away. This time, she beckoned to him with an imploring look. Did she already know Flint was inside?

That all the books would burn? And that she would, too?

The bees came first, flying so close that he had to close his eyes.

When he opened them, Buzz was at his side.

"Hail, Young Worm," said his counselor.

"The lava," said Clay. "It's real; it's not magic."

"It's real. *And* magic."

"I don't believe you," said Clay, willing it to not be true. "And I don't believe Flint is really going to burn down the library."

Buzz looked him in the eye. "Is that a risk you want to take?"

"You guys wouldn't let him," Clay insisted. "You wouldn't let him hurt Mira."

"Maybe not," Buzz said levelly. "Or maybe we have faith that you will stop him in time."

"But how?" asked Clay, miserable. "There's no way I can get in."

"Sure there is. The library doors are right in front of you."

"I'm supposed to walk across the lava?" Clay looked down at his sneakers. The rubber soles were almost worn out already. "My shoes will melt in seconds."

"True. If you wear them."

Buzz put his hand on Clay's shoulder. "Just remember, you have to mean it."

"Mean what?" asked Clay.

"The magic," said Buzz. "Remember, you're every bit as strong a magician as Flint is. You just have to trust in yourself."

Clay looked at the moat again, hoping vainly that he would see a way through that he'd missed.

When he looked back, Buzz was gone. Clay's only companions were the bees. Clay blinked in surprise. It was as if he had hallucinated the conversation.

Was he really supposed to walk barefoot across the lava? Flint had done it at the lava feast. But Flint was insane. A pyromaniac with a death wish.

And yet if Clay didn't walk...? Clay thought of

Price's niece, the original Mira, who had burned in Price Palace. It wasn't so much that Flint had been rewriting Price's story, but that he, Clay, was reliving it—with a twist. He was being asked to right the wrong, he now understood. To reverse history. It seemed impossible, fantastical, but he had to try.

The whole summer, his whole experience at camp, it had all been leading up to this moment—this moment when he would use magic to enter the library and save Mira.

But what magic?

There was that strange word he remembered Flint pronouncing, the word that sounded like it was part of no language he knew.

Was it a magic word—a bad word, as Clay and his brother used to call them? For Flint, it sure seemed to work like one.

According to Buzz, it wasn't enough to say it; he had to mean it.

Could he mean it? Until now he'd assumed Flint's magic tricks were just that. Tricks. Illusions. Stage magic, even if they weren't on a stage. Like Clay and his brother used to do.

Now he was being asked to believe the magic was something else. Something more than cheese-wizardry.

Just say it, he told himself.

He spoke the word loudly, emphatically, trying

his best to mean it, even if he didn't know what the word meant.*

He looked at the lava; it was unchanged. But on the stone wall of the library was the word he had just pronounced—in his handwriting, but in big letters. Much the way *MAGIC SUCKS!* had appeared on Mr. Bailey's wall at school.

As he marveled, the word disappeared. It was time.

He pulled off his shoes and socks, and took a tentative step—

"Ow!"

—and recoiled.

He tried again. The lava felt hot, painfully hot. But asphalt-in-the-sun hot, sandy-beach-in-summer hot, not molten-rock hot.

Girding himself, he started walking. Quickly but not so quickly that he was running. He made himself think cold thoughts. He imagined the snow on top of Mount Forge coming down the mountain in an avalanche and covering all the lava. Amazingly, the lava seemed to cool beneath his feet. By the time

---

* I'M SORRY I CAN'T TELL YOU THE WORD CLAY USED, OR EVEN WHAT LANGUAGE IT WAS. (HINT: IT'S NOT A LANGUAGE CURRENTLY SPOKEN ANYWHERE IN THE WORLD.) THIS IS PARTLY BECAUSE I DON'T WANT YOU TO TRY WALKING ON LAVA. IF THE SPELL DIDN'T WORK, YOU WOULD BE BURNED AND I WOULD FEEL BAD. WORSE, IF THE SPELL WORKED, AS IT VERY WELL MIGHT—WELL, I CAN'T IMAGINE WHAT WOULD HAPPEN THEN.

he got to the other side of the moat, it felt icy cold. He could feel snow between his toes.

"Help! Clay!"

Mira was crying for him from inside.

In a kind of dream state, he pulled open the heavy library doors. He expected to hear more cries. Instead, he heard cheers.

CHAPTER
TWENTY-NINE

CURTAIN CALL

Everybody was there.

They all stood around the checkout desk, applauding, big grins on their faces. Leira in her newsboy cap. Buzz in his beekeeper outfit. Nurse Cora in her hair. The Worms wore makeshift party hats and Mardi Gras necklaces. Caliban wore a flower lei. It looked to Clay as though he had interrupted a going-away party or a birthday celebration.

"Hi, were you looking for me?" Mira stepped up to Clay, back in her polka-dot dress. She offered him a glass of something pink. "Punch?"

Overwhelmed, Clay automatically took it. He held the glass in his hand, not drinking, just staring.

"Why is everybody here?" he asked, his voice coming out in a whisper. "Why are they clapping?"

"They're clapping for you, silly," said Mira. "That's what you do when the show is over."

Clay blinked, trying to absorb what she was saying. "You mean it never ended? It was always still... on? The play, or whatever it was."

He had suspected this might be the case, but he couldn't quite believe it, even now.

Mira nodded. "This is the cast party and curtain call rolled into one. You should take a bow."

"But I didn't do anything. I'm just the audience, remember?"

Mira laughed. "What do you mean? You're the star of the show."

Clay looked around, stunned. The library was much brighter than it had been the last time he was inside. It was like they'd turned on the houselights, now that the show was over.

Clay's fellow Worms were smiling and nodding at him.

"That was awesome," said Jonah.

"Yeah, you really pulled it out in the end," said Kwan.

Pablo raised a fist. "Way to go, man." Caliban, standing next to Pablo, raised a fist as well.

Still trying to take it in, Clay half raised his fist in response.

"My turn," said Leira, pulling her sister away from Clay. "Welcome back."

"Uh... thanks, I think?"

"You dropped something up there—"

She handed Clay his wallet. He looked at it blankly.

"What—? Oh, right, heh." He forced a smile.

Skipper, the pilot, was next. He stepped up to Clay—"Nice job, Shakespeare"—and pulled off his gray-ponytailed wig, revealing himself to be Uncle Ben, the old custodian.

"Hey, Skipper—I mean, Uncle Ben," Clay managed. "So you were part of this, too?"

"The name is Owen." The bald man took a rag out of his pocket and started wiping off spots and scabs and wrinkles. The octogenarian quickly became a man of thirty—with a shaved head. "And Gilligan—well, that's what he's actually called."

Gilligan the bulldog, not exactly docile, but much sweeter than he'd ever been before, nuzzled Clay's leg. Clay distractedly scratched behind the dog's ear, and the dog licked his hand.

Buzz stepped up, a warm smile on his face. "Congratulations, Worm. We knew you had it in you."

Behind Buzz, lurking in the background, was Flint. He nodded at Clay, but he didn't break a smile. Evidently, he was part of the show, too, but he didn't seem altogether pleased with the way things had gone. Clay wondered how much of Flint's animosity toward him had been real, how much scripted.

"And here at last is the director of our camp—" Buzz gestured toward a short hobbit-like man in sandals and mismatched socks.

"Hiya, Clay," boomed a familiar voice. "I know it's a little late, but welcome to Earth Ranch."

"Mr. Bailey?" Clay was surprised to see his language arts teacher... but not very surprised. Nothing surprised him very much anymore.

"Call me Eli," said Mr. Bailey, beaming. "Great performance. *Bravissimo.*"

"You were watching?"

"From the back row, you could say. Hard to guide the action if you can't see anything."

Clay thought of Over There, the mysterious moving teepee—and the sense he'd often had that the director was just around the corner.

"So you're not just the director of the camp—you were the director of the show?" said Clay. "Just like at school."

Mr. Bailey shrugged his shoulders. "We don't think of it so much as a show. More of a game."

Clay's big eyes narrowed. "What kind of game?"

"The Hero Game, we call it. Everybody here has played—their own versions, of course. For Kwan we made up a junior poker championship. Pablo we threw into an imaginary civil war. I don't think we've ever used Shakespeare before...."

"So everything that happened—the ghost, the journal, the lava—it was all like game levels or something?"

A feeling that was part anger and part disappointment had been building inside Clay ever since he entered the library. It was like a stomachache he was trying to ignore. His leg jiggled.

"What about Gideon? Did he really write on your wall, like you said in your letter?"

Mr. Bailey shook his head. "No. Sorry about that. I couldn't think of any other explanation...."

"And those guys—" Clay nodded toward the other campers, the people he'd thought were his friends. "Even at the end, they were just acting like we were all in it together?"

"It wasn't like that—" Jonah protested.

"Right. Nothing's really like anything here, is it?" said Clay, a sour taste in his mouth. "Nothing here is real."

"Nothing in the Hero Game is real or unreal," said Mr. Bailey. "Remember what we said about fiction in class? It's a lie that tells the truth."

Clay nodded—slightly. Sure he remembered. But he also remembered what he'd thought at the time: A lie is a lie.

"And what about—" Clay could barely bring himself to say it aloud. "What about the magic?"

"What about it?" asked Mr. Bailey.

"Never mind, it doesn't matter," said Clay, humiliated.

Of course magic wasn't real—no more so than his friendships with the other campers.

He, Clay, the cynic, had been duped. Tricked into believing in something that didn't exist. Flint and Buzz were just expert illusionists, that was all. Earth Ranch was like one big Las Vegas magic show with lava and bees instead of dancing girls and tigers.

He should have been relieved to learn the magic was a hoax; after all, he was the guy who wrote *MAGIC SUCKS!* in his journal. So why were his eyes filling with tears?

"I guess you proved your point, didn't you?" said Clay, his emotions bursting to the surface. "I'm just as dumb as everybody else. Everybody falls for magic tricks in the end, right?"

"You didn't fall for magic," said Mr. Bailey quietly. "You found it. In yourself. That's how we know you're ready."

Clay glared at his teacher. "Ready for what? To be conned again?"

"To be a magician."

"You think I want to be a magician?" Clay snorted. "After what you guys did? You're just like my brother. A bunch of fakes."

"That's what Max-Ernest thought you would say," said Mr. Bailey.

Clay froze. "Wait—what did you say?"

"I said, that's what Max-Ernest thought you would say."

"You—you know my brother?" Clay stammered.

Mr. Bailey nodded. "He helped write your game. He even named it."

He pointed to a banner hanging above the checkout desk.

it said in glittery gold letters. In his delirium, Clay had missed it earlier.

"The kids wanted to change it to *MAGIC SUCKS!*," said Mr. Bailey. "But as a teacher, I just couldn't—"

"Where is he?" Clay demanded.

"At the moment, I don't know."

"But he's my brother!"

"I'm sorry, Clay," said Mr. Bailey. "You just have to trust him."

Clay looked at his teacher, tears trickling down his cheeks.

"You know what, forget it," said Clay, a deep despair taking the place of the emotions that had been roiling inside him. "He obviously doesn't want

to see me, anyway." He just wants to play tricks on me, Clay added in his head. "I should have known. This whole thing—it's something only Max-Ernest would do."

Wiping his eyes, Clay turned toward the exit. "Uncle Ben, Skipper, Owen, whatever your name is— I'm going to go wait by your plane."

Mr. Bailey put his hand on Clay's shoulder. "I understand how you feel, Clay. But before you go, there's something you might want to see—"

The banyan tree that grew out of the bottom of the library seemed even larger to Clay when he stood at the base. The trunk was so wide that there was almost no space to walk around it. And so many roots dangled from the tree that it was almost impossible to see more than one or two feet ahead. He wasn't sure what he was looking for—Mr. Bailey had merely pointed him in the direction of the tree—and he was half-inclined to give up the search and exit the library as he'd planned. Instead, he pushed his way through the roots, circling the tree.

He'd almost made a full circle when he noticed a faint buzzing sound coming from the tree trunk. Another beehive? Cautiously, he stepped closer, and saw it: a small round door at the base of the tree, surrounded by roots on all sides. In the middle of the door was a brass knob.

The buzzing grew louder.

Clay remembered Uncle Ben—Owen, he reminded himself—saying something about a vault underneath the tree. A vault that contained Price's most precious books. Is that what this was? Then why the buzzing?

Clay tried the knob, but the door was locked or stuck. Or maybe it's fake, Clay thought. Like everything else on the island.

"It was locked by Max-Ernest," said Mr. Bailey, who had walked up beside Clay. "Only you know the word that will open it."

Clay frowned. "How would I know it?"

"He said it was the first magic word you ever learned. He wouldn't tell us what it was."

Clay studied the door for a moment; he couldn't imagine which word—of all the magic words that they had spoken to each other—Max-Ernest might have been thinking of.

What was strange was Max-Ernest calling it a magic word instead of a bad word, as they usually did.

Then, suddenly, Clay grinned. That was the clue. Max-Ernest loved reversals. If *bad word* meant *magic word*, then *magic word* meant *bad word*. The magic word Clay needed now wasn't the first magic word he ever learned, it was the first bad word he ever learned.

The old kind of bad word. The bad kind.

Clay stood as tall as he could.

"#⟨*%!!!..."

he said, perhaps not quite as loudly as he had in that elevator when he was three years old, but with no less feeling.

No sooner had Clay spoken this terrible word than it appeared on the tree trunk in front of him. It looked as if it had been burned into the tree by a thoughtless vandal.

Mr. Bailey looked at Clay, aghast. "What have you done, young man? If you were in school, I'd expel you all over again!"

"Sorry," said Clay, mortified. "I didn't know it would do that."

"Oh, it's okay, just this once," said Mr. Bailey, the ghost of a smile on his lips. "Look—"

The offensive letters were already fading; the tree trunk was restored.

As Clay watched, the small round door swung open, exposing the top of a steep ladder.

CHAPTER
THIRTY

THE LIBRARY INSIDE
THE LIBRARY

From above, the vault looked an awful lot like a dungeon.

As he climbed down the ladder, Clay heard a cacophony of unnerving sounds. Not just buzzing. There was humming. Rustling. Fluttering. Squeaking. It didn't sound like bees. Or not only bees. Maybe bats?

There were no bats. Nor even any bees.

Only books.

It was chaos. They floated in the air, some gently swaying, some flapping like birds. Some were stuck in the roots that grew out of the ceiling. Others lay in piles on the stone floor. There were big books and small books. Old books and new books. But they were all, it was impossible not to see, magic books.

It was a library inside the library. A magic library.

"A bit less organized here than upstairs, isn't it?" said Mr. Bailey, descending the ladder. "Magic is like that."

As he stared dumbfounded, Clay saw a familiar red leather book flying toward him, pages flapping wildly. Clay grabbed it out of the air and opened it.

As he expected, he saw his own writing inside. *MAGIC SUCKS!* But a second later his bubble letters started to dissolve as if he'd poured water on them, and *The Memoirs of Randolph Price* came into focus. So there had been only one journal after all—one magic journal!

No sooner had Clay come to that conclusion, however, than Price's writing started to melt away, revealing another layer of writing hidden behind it.

The Book of Prospero

it now read on the title page.

Clay paged through quickly. It was just as Price had described, full of strange drawings and spells and magical potions. A *grimoire*. The red journal wasn't just a magic book—it was also a book of magic.

And that wasn't the only surprise: Folded inside was a letter—in handwriting Clay hadn't seen in a long while.

Happy birthday, Clay!

I hope you didn't think I forgot!
I would never forget your birthday.
Okay, so I forgot last year. I'm
sorry, I was very busy with—never
mind, there's no excuse, I'm just
sorry. And I'm sorry I cannot be
there today. Try not to hate me.
And if you have to hate me, don't
hate magic. Magic is not a bad
word. Or if it is, it's our kind of bad
word. The good kind.

I hope you've figured out by
now what a great magician you
are and will be. I knew you were a
natural from the time you did that
rope trick when you were five. I
should have acknowledged it then.
But the truth is, well, I was jealous.
I know it's nuts to be jealous of
a five-year-old, but there you
are. This may come as a surprise
to you, it comes as a surprise to
me, but I've never been a great
magician. Too clumsy. Too anxious.

You may think that rope tricks have nothing to do with "real" magic, but stage magic and real magic are a lot closer than most people suppose. That's something I learned from an old man named Pietro, whom I will tell you more about someday. *Magic, it is what is left when you stop pretending to understand,* he told me. My problem is I can't stop pretending to understand. But you—you don't pretend at all. You're the most honest person I know.

Why did I run away? The answer is: you. Not to get away from you. To protect you. I see now that my absence is not enough. In fact, ignorance may harm you. I'm not going to say magic runs deep within you or anything like that, because I know you would say it was cheesy or cheese-wiz-y or whatever it is you say, but believe me when I say the magical world is

going to catch up with you one way
or another. Not just because you
are my brother, but because you
are you.

I cannot spare you—it's time
to join the fight. The Other Side
is in danger from people who
would twist it to their own ends,
no matter what the cost. We must
stop them.

I will see you soon. You are in
good hands until then.

Love, your proud brother,
M-E

Clay looked up from the letter, his eyes wet. He
had been so absorbed in what he was reading that
he almost forgot he was in a room full of floating
books.

"Well, are you in? Will you join us?" asked Mr.
Bailey, who had been standing at a respectful distance while Clay read.

"Yeah, dude, will you?" "Come on, man!" "Just
join!"

It was the Worms, crowding around the trap-
door above. They grinned down at Clay.

"Join what?" he asked, confused.

"SOS: The Society of the Other Side," said Mr. Bailey. "That's who we are. Everyone on the island."

"SOS..." Clay repeated. "So that's what the message on the printing press was about?"

Mr. Bailey nodded.

"And the sign on the beach?"

"A way to identify the island," said Mr. Bailey. "Not a plea for help."

Clay held up the letter from Max-Ernest. "This society, does it have something to do with the fight my brother was talking about?"

"The fight to protect the Other Side, yes," said Mr. Bailey. "So what do you say? If you like, Owen will fly you back this afternoon. But if you want to stay, well, I think you'll find my language arts class a little more exciting here than at home!"

"Just say yes!" "Don't be a loser!" "Stay and play with us, you dork!" the Worms chorused from above.

Clay nodded, unable to stop the big smile forming on his face. Maybe they really were his friends after all, not just the best actors he'd ever met. "Okay, okay, I'll stay. I just have one question. What's the Other Side?"

Mr. Bailey pointed to the ladder. "Why don't you go outside and see?"

As Clay left the library, he was almost blinded by sunlight. For the first time since he'd been on the island, the vog had completely lifted. There was not a cloud in the sky.

"The Other Side is not another place," Mr. Bailey was saying behind him. "It's another perspective on the place you already are."

"You mean, it's like the magic side of the world?" Clay asked, struggling to understand.

"You could call it that. To me, it's the world of potential. The world where the answer is always yes instead of no."

The lava moat was gone, if it had ever really been there, replaced by a ring of flowering bushes. The bees danced around the flowers, and then rose together in a waving ribbon formation. They circled Clay once, then flew off toward camp, as if leading the way for him.

"Think of a kid who gets dismissed as a problem—you know, a bad kid," said Mr. Bailey. "If you expect nothing from him, you get nothing. But if you give him a chance, you never know what he's got up his sleeve."

"So every juvenile delinquent is secretly a magician?" Clay scoffed.

"Why not?" Mr. Bailey looked into Clay's eyes.

For once, Clay was the first to look away.

In a daze, Clay almost walked right into the director's teepee, Over There. It was sitting among the ruins of Price Palace. Or rather, hovering.

"Walk or ride?" asked Mr. Bailey, his eyes twinkling.

It took a second for Clay to understand that Mr. Bailey meant the teepee. "Uh, ride?"

Mr. Bailey bowed. "After you."

Entering the teepee felt a little like entering an inflatable jumpy house. It was difficult to stand without wobbling. Clay was glad Mr. Bailey suggested he sit.

As far as Clay could tell, the teepee worked like a hot-air balloon. A magical, vanishing, cone-shaped hot-air balloon. The heat came from a camping stove, and Mr. Bailey steered with a system of ropes and pulleys.

Soon they were floating over Earth Ranch at a height that just cleared the tallest trees.

Almost everything looked the same; and yet everything was different.

There were some obvious things. The rainbow on the outside of Art Yurt rippled like water. The dome over the fire pit pulsed with an electric glow. The trees and bushes and even vegetables moved slowly back and forth and up and down, as if they were all joined in a long synchronized dance.

But it was the less obvious things that astonished Clay the most. Things that he didn't see so much as feel. The more melodious singing of birds. The bluer blue of the lake and the greener green of the trees. The sense of warmth and well-being that radiated from the cabins and the yurts. The sparkling glow that seemed to pervade the very atmosphere of the camp. It was as if Clay were suddenly experiencing the world through the eyes and ears of a different species, perceiving colors and sounds outside the normal human spectrum.

"When did—was all this there?" Clay asked.

"The whole time, yes, right under your nose," said Mr. Bailey. "You didn't see it before because your mind wouldn't accept it."

Mr. Bailey lowered the teepee slightly as they passed the blue barn. Clay could see Como at the fence, straining his neck to watch them.

"He wants to come with us," Clay said.

"How do you know?"

Clay shrugged. "I guess I don't."

"Yes, you do," said Mr. Bailey earnestly. "You've been communicating with that llama since you first got here. You just never believed it. . . . Sadly, he's a bit too heavy to ride in the teepee with us."

Clay waved at the llama. "Sorry, he says you're too fat, amigo!"

As they started to float over the long crescent-shaped lake, a flock of blue parrots flew next to them, squawking loudly. For a moment, they were only a few feet away. Clay listened intently.

"I didn't say you were going to suddenly turn into Dr. Dolittle," Mr. Bailey teased.*

"Who?"

"I just meant it might take a while before you're communicating with all the animals."

"Oh," said Clay, embarrassed. The parrots flew on.

"But there's no harm trying," said Mr. Bailey reassuringly.

They were past Egg Rock now, floating toward the waterfall. Clay could hear its roar and feel its spray blowing in the wind. The waterfall looked less milky than he remembered, and more pearlescent; there seemed to be a rainbow of colors in every splash. Before they got too close, Mr. Bailey pulled a rope and the teepee started to ascend higher and higher, as if they were chasing some of the clouds of vog that had cleared away.

Clay thought perhaps Mr. Bailey planned to head for the volcano, but just then the ribbon of bees flew toward them and started circling the teepee.

Mr. Bailey frowned in concern. "I think they

---

* DR. DOLITTLE IS THE TITLE CHARACTER IN A CHILDREN'S BOOK SERIES NOW ALMOST ONE HUNDRED YEARS OLD. (AND HERE I THOUGHT I INVENTED THE IDEA!) IN LIEU OF HUMAN PATIENTS, HE TREATS ANIMALS, TO WHICH HE SPEAKS IN ODD ANIMAL LANGUAGES. OTHER CHARACTERS INCLUDE THE PUSHMI-PULLYU, A TWO-HEADED GAZELLE-UNICORN, AND GUB-GUB, A PIG WHO IS THE PURPORTED AUTHOR OF MY FAVORITE BOOK IN THE DOLITTLE SERIES, GUB-GUB'S BOOK, AN ENCYCLOPAEDIA OF FOOD.

have a message from Buzz. I hope everything is okay."

"Everything's fine. Look—" Clay pointed.

The bees had changed formation to deliver their message:

HURRY UP
TIME 4 DINNER

"They aren't guard bees," said Clay, laughing. "They're spelling bees!"

It was just the kind of silly joke Max-Ernest would have loved. Someday, Clay hoped, he would get the chance to repeat it for his brother.

Eventually, of course, he would get that chance, but by then he would have many more jokes—and many more adventures—to tell me about.

THE END

APPENDIX

GRAWLIX (pl. grawlixes)

Often found in the funnies section of a newspaper,* a *grawlix* is a series of typographical symbols employed in place of an offensive word or phrase.

Like this: $#%@!

The term *grawlix* was apparently invented by the cartoonist Mort Walker, who also defined a set of symbols, called *symbolia*, that you have no doubt seen in comic books and cartoons without having any idea they had names:

agitron: *a wiggly line that means an object is shaking*

---

* Newspapers are printed publications (usually issued daily or weekly) consisting of folded unstapled paper sheets and containing news, feature articles, advertisements, and so on. They were once very common.

briffit: *a cloud of dust that means a character has left in a rush*

emanata: *lines emanating from a character's head that means he or she is surprised*

plewd: *a drop of sweat that means a character is hot or stressed*

squeans: *asterisks that mean drunkenness or dizziness*

waftarom: *a wavy line that means something smells foul*

ONE POTATO, TWO POTATO...

A potato robot is another matter, but it's not difficult to make a potato battery. To turn a potato into a battery, you'll need these items:

two full-size potatoes
(it helps to label them 1 and 2)

two copper pennies or some copper wire

two galvanized nails

three pairs of alligator clips (each pair connected by wire)

one low-voltage device, such as an LED light or a clock

one adult*

1. Insert a penny into potato number one, pressing the penny in as far as possible to maximize the surface area touching the potato. (The copper will make contact with

---

* FOR THE SAKE OF APPEARANCES, IT'S BEST TO HAVE AN ADULT "SUPERVISOR" AROUND WHILE PERFORMING THIS EXPERIMENT (ALSO WHILE PERFORMING THE ROPE TRICK BELOW). NATURALLY, I AM NOT SUGGESTING THAT THE ADULT WILL DO ANY REAL SUPERVISING, ONLY THAT SHE OR HE WILL PROVIDE COVER FOR YOU. WITH AN ADULT AROUND, PEOPLE ARE MORE LIKELY TO ASSUME YOUR INTENTIONS ARE INNOCENT. SILLY THEM.

the phosphoric acid in the potato juice. The penny is the anode.)

2. Take the galvanized nail and drive it into the potato, *as far away from the penny as possible*. (It is the cathode.)

3. Do the same with your second potato.

4. Remove the battery from your low-voltage device. Let's say it's a clock. (That way we can see how long this potato battery works.)

5. Attach one pair of alligator clips to the penny in potato number one and to the positive (+) terminal of the clock's battery compartment.

6. Attach another pair of alligator clips to the nail in potato number two and to the negative (-) terminal of the clock's battery compartment.

7. Use the third pair of alligator clips to connect the nail in potato number one to the penny in potato two.

You should now have power. Set that clock! Time's wasting. It's not made of potato juice, you know.

CLASSIC ROPE TRICK

Note: This trick works much better with real rope than with licorice.

Here's how to do the old cut-and-restore rope trick. A rope about four to five feet long works best. And you'll need a pair of scissors.

1. After demonstrating to your audience that your rope is just rope, nothing tricky about it, your first step is to make a square knot very close to one of the ends of the rope. When you're done, your rope should look like a lasso—or, if you prefer, a letter *P*—with a loop at one end.

2. To make a square knot, lay your rope on a table. Take the left end and place it over the right, bring the (old) right back over the (old) left, then the (same old) left back over the (same old) right. (You should practice this a few times before attempting the knot in public; look in a book of knots if you're confused.)

3. When your knot is complete and you have a nice loop at the end of your rope, show it to the crowd. Then grab your scissors and announce that you are going to cut the rope in half.

4. Then cut into the loop of rope. Try to cut very close to the knot and the short end of the rope. After you cut the rope, it will look as if you have two pieces of rope tied together with a knot. (In reality, it is just one piece of rope, and a knot that can be pulled off the end.)

5. Now is the time to say a magic word. Wave a wand. Blow pixie dust. Whatever inspires you.

6. Wrap your hand around the knot and pull it off the end of the rope. You should have a short piece of rope left in your hand—hide it.

7. Let the rest of the rope fall, or stretch it between your hands. Voilà! The rope is restored. You are a master magician.

Didn't work the first time? Take heart—it never does. Keep trying.

A WAGER

It strikes me, as I bring this book to a close, that while I have discussed magic again and again, and even told you how to do a rope trick, I haven't actually shown you any magic. A terrible oversight.

As a remedy, I propose to perform a magic trick for you right here, right now.

Don't believe I can? Okay. Let's make a bet.

Not for money. Just for fun. Although if you want to throw a few pieces of chocolate into the mix, that's fine, too.

I bet I can make you obey my command, no matter how hard you resist, no matter where you are reading this book.

Are you prepared to be amazed by my magic powers?

Turn the page....

I win.

What? I wasn't playing fair? That wasn't the kind of magic you were thinking of?

Fine, let's try again. This time, I promise, no funny stuff. You will follow my next command as soon as you read it. If you don't, I will eat my top hat.

Ready?

You will find the command on the next page. (Don't worry—it has nothing to do with turning pages.) Drumroll, please...

Here's the command:

Read this sentence.

Ta-da!

And there you have it, my friend. Magic. Right in front of your eyes.

It's in every book if you know where to look.

Of course, there are some books that are more magical than others.

And some authors.

Now let's have some chocolate.

DON'T MISS THE NEXT ADVENTURE IN
THE BAD BOOKS
SERIES!

Read on for a sneak peek of *Bad Luck*.

The *Imperial Conquest* had five swimming pools, four gyms, a three-story waterslide, a two-lane bowling alley, an outdoor movie theater, a giant climbing wall, a miniature golf course, an ice-cream parlor, a pizza parlor, a sushi bar, a taco stand, a twenty-four-hour arcade, an eighteen-and-under dance club, a full-service spa, and a multi-floor luxury shopping mall, but so far the thing Brett liked best about this gigantic cruise ship was the Jell-O parfait at the Lido Deck Snack Shack.

Jell-O and whipped cream. It was the perfect combination. Sweet and tangy. Rich and soft. He couldn't believe it had taken all twelve long years of his life to discover it.

Eating slowly to make his parfait last, Brett waded through the sea of sunbathers. He was the only person around who was fully clothed, not to mention wearing a bow tie (sometime in the sixth grade, Brett had decided that bow ties would be his "signature accessory"), and as usual he got some funny looks.

A sunburned boy pointed at him. "Hey, penguin, wrong cruise—North Pole is the other way."

"You mean South Pole," Brett replied automatically. "No penguins in the North. Just...elves."

And next time, try a higher SPF, he thought. *Lobster.*

A woman squinted at him from behind her sunglasses. "Are you my waiter? Where's my drink?"

"I don't know," said Brett. "Maybe you drank it?"

By the way, I'm not your waiter; my dad owns this ship, he almost added. But she probably wouldn't have believed him anyway.

Even though it happened to be true.

All he wanted to do was to return to his stateroom and eat his parfait in peace. Was that too much to ask? Well, maybe just one more bite before he—

BEEP! BEEP! BEEP!

He almost choked when the alarm sounded. Three high-pitched beeps so loud they made his head hurt.

Brett looked down in dismay—a dribble of green Jell-O had landed on his tie. He could barely see over his chin, but he wiped it away as best he could.

"*This is your captain speaking*," said a woman over the ship's intercom. Her voice had a distinctive accent—Australian, it sounded to Brett. (A good sign, he thought; Australia was the home of the Great Barrier Reef, and if she could navigate the world's biggest coral reef, she could probably navigate anywhere.*) *"Please report to your assigned muster room immediately. This is only a drill...."*

Brett's muster room, the Shooting Stars Nightclub and Casino, was five floors down. As Brett entered, still clutching his parfait glass, a uniformed crew member stood onstage, trying to entertain everyone with a less-than-successful rendition of Michael Jackson's "Beat It."

The crowd booed happily.

"Oh, so you guys think you can do better, huh?" said the crew member, pretending to be insulted. "Well, our karaoke contest is tomorrow night, right after the magic show!"

He nodded to the poster behind him. It showed a big pair of bunny ears sticking out of a top hat:

NOW YOU SEE HIM...
NOW YOU DON'T!
AN EVENING OF MAGIC AND MYSTERY

Another crew member, whose badge read MIGUEL, PHILIPPINES, scanned Brett's cruise ID card, and Brett saw his own image flash across a small video screen, along with the words VIP—ALL ACCESS.

Miguel looked down at the husky, overdressed twelve-year-old in front of him. If he was suspicious of Brett's VIP status, he didn't say anything about it.

---

* IN FACT, AS I'M SURE BRETT WOULD BE THE FIRST TO TELL YOU, THE GREAT BARRIER REEF IS NOT JUST ONE CORAL REEF; IT IS A GROUP OF REEFS THAT TOGETHER MAKE UP THE BIGGEST STRUCTURE IN THE WORLD TO HAVE BEEN BUILT BY LIVING ORGANISMS—SO BIG IT CAN BE SEEN FROM A SPACESHIP. OR SO THEY SAY. I MYSELF HAVE NEVER SEEN IT FROM A SPACESHIP, ONLY FROM A SUBMARINE—AND ONCE, MEMORABLY, FROM THE MAST OF A CATAMARAN.

"I was wondering, Miguel," said Brett. "Why do they call this a muster room? Is it because you have to muster your courage when the ship is sinking?"

"Sorry, sir. I have no idea."

Miguel didn't look sorry. In fact, he looked irritated. Brett often had this effect on people. He wasn't sure why.

"Well, if I were you, I would look it up," Brett said helpfully. "Mustering is your job, after all."*

Before Brett could find a place to sit, Brett senior walked over with his smiling young fiancée, Amber, in tow.

"Junior! What took you so long?" he bellowed loudly enough to cause people to turn. "Good thing there isn't a real emergency!"

Brett cringed in embarrassment. It looked as though his father had come straight from the pool; he was wearing an open shirt and one of his just-a-little-too-small bathing suits. A gold chain hung from his neck, snagging on his hairy chest. At his side, the always-sunny Amber was dressed in sparkly yellow workout clothing. It seemed to Brett that she had an entire rainbow's worth of yoga pants. Both his father and Amber wore life vests around their necks.

"Where's your vest? Never mind—" Brett's father turned to Amber, who was busy applying strawberry lip balm to her already-balmy lips. "Can you grab him one, princess?"

---

* ACTUALLY, THE REASON A MUSTER ROOM IS CALLED A MUSTER ROOM IS NOT SO MUSTERIOUS. *TO MUSTER* IS TO ASSEMBLE—AS IN TO ASSEMBLE TROOPS, OR IN THIS CASE TO ASSEMBLE PEOPLE ON A SHIP. SIMILARLY, *A MUSTER* IS A GATHERING OR AN ASSEMBLY OF PEOPLE, USUALLY IN THE MILITARY. THUS, *TO MUSTER ONE'S COURAGE* IS SIMPLY TO GATHER ONE'S COURAGE. *TO CUT THE MUSTARD*, MEANWHILE, MEANS TO SUCCEED OR QUALIFY, AND LIKELY HAS NOTHING TO DO WITH MUSTERING AT ALL. SO WHY MENTION IT? BECAUSE I WANT TO OFFER THIS INVALUABLE PIECE OF ADVICE FOR ALL WHO FIND THEMSELVES MUSTERING IN A MUSTER ROOM, OR INDEED WHO FIND THEMSELVES SHARING ANY SMALL SPACE WITH OTHER PEOPLE: IF YOU WANT TO CUT THE MUSTARD, PLEASE DON'T CUT THE CHEESE.

"Of course, my knight."

My knight...? That was even worse than *princess*, Brett thought. Couldn't they keep their pet names private?

Amber picked up a vest from a pile and handed it to Brett. "Here, honey."

"Thanks, orange is my favorite color," he said, unable to keep the sarcasm out of his voice. Amber had never been anything but nice to him—almost too nice—and yet he couldn't bring himself to like her.

Brett's father eyed the parfait glass in his hand. "Didn't you already have one of those Jell-O things this morning?"

"So? They're free."

"That's not the point. You haven't even had lunch yet. No wonder—" His father stopped himself before finishing his sentence.

"No wonder what?" *Go on*, thought Brett. *Say it.*

"Do you want to be like all the other overweight losers on this ship?" said his father, lowering his voice. He smiled broadly for the benefit of their fellow passengers.

"If that's how you feel, why did you buy this ship in the first place?" asked Brett, stung.

His father shrugged. "I like big things."

"Yeah, except for me," said Brett under his breath.

Brett senior's scalp reddened underneath his new hair plugs. "It doesn't matter whether *I* like you," he said, struggling to control his anger. "It only matters whether *you* like you."

Amber put one soothing hand on Brett's shoulder and one on his father's. "All your father is saying is that you need to take care of yourself," she cooed to Brett in her unnervingly sweet voice. "There are so many great exercise classes on the ship.... Pilates ... Jazz-aerobics ... Why don't you try one? Or at least go for a swim. Your father says you used to be a very strong swimmer."

"Yeah. Emphasis on *used to be.*" Brett hadn't voluntarily

taken his shirt off in public since he was ten. (Or, to be more exact, since the day Mitch Poll had started making fun of Brett's "boy boobs" at their class swim party.)

Mercifully, a neighboring passenger shushed them. A diagram of the ship was being projected onto a screen above the stage. Red circles were drawn around the lifeboats.

*"In the unlikely event of an evacuation, you will be escorted to a tender. Do not attempt to board without a crew member...."**

The emergency training session had begun.

Brett's father was always buying things: oil rigs, construction companies, sports teams. Still, Brett had been a little surprised when, a few weeks earlier, at the same time his father announced his engagement to Amber, he also announced that he had bought a cruise line. As far as Brett could remember, his father had never expressed much interest in sea vessels or even in the sea itself.

Why buy an entire fleet of cruise ships?

But what had really surprised Brett was that his father wanted to take *him* on a cruise. In the old days, when his mother was still alive, they'd traveled all the time, but his father rarely took Brett away for a weekend anymore, never mind a weeklong vacation. Brett now suspected Amber's influence. She might not care much about Brett one way or the other, but at least she had some idea about the way families were supposed to behave.

---

* FOR SUCH A SOFT AND DELICATE LITTLE WORD, *TENDER* HAS MANY MEANINGS. YOU MAY TREAT PEOPLE WITH TENDERNESS BECAUSE YOU FEEL TENDERLY TOWARD THEM, OR SIMPLY BECAUSE YOU ARE TENDERHEARTED. IF YOU HAVE DONE A JOB, YOU SHOULD BE PAID IN LEGAL TENDER (I.E., MONEY). IF YOU AREN'T, I SUGGEST YOU TENDER YOUR RESIGNATION (I.E., QUIT). IF A SHIP IS TENDER, IT TIPS EASILY. LARGER SHIPS ARE USUALLY MORE STABLE, BUT THEY ARE LIKELY TO HAVE A TENDER OR TWO ABOARD. *A TENDER* IS A SMALL BOAT USED TO CONVEY PEOPLE OR THINGS BACK AND FORTH FROM A LARGER SHIP TO THE SHORE. ON CRUISE SHIPS, TENDERS DOUBLE AS LIFEBOATS.

Unlike his father.

He hates me, Brett thought. *He really hates me.*

His father had practically admitted it to his face.

After quitting the muster room, Brett found himself back on the Lido Deck. Another parfait. It was the only answer to the terrible pit that had opened in his stomach. But when he reached the Snack Shack, it was closed. The dessert case was empty.

Now, this is an emergency, he thought.

As Brett considered his options—pizza? gelato? those twisty croissant-y things in the Tahiti Dining Room?—he noticed an open door next to the café. Inside was a gleaming stainless-steel world of counters and refrigerators and ovens and heat lamps. Standing in a corner, beckoning to Brett like a diamond necklace to a jewel thief, was a rolling rack stacked with Jell-O parfaits. Dozens of them. In every color. Each topped with a bright red maraschino cherry.

Glancing only briefly at the STAFF ONLY sign, he walked straight through the door. The parfaits were free anyway, he reasoned. And if he got caught, well, his father owned the ship. Basically, he was stealing from himself.

He was in the middle of his second parfait—fourth if you counted the two he'd eaten earlier in the day—when a muffled noise caught his attention. It sounded like cars caught in traffic, honking and revving their motors, and it came from behind a steel door at the far end of the kitchen.

Above the door: a blinking red light and the words ACCESS RESTRICTED.

Ordinarily, Brett was a cautious fellow. True, he often spoke without thinking. He was especially bad at holding his tongue when he was being bullied (a twice- or thrice-daily occurrence). But when it came to serious risk taking, let's just say he preferred the comforts of a couch and a touch-screen device. Today was different. Maybe it was his anger at his father, maybe the Jell-O in his bloodstream, or maybe all that red dye in the cherries; whatever the reason, Brett felt bold and reckless. He inserted his all-access ID card into the slot.

Stepping through the door, he found himself at the top of a stairwell. At the bottom was an enormous storage area—a warehouse space that would have seemed large enough on land, let alone at sea—filled with boxes and crates of all shapes and sizes.

As soon as Brett walked in, he identified the source of the traffic sounds: not cars but animals. Live animals. Goats. Sheep. Pigs. Chickens. Even a few cows. All squeezed into pens. It looked as if an entire farmyard had been airlifted onto the ship.

It smelled like that, too.

Why animals on a cruise? For a petting zoo? Maybe a *tableau vivant* of Noah's Ark?* Brett didn't know anything about farming, but the animals sure didn't look happy.

Behind them sat a rusted steel shipping container the size of a city bus, with airholes drilled into its sides. Next to the shipping container was a rack of fire extinguishers, as well as a locked glass case filled with weapons—stun guns, spearguns, rifles—enough to take down a blue whale or a herd of elephants.

No, probably not a petting zoo.

Suddenly, he heard people entering the room, arguing.

Trying not to panic, Brett stepped behind the shipping container and listened. A woman was complaining that the ship's crew was unhappy about having live animals in the hold. "They're smelly and only encourage the vermin!" Brett recognized her voice from the intercom.

"Not your business, lady," a man growled. "This space

---

* *A TABLEAU VIVANT IS A "LIVING PICTURE" WHEREIN HUMAN—OR, IN THIS CASE, ANIMAL—ACTORS POSE WITHOUT MOVING, STAGING A SCENE FROM HISTORY OR LITERATURE OR ART. JUST A MOMENT AGO, FOR EXAMPLE, WHEN I WAS SITTING AT MY DESK, STARING INTO SPACE, WITH A PEN FROZEN IN MY HAND, I DID NOT HAVE WRITER'S BLOCK; I WAS MERELY CREATING A TABLEAU VIVANT OF L'ÉCRIVAIN AU TRAVAIL. THAT'S "THE WRITER AT WORK" FOR YOU HELPLESS NON-FRANCOPHONES.

He held his breath. *One . . . two . . .* Silently, he himself, as if he were waiting for a bomb to explode. *four . . .* Had he averted discovery?

Then—

"Brett!"

His father stared at him from the doorway, more furious than surprised.

"Um, hello," said Brett numbly.

The captain stepped up from behind Brett's father. "What in the world . . . ?" Horrified, she stared not at Brett but at the contraption in front of his feet.

Brett glanced down again. The muzzle was a brutal piece of hardware, all right, made of steel thick enough to hold the biggest, strongest animal on earth. On the inside were spikes so long and so sharp they would keep King Kong from opening his jaws.

This cage he'd stumbled into—it wasn't meant for a magician.

It was meant for a monster.

What's next for Brett?
Will he find his way to Earth Ranch?
And what's in store for Clay and
his vog-weathered friends?
All I can tell you is that NOTHING GOOD is
going to happen in

Available February 2016!

e except Mr. Perry and the staff of

wallowed. Mr. Perry was his father, Brett senior.
n who was speaking sounded like Mack, the ex-boxer
worked as his father's bodyguard and chauffeur. Brett
ked around the corner: Sure enough, Mack was there, and
tt's father, too. (Thankfully, his father was now wearing a
awaiian shirt and tan pants. Not a great look, but Brett
referred it to the bathing suit.) Walking with them was a tall
woman in uniform.

"I'm the captain of this ship, you moron," she said, incensed.
"No space is off-limits to me!"

"And I'm the owner of this ship," Brett's father reminded
her. "Your employer."

"I am still responsible for two thousand passengers. Never
mind a thousand crew members. What is this 'Operation St.
George'?"

Brett stepped back out of view. He couldn't risk his father
seeing him now. He'd had more than enough parental disap-
proval for one day. The container door was open. He slipped
inside—

What the...?

Bolted to the floor were a half dozen iron chains attached to
an equal number of manacles. The chains looked so heavy and
barbaric that at first Brett was sure they were fake. He thought
of the magic show that was supposed to take place the following night. Could the chains be props for a Houdini-style escape
routine? Perhaps the entire container was a magician's set—
a cage for a stage.

Maybe the farm animals were part of the show, too?

Then Brett spied the massive steel muzzle on the floor. Leaning in for a closer look, he accidentally brushed against one of
the chains. It clanged loudly against the side of the container.

Oops.